Young Again

About This Book

When a small Midwestern university thinks the key to retention is to have a small cadre of faculty live among its students, dormitory life becomes the blueprint for *carpe diem* gone wrong. As hedonists collide, commingle, and sometimes collude, the dorm becomes the place where the awkwardness of adolescence meets head-on the awkwardness of middle age, and both groups learn lessons along the way. Gretchen Johnson's *Young Again* slyly reminds us that, while we're young only once, we can be immature forever.
    Jerry Bradley, author of *Collapsing into Possibility*

I loved the characters, the pacing, the way the author doesn't lecture you on anything yet clearly gets her points across.... And (maybe) not just because I'm at the right age and have the right background to enjoy middle-age academics and their antics, it's really hard to pick favorite parts. There were just too many. The way she jumps in and out of each character's POV, just as the tension tightens–it's so impressive! ... The details keep adding layers and more layers while never getting dull because they're so precise and witty.
   Rachel George, Old Books on Front Street, Wilmington NC

Young Again

by

Gretchen Johnson

Golden Antelope Press
715 E. McPherson
Kirksville, Missouri 63501
2021

Copyright ©2021 by Gretchen Johnson
Cover Painting by Michelle Lansdale
Cover Design by Russell Nelson

All rights reserved. No portion of this publication may be duplicated in any way without the expressed written consent of the publisher, except in the form of brief excerpts or quotations for review purposes.

ISBN   978-1-952232-60-2

Library of Congress Control Number: 2021944654

Published by:
Golden Antelope Press
715 E. McPherson
Kirksville, Missouri 63501

Available at:
Golden Antelope Press
715 E. McPherson
Kirksville, Missouri, 63501
Phone: (660) 665-0273
http://www.goldenantelope.com
Email: ndelmoni@gmail.com

Dedication:

*For academics everywhere
and for my love, Tom*

Acknowledgments:

I could never have written this book without the love and support of my husband, Tom Sowers. His willingness to read and give constructive criticism on early drafts was so valuable, but, more than that, I'm thankful for the way he takes care of so many of the boring parts of life (like cooking and washing dishes) and gives me space to be creative.

I'm forever grateful for the team at Golden Antelope Press, especially Betsy Delmonico. Their dedication to the publication process, from the initial submission to the final product, makes working with them such a joy. I'm so thankful that they saw potential in *Young Again*.

I'd like to thank my talented friend, Michelle Lansdale, for allowing her beautiful painting to be used as the book cover image.

I'm thankful for my parents, Brian and Lois Johnson, and the rest of my Minnesota family: Alex and Jes Johnson, Emmett, Paige, and Brooks. They've always supported me in every way imaginable.

I am lucky to be surrounded by a wonderful collection of academic friends: Brian Williams, Terri Davis, Jerry Bradley, Jim Sanderson, Don Price, Sharon Joffe, Adam Nemmers, Casey Ford, Brendan Gillis, Jennifer Ravey, T J Geiger, J.P. Nelson, Bin Wang, and Charles Popp. Being around all these talented people helps push me to keep writing.

Lastly, I'd like to thank Lamar University for the summer research fellowship I received that allowed me to finish this book. I am grateful to have been selected by Dr. Maurer and Dr. Lei for that opportunity.

Young Again

Chapter One

A week before her thirty-eighth birthday, Lyla Benson moved back into the dorms. Unlike the move-in twenty years earlier, this time was met with the shadows of shame that seemed to accompany all of her decisions since the divorce. As an adjunct faculty member struggling to survive on a tiny income, she had jumped at the chance to get free room and board when the idea was first presented at a sparsely attended faculty meeting the year before.

"The idea is retention, keeping the students around all four ... or five ... years, and what's the best way to retain students?" John Ulder, the chair of the history department, had asked the few present.

"How about you just tell us? I know we could drag this thing out the full hour, but it's Friday afternoon, and I have a long drive back to Sioux Falls," Janet pleaded before coaxing her green-rimmed glasses back onto the bridge of her bony nose.

"I only have you for an hour. At least give me that," he joked. "So the idea is that faculty involvement will help retention, and how can the faculty be more involved?"

"I know how we can be more involved," Jesse said and winked at Lyla for reasons she chose not to acknowledge.

"Be serious, Jesse. Come on. Can't we just get through one meeting, just one meeting where we're not at risk of violating some HR policy? Seriously—can't we just do that?" John said, and shot Jesse a stern look. "But back to the point—how can we make a real effort to get to know these guys, to make a real impact on their lives? Anyone?" he said and paused. "Anyone?"

"Just tell us," pleaded Janet.

"Just try one guess," John said.

"Okay, I'll give it a go," said Ted, a retired lawyer who decided to finish his master's in history and teach part-time instead of heading south like most of his friends. "Activities with our students? Like field trips to museums?"

"No, no, we've tried that. It's not enough. Think deeper," said John.

"We've gone deep enough. We guessed. Just tell us and take volunteers, and let us head home for the weekend," Janet said as she shuffled impatiently in her chair.

"One more guess."

"Fine. I'll guess. You want us to follow them everywhere, to eat with them, shower with them, be there every step of the way in order to force them to give a damn about this second-rate school they're only attending out of a lack of other options. That's got to be it, right?" Janet piped in with obvious sarcasm, the kind of sarcasm that can only be employed by those lucky enough to possess the safety of tenure.

"You're actually pretty close," John said with a sly smile forming on the sides of his thin mouth. Lyla noted that his smile almost made him attractive despite the tired features that normally gave him the look of someone who stayed up all hours of the night worrying about silly things, like whether or not the trash was placed on the correct side of the stoop.

"Just tell us," Janet said, clearly enjoying the process despite the urgency she felt to get on the road before the timing would place her right in the middle of Sioux Falls' mild rush hour traffic.

"Okay. Okay, but I want everyone to keep an open mind on this. I want everyone to actually take a minute to let the idea settle before immediately dismissing it," John pleaded while Janet rolled her eyes and turned to look at Ted. "The proposal is to allow faculty to live in the dorms."

"Who the hell would do that?" Janet half shouted.

"Let me finish, would you? There are benefits, benefits to everyone really. The students—"

"No, no, you don't. Don't start there. We all want to know the benefits for *faculty*. I'd like to see you bring *those* out for everyone to see because we all know damn well that there aren't any," Janet said.

"There are. If you'd let me finish ... if you'd ever let me finish." He looked at her for a minute to ensure her mouth was in that sewn-shut position she mimicked with curled-under lips when she wanted to act like she was showing respect but was actually mocking the speaker. She did this, and he went on. "Free room and board. Need I say more?"

"Yes, you need to say a lot more. Who the heck cares about free room and board? We're adults with full-time salaries. Well, most of us," she said and smiled awkwardly at Ted. "We don't need room and board anymore."

Lyla sat and listened to all this and started doing calculations in her head. Her salary was $24,000 a year, rent was $690 a month, and she figured she must be spending at least a couple hundred on food each month. As everyone else ridiculed the idea, she sat and waited for Dr. Ulder to expand on it.

"It honestly doesn't matter what your opinion is, Janet. This is already a done deal. The provost and president voted yes, and it spent all spring semester in the student retention committee. Chairs all over the university are having this same conversation with their faculty as we speak. The administration is going to find their seven volunteers, and those faculty will make up the first cohort of the program. It's happening." Janet folded her arms and slumped to the back of her chair, suddenly giving off the appearance of a disappointed child, a comical appearance for a woman nearing sixty to possess. "The bottom line is that this is not something we're forcing on anyone, of course not. This is not, in any way, a mandatory appointment. We're not taking turns or drawing straws or anything like that. It's completely optional.

Beyond that, despite what *you* might think, this could be a great opportunity for those faculty members—" (he stopped and looked at Julie Spivey, the new hire from New York) "—who are looking for a way to stand out and be real advocates to the students we have on campus." Lyla noticed a glint of disappointment in Julie's eyes. "So, if anyone wants to know more about this or is ready to sign up for what is basically a big raise, chat me up after the meeting today. Now, onto the next order of business – sadly, we're not going to be able to provide paper clips or pencils for faculty anymore. Just got the word from the higher-ups this morning."

*

And a year later Lyla stood alone in her single room, down at the end of the hall of Homestead co-ed dormitory. After hiking boxes and bags and armloads filled with casual and teaching clothes up three flights of stairs all afternoon, she was exhausted and stood silently, staring out of the small slatted window onto the pavement below. There they were. The freshmen class. The reason she had been allowed to fulfill such a humiliating role with the promise of free rent and food. Even from three stories up, she could see their thin waists, toned thighs in tiny shorts, and breasts that sat proudly under the fabric of their fitted sundresses. She wondered if they knew she would be here, wondered how they would feel when they found out, could almost feel the disgust in their voices as they gossiped in hallways and bathrooms about the pathetic professors who were living amongst them, watching their every move, tainting the freedom of their college days. Lyla's boxes were still unpacked, the Faculty Dorm Dweller contract still unsigned. She could just skip the orientation meeting, rest for a bit, get a slice of pepperoni and a coke at Stone Willy's Pizza, come back, repack her car, and head downtown to beg her old landlord to let her sign another year's lease at the apartment she had just given up. Surely someone else could take her place in the Faculty Dorm Dweller program if she decided it was all just too much for her to handle.

"I'm barging in. I'm barging in," called a boisterous woman with platinum blonde hair piled high over her heavily made-up face. "Sorry, don't know what to say when the door's already open and knocking's not an option. You're Lyla, right? Don't ask how I know that. I don't know much else. I mean, it's obvious that you're not a freshman ... no offense. I'm not either, in case you were wondering." She didn't chuckle or smile, leaving Lyla to wonder if this woman was delusional or making a joke. "There's a meeting, right? I thought I heard something about a meeting. I found a couple of freshman guys to help move my crap ... kind of cute ... I'm sure you noticed, but that is one of the hidden ... or not so hidden ... benefits of this whole gig, right? That and easier access to weed. I'm just kidding. Of course, I'm kidding," she said; but then she winked. "So when is this meeting?"

"I was just about to head down there," Lyla said and suddenly felt the momentum of her decision to quit the Faculty Dorm Dweller program losing steam.

"Oh, good. I'll walk down with you. I'm Juanita Jane, by the way. For a while, people called me JJ, but I don't like that anymore, so now I'm back to my roots, back to where it all began," she explained, and Lyla caught a whiff of whiskey on her breath as Juanita Jane reached out to hug her new dorm mate. "Can you believe only four of us signed up? Crazy, right? I thought people would be clawing the shit out of each other just to get a chance at this, but no. Turns out it's just gonna be the four of us," she repeated as they descended the stairs, both of them nearly out of breath by the time they reached the bottom.

Down in the student lounge area sat the other two Faculty Dorm Dwellers and some administrative people Lyla had never seen before.

"Okay, everyone's here. Let's get started," Mr. Administration said lifelessly while motioning for Lyla and Juanita Jane to sit down next to a fiftyish Hispanic man.

"Congratulations. You four are the first round of what will hopefully become a very successful run of the FDD Program."

"FDD?" Juanita Jane asked.

"Faculty Dorm Dwellers," he responded flatly. The mere mention of an acronym made Lyla's bullshit meter spike, but she wasn't sitting there for student retention purposes. She listened to this man drone on about the "immense possibilities of the FDD program" and reminded herself that even the rent on her crummy studio apartment over the movie theater in downtown Marshall was barely financially feasible. Like her grandfather who only enlisted in the army because of the promise of free clothes and some world travel, she was there for the free room and meal plan.

Twenty years earlier she had sat in this same lounge, on one of the same wooden benches, as her resident advisor droned on about dorm safety and the importance of avoiding date rape. She never intended to return to Marshall, Minnesota, a town of only 12,000 people out on the prairie on the western edge of the state, but after a three year escape to graduate school in Tallahassee, her only job offer took her back to the place she had started.

"And one of the most important rules," Mr. Administration said—accompanying the word *rules* with the hand air-quotes that have come to represent sarcasm or inauthenticity of some kind—"is to never sleep with a student."

"I thought the purpose here was to retain the students," the Hispanic man next to Lyla whispered in her ear. She faked a stifled laugh and wondered why this man was there. *What would the students think of him?* She looked down at her newly wrinkled wrists and again wondered what an eighteen-year-old freshman would think of *her* living in the dorms.

"Just think of it this way," Mr. Administration continued. "You're not their parent. You're not their friend. You're not their teacher, once you enter the dorm doors. You're not their counselor. You're not their coach. You're not a dorm cop. You're not a spy." Lyla wondered what role this guy thought she was supposed to fill. "You're just someone to be *there*. The research has shown that just the presence of a faculty member in a non-classroom setting helps students to see that what happens in the classroom extends far beyond its borders. If a student sees you walking around in their halls, eating the food in their dining hall, just making it through the daily routine just like them, that student is less likely to villainize you. You become a human being and not something to be feared." Lyla scanned the room and decided that none of the people sitting there looked particularly scary, not even to the eighteen-year-old version of herself. If anything, she felt they looked a bit pathetic. Juanita Jane had the air of an aging stripper with her platinum ringlets, sun-damaged skin that resembled bread kept too long in the toaster, and dark crimson lipstick she couldn't quite contain to the confines of her thin lips. The woman across the table reminded her of a gullible babysitter her parents had hired once who allowed Lyla and her younger sister to order the expensive takeout Chinese food with the money their mother had hidden in a jewelry box upstairs. And the man who had spoken to Lyla looked totally out of place sitting there in trendy sneakers with a backpack resting against his bare legs. *Why would someone his age have to move back into the dorms for free rent?*

"So just be there," Mr. Administration said.

"Oh, I'll be there," said the Hispanic man as he jabbed Lyla in the side in a failed attempt at comedic timing.

"Let's just go around the room and have you each introduce yourself. Tell us where you're from originally and why you signed up for the FDD program," said Mr. Administration.

Juanita Jane started. "I'm Juanita Jane. I used to go by JJ, but I'm back to Juanita Jane now, back to the beginning, back where it all started, and, frankly, I'm pretty damn excited about that. Let's see ... I'm from Baton Rouge originally but have lived just about everywhere between relationships with various lovers and many jobs and interests and random extended house-sitting stays.... You get the point, so here I am, an FDD, ready to meet these guys and keep them on the path to graduation. And that's me," she said and nodded at the man next to her.

"I'm Humberto Rojas, but everyone calls me Bert. I'm from Madison, been teaching here for almost twenty years, and I thought this sounded like a nice change from day-to-day life. It's nice to meet you all and join the FDD group as the token—"

"Hispanic guy," Juanita Jane chimed in before he could finish.

"I was just going to say guy, the token guy, but that's true too."

"Oops. Shit. Always putting my foot in it," she said and somehow pulled her red high-heeled foot all the way up to her mouth while letting out a huge "Ha!"

"Just glad it's not me this time," he said and smiled.

"Funny thing is, you'd think it was me too," Juanita Jane said.

"Meaning?"

"I'm Juanita. I'm white as the skin on her ass," she said and nodded in Lyla's direction. "But the name sounds Hispanic, so people always assume, before they meet me, you know?"

"Ha! Yeah, so we have the token Hispanic guy and the token white-woman-with-a-misleading-name, and I haven't categorized these other two just yet—"

"Okay, okay. Let's keep going," interrupted Mr. Administration.

"I'm Lyla Benson, from here – Marshall. I actually went here for my undergrad too, and I've been back teaching here for almost ten years." She thought about telling the truth, that she needed the extra money that would be saved by not having to pay for rent and food, but instead said, "I thought it sounded like a cool idea and wanted to help out."

"I'm Joy McPherson, from Devil's Lake, North Dakota—"

"How old are you? You look like a teenager?" Juanita Jane interrupted.

"I'm twenty-nine."

"Shit! That's some crazy shit! Wouldn't have guessed it!"

"I'm honestly just here to give my boyfriend some 'space.' His words, not mine. Also, my chair pretty much guaranteed me tenure if I'd do this for a year."

And there they were, the four fools who had signed up for a lack of privacy and integrity for a semester, and all for the promise of free things, promotions, and a change of pace from the monotony of regular life.

Chapter Two

"I can't believe we have *den moms* in the dorms this year! What the fuck? If I had known Prairie State College was going back to the fifties, I would've gone somewhere else."

"I know what you mean. Total bullshit."

Juanita Jane sprang up in her twin dorm bed upon hearing these voices in the hall and raced to the peephole to try to see the faces of the gossiping girls, but she was too late. All she could see was the white concrete wall beyond the door.

"Damn it," she whispered. A *den mom*? She was *not* a den mom, whatever that was. She was an associate professor of English. She was only doing this stupid FDD program to appease her boss after unknowingly flirting with the woman's husband at a faculty Christmas party. She was not a joke, as these girls seemed to think. She had won awards, published poems in journals, taught for over twenty years. They should be *lucky* to be living in close proximity to her.

She pulled the pink silk robe tighter around her still mostly slim waist, licked her thumbs, and used them to wipe away the remnants of yesterday's eye liner that hadn't rubbed off on the pillowcase during the night. For the past few years, she had gotten into the habit of never staring straight into a mirror before her morning shower, but she suddenly realized that the new reality of living in a college dormitory was going to shatter that routine. She would have to look before venturing into the hallway and down the half flight of stairs to the community bathroom. She couldn't risk going out there in an unkempt state. This was a part of the FDD program that was conveniently left out of the faculty meetings and certainly not discussed at the orientation meeting the week before moving in. This was terrifying.

She moved slowly to the long mirror glued to the back of the closet door, and there she was. Somehow her face appeared to have tied itself into knots during the night. Where her lips had appeared larger and more relaxed under the veil of berry gloss the night before, the morning left them wrinkled and old and dull. The skin around her nose sported red splotches that needed to be evened out with foundation, and her eyes looked like they required great effort just to stay open. With her hair pinned up tightly for sleeping, she noticed that her hairline appeared to be receding. *When had that happened?* She had no idea women had this issue too. It was worse than she feared. She was getting old. Still, she told herself, fifty-one is the new thirty, right? But even thirty would seem old to these college freshmen.

She grabbed the purple shower caddy she had awkwardly purchased at Walmart a few weeks back and remembered how the salesgirl had asked if her daughter was starting college. "No," she had said. "It's for me."

"Oh, wow. Good for you! Going back at your age. That takes courage," the girl had said, and because Juanita Jane didn't want to extend the conversation, she simply smiled and nodded and left the store.

When buying the carrying case for her soaps and shampoos that day, she hadn't thought about how hard it would be to shower in the dorms, hadn't considered that the Walmart conversation wouldn't be the awkward part. She stood by the door holding a beach towel and the shower caddy for a moment before cracking the door to see if anyone was coming down the hall. It was clear, so she grabbed the keys and made a run for it.

*

Chapter Two

In class that morning, Juanita Jane knew something was off, that her confidence had not survived the long stare into the mirror earlier that morning. She looked out at the rows of freshman students and realized she hadn't felt this way since she was a freshman. *Had moving back into the dorms sent her right back to that place?* She shuddered to think so and forced an appearance of poise as she wrote her name and the course title on the dusty chalkboard.

When the day-one ritual of having students each say their name, their home city, and their major was underway, Juanita Jane was almost sure that the blonde with the Disney princess eyes and perfectly tanned legs in the third row owned the voice she had heard mocking her that morning. *Who did this bitch think she was? Juanita Jane was way more of a knock-out in college than this girl. This girl would have to run circles around Juanita Jane to get the same guys she could get back then.* As the guy next to Disney Eyes took his turn to speak, Juanita Jane kept her attention on the girl. She would make sure this girl knew who the top dog was. Disney Eyes might be the pretty one now, but Juanita Jane could pass out the grades, and ultimately that would win out.

*

In her office that afternoon, Juanita Jane felt restless. She kept taking the compact mirror out of her top drawer and inspecting her face. With the help of cooling cream and bronzer, she decided her skin was presentable but no longer striking. She sat back in the torn leather chair and wondered when it had happened, asked herself to recall the exact moment when she no longer looked like that younger version of herself she was so used to.

The problem with being a college professor was being constantly surrounded by youth. In a county clerk's office, she might be the cute middle-aged woman, might even be the object of midday sexual fantasies played out in the mind of the balding forty-something man across the way, but at a university she went unnoticed. She stared hard at the face in the mirror and decided she needed a darker lipstick, a little more eyeliner, and a heavier hand when applying the blush strokes beneath the eyes. She knew there had to be a way to paint back that version of herself who had received all those flowers, marriage proposals, expensive dinner dates, and weekend getaways to resorts she couldn't remember the names of.

She knew that, as usual, no students would come to her scheduled office time until the last week of the semester when they were desperate and fraudulently remorseful, so she decided to leave early.

Out at the edge of campus, was the Prairie Preserve Nature Trail. To the faculty members coming from places like New York or Montana, the nature trail was a sad excuse for a walking path that didn't offer much of a retreat from the uninspiring regional campus with its boring brick buildings and treeless landscape. Juanita Jane had heard the half mile path mentioned frequently at sustainability meetings and local radio shows, a testament to the lack of entertainment options in Marshall, but she had never stepped foot on it. While renting the basement apartment of a historic house a mile east of campus, she never spent time at work unless she was being paid for it, but now her entire life would exist within the confines of the campus. She couldn't go to the parties in the student dance club, couldn't hang out in the student rec room playing table tennis and air hockey with co-eds, wouldn't hang around the dorm lounge watching community cable television with the residents of her assigned building, but she felt comfortable taking a hike on that walking path.

Since she hadn't worn a pair of pants in over a decade and didn't own anything other than high heels and one pair of semicomfortable flip flops, the idea of a hike should have struck her as ludicrous, but on she went anyway. Somehow, in the middle of an entire region of prairie grasses and corn fields, the first stretch of the Prairie Preserve Nature Trail was lined with birch and oak trees, probably planted along the half mile loop decades ago when the path was first devised. Like most ideas in Marshall, the original project had clearly been scaled down as funding and interest waned. At the start of the trail, a worn wooden boardwalk stood only a few inches off the ground, giving the appearance of a path over a body of water or at least an uneven surface below, but the terrain beneath the boardwalk was a long even trail that stretched out smoothly past the tree-line and out to the open field beyond.

She yanked the elastic waist of her knee length skirt up under her bra line in order to expose most of her thighs to the late-day sun, contemplated taking her heels off, but, fearing splinters or the presence of a garden snake, decided to keep them on, and she was off.

Maybe this wouldn't be so bad, she thought. She was already doing better than she would have in the old house. Instead of finishing off a sleeve of Oreos and a bottle of Walgreens white zin, she was going for a walk. Instead of waiting for men she had never met in person to compliment her latest Facebook selfie, she was out getting a tan and inhaling the last of Minnesota's summer heat.

She stepped carefully, avoiding the cracks between boards so as not to accidentally lodge her heel or, worse yet, break an ankle, and wondered why her knees were hurting so much after just a few minutes of leisurely walking. She stopped to watch a doe luxuriating in an endless supply of summer leaves and grasses, and she decided that this year would be different. She would finally get her life together, would finally visit the dentist and get that crown she was supposed to schedule an appointment for years back. She would schedule all the appointments she just never got around to making. She would make this walking thing a habit, not break the no-alcohol-in-the-dorms rule (after that last bottle of vodka was gone), and stop having sex with Sean just because he sometimes bought her drinks and once called her the "sexiest piece of ass in Marshall." She would do it.

And just then she saw them: a young couple holding hands in the clearing beyond the end of the path. And he was the kind of handsome she used to spend time with – heavily muscled legs, shaggy sandy hair, broad shoulders, and the confident posture of a man who knew he was going places and always would be. And she was the kind of girl Juanita Jane used to be – tanned limbs effortlessly extending beyond the flowing fabric of her yellow tank and cream shorts, long honey locks just slightly disheveled in that way that looks stylish at twenty and stupid at fifty, and flat feet standing expectantly with the heels slightly raised above the bottom of her tan flip flops. And then he was twirling her around, dancing to nothing, as only those unjaded by the knowledge of what a colossal break-up feels like can do. And then she was giggling, and he was kneeling down on the bed of warm prairie grasses, and her shriek, and a "yes" that Juanita Jane could only ascertain by the exaggerated nod, and then they were gone, walking briskly through the field, back to campus to tell everyone. And Juanita Jane was alone, left to remember the last time she almost had the thing this girl now possessed.

*

In Juanita Jane's younger years, she was a Houdini of relationships. She enjoyed putting herself into situations nearly impossible to get out of, liked to tie the knots as tightly as possible and later attempt to somehow wriggle out of the trap she herself had set. She did it time and time again, leaving a line of angry and disillusioned men behind her, swearing to herself that this was the last time but knowing it probably wasn't.

She never went into a relationship with the intention to leave, but it always struck her, the further she got into something, that there might be a better option waiting somewhere just out of frame, that if she just escaped the current man, she could go searching for something superior, something she would always regret not looking for if she stayed.

But when her forty-fifth birthday arrived, she stayed up past midnight to usher it in and decided it really had to end, that Kyle might be her last chance, that she couldn't do to him what she had to the others after he put six years in and stayed with her through two intense and messy affairs. As Kyle slept through the weather channel forecaster doling out advice for hurricane preparedness, Juanita Jane promised herself that she would accept the marriage proposal she knew was coming the following day.

But in the months leading up to the wedding she grieved, grieved in a different way than she had before, the kind of grieving done in secret, the kind they say only a man does before his wedding day. She grieved for the end of things, for knowing strangers would never call her beautiful again, for no more first dates, first kisses, no more nights of the madness of great passion when she stayed up late in her basement apartment dancing with imaginary suitors. She grieved for all of it, for knowing he would only become more ugly to her, that his drooping eyes would only slip further down his face and his pursed mouth only lose more and more of its power as the years ticked on. She hated him for taking the possibility of future lovers away from her. She hated herself for wanting them, for still desiring the dreams of unmade decisions. And as the wedding drew closer, the panic set in deeper. She found excuses to not see him, sicknesses and work exhaustion and places she needed to be. She was afraid that if she spent too much time with Kyle she would suddenly blurt it out, that she would say, "I can't do this. I have to get out. I'm sorry" as she had before.

Her friends scolded her. "Kyle is perfect for you." "You're insane." "Come on, JJ. You know he's the one." "I would be thrilled to have a guy like him. Don't throw this away." "No, it's not like Ryan or James or Kent. It's different with Kyle. You'll see."

But the more they encouraged her, the more she felt like she was being pulled into a huge trap. She had to get out, but she knew she couldn't.

The wedding rings were ordered, the church booked, cake paid for, dinner at the golf course decided upon, deposits paid, and then the invitations went out, and the balances paid off.

She was nearly twenty-grand into something she didn't want, the hardest trick to get out of to date.

She somehow made it through the rehearsal dinner, downing glass after glass of wine, sitting silently in a black lace dress that hung too loosely on her hips and constricted the skin over her collarbone as people swirled around her chatting about the weather and the out-of-town travel complications they had endured to be there. She told herself that she only had to show up the next day, say a few words, smile for some photos, and then it would be done. She would have made her decision and could settle in to the life that waited on the other side of it.

And on her wedding day, after the hair appointment, she got in her car but didn't stop at her house to put the dress on and head to the church. Instead, she kept driving, out past the population sign, down Highway 59 toward the Iowa border. She imagined them waiting for her, tried to convince herself to pull over and turn around, but kept going until she flew past the state border. She felt the nausea of unearned freedom racing through her and opened the windows to breathe the cold January air beyond the car in an attempt to distract herself from the knowledge of her cruelty. She could see Kyle waiting at the church. She could feel his fear rising as she put more and more miles between the things she had agreed to and the life he had planned out with her, but she kept driving. She drove and drove as the clock in the church she was fleeing ticked closer to the wedding start time, and when she reached Council Bluffs, nearly out of gas and exhausted from the efforts of her escape, she pulled the car into the nearest gas station, dragged herself out of the car, and stumbled in with the ridiculous wedding hair piled in ringlets on the top of her sore head.

She looked around at the stale gas station filled with men less attractive than Kyle and started to sob.

"It's okay, Miss. We can cover your gas if you're short on funds," said an elderly woman patron standing in line to pay.

"It isn't that," Juanita Jane said. "I have the money. I just don't have anywhere to go once I fill up." She expected an attempt at comfort from the stranger, but the woman just nodded, said nothing, paid for her beef log and air fresheners, and left the station.

Back in the car, Juanita Jane looked at her cell phone for the first time since leaving the hair appointment. She had heard the ringing and dinging in the backseat as she drove, but it became so predictable that she stopped hearing it, like the slight whistle in the back wheels she had been ignoring for over a year. Thirty-seven missed calls. Eighteen text messages. Fourteen voicemails. And just then another text came in:

Are you okay? Did you die? I'm about to have a heart attack if you don't contact me soon.

And then another one:

Seriously.

It was her mother. Juanita Jane knew this would happen, had fully anticipated the storm of consequences her decision would produce, but she somehow hadn't factored in her mother's reactions. She knew she would hide from Kyle as long as possible, but she had to call her mother back, and so she did.

Before Juanita Jane even heard the ring on the other end, her mother's voice was there. "What are you doing? What the hell are you doing? Where are you? The wedding was supposed to start forty-five minutes ago ... no ... fifty now. Where are you? You were supposed to be here for pictures at one. What the hell are you doing? Are you okay?"

"I couldn't do it," Juanita Jane said in a defeated tone.

"What the hell do you mean *you couldn't do it*? You *can* do it. You *will* do it. You promised Kyle you would be here. We have all these people from Louisiana here. They flew in to see you get married. What the hell are you doing?"

"I thought I could. I really did think I could this time, but I can't. I tried to drive home after my hair thing. I did. I tried. I just couldn't do it."

"Listen," her mother said in an authoritative voice Juanita

Jane hadn't heard in years. "You listen to me. I don't know what the hell is going on in your mind, but I need to talk some sense into you. You're a forty-five-year-old God-damn woman, and there are two-hundred of your friends and family waiting for you, sitting here waiting for you to finally do the right thing in your life. I don't know where you are. I don't know what you're thinking, but turn your fucking car around, and get your ass down here."

She could picture her mother standing in the corner of the church narthex, back behind the coat rack, whisper-shouting into the phone, foolishly believing no one was listening. "I'm in Southern Iowa. I'm not coming back. I'm sorry," she said and hung up the phone, leaving her mother to face the horrible scene she had created.

Chapter Three

Marshall, Minnesota, was a small town by almost anyone's standards, anyone but the people who lived in the even smaller towns surrounding it. Marshall had all the things a town should have but not much more. To those from Minneapolis and St. Paul, it was a nearly uninhabitable region, but to the other towns in the Southwestern Minnesota region, with their populations always hovering between three-hundred and three-thousand, Marshall had it all. There was a grocery store, funeral home, coffee shop, movie theater with two screens, Walmart, a splattering of fast food chains along the road by the college, a high school, middle school, three elementary schools, seven churches, eight bars, four gas stations, a regional hospital, an Applebee's, and even a new Mexican restaurant that had just opened and was run by a few of the most recent immigrants to the area. But to Bert Rojas, it wasn't enough.

The plan had been to get out of Madison and finally go somewhere bigger, more diverse, more filled with the life he had imagined during his long high school and college years when days seemed to stretch on forever as his mind plotted out a life beyond the mundane world of Wisconsin.

"Remind me again why we're doing this," Lyla Benson asked him, taking a seat beside him at the dining hall.

"Is this conversation safe?" he asked.

"Safe?"

"Yeah. Am I talking to an equal or to someone who is going to speak with the administration about—"

"Oh, no. Of course I won't. Tell me whatever."

"I had to get away from my wife," he said and took a bite out of the stale dinner role.

"Seriously? You're married? You're married, and you're doing this?"

"Oh yeah. I had to get out, had to get away from it all for a while, all the bullshit of married life. We've been married forever. That woman was driving me insane. You understand," he said. She didn't.

"And your wife—" she started and made the so-on-and-so-on hand motion to get him to fill in the blank space with a name.

"Jean."

"Your wife, Jean, was okay with this?"

"Of course not."

"So how did you convince her?"

"I put a good spin on it."

"Spin?"

"Yeah, I told her it was either this or do a semester with the study abroad program. Made it out to be a take-my-turn-or-get-fired situation."

"And she bought it?"

"Probably not, but what's she gonna do? Sometimes I gotta wander a bit. She's been with me long enough to know that," he said with a bit of a huff in his voice.

Lyla couldn't believe he was telling her all this, just sitting there so casually with students surrounding him in easy earshot, but then she remembered Mr. Administration explaining that they should act like the students, should just live their lives in the dorms and dining hall right alongside them, and she wondered if *she* was the one in the wrong for questioning the conversation.

"Besides," he said. "She'd much rather have me a couple miles away than halfway around the world for a semester." As he spoke, Lyla studied his face. She wanted to be disgusted with his story, but there was something kind in the way his eyes stayed closed just a moment after he blinked, and it reminded her of the way a fat cat she had as a child always looked at her. "So why are *you* here?" he asked. "And I don't want that bullshit story you told the day of orientation. I want the real deal because, let's be honest, this FDD program is basically a curtain call for the unhappies, misfits, crazies, and destitutes among the faculty."

"I'm that last one," she said and scanned the room for students currently in her classes.

"Destitute?"

"Pretty much."

"Adjunct?"

"Yep."

"Let me tell you something," he started, stopped to scoop some cheesy potato casserole into his mouth and continued. "That whole adjunct thing is bullshit ... should be criminal. Now, don't ever repeat what I said to anyone. Don't say *I* said it. Don't *you* say it. Just don't ... because we all know the whole construct of that faculty pyramid that is just barely holding together is dependent on you getting fucked. You have to work for shit pay so that I can make ninety a year doing nothing. It's total crap." She was surprised by him and wondered if this Jean person really was at fault for driving him out of the house. After all, he was being honest, something that seemed lacking among the other senior faculty she had spoken to.

"Yeah, so that's why I'm here, but I'm really wondering if I made the right choice. I mean, it feels like I'm going backwards in my life, like I spent all this time away from being a college student, and now I'm right back to a single room with only a couple of boxes of belongings and all my real stuff in storage at my parents' house," she said.

"Nah. The thing you got to realize is that there is no such thing as 'going backwards.' It's not a real thing, just a bunch of bullshit the world made up to push their agenda on you."

*

In his office, Bert felt like nothing had changed, like he hadn't recently left his house in the middle of a shouting match to drive to a tiny dorm room and move in alongside his students. In his office, those disorganized stacks of books and papers lining the metal shelves still covered the walls. The ceramic Eiffel Tower, seashell seahorse, bobble head collection of minor league baseball mascots, superhero Pez dispensers, and Louis Armstrong figurine were still standing in front of his printer and shrouded in a decade of dust. He still hadn't recycled the ever-growing box of crushed pop cans, and the vanilla scented plug-in air freshener had long ago dried up but was still plugged into an outlet by the door.

He scanned the room, searching for the safety of familiarity but mistakenly stopped on the one thing he didn't want to see, the framed photograph of Jean and him standing in front of their house right after they bought it, back when they were in their late twenties. Over the years it had slowly migrated from the front of his desk to a shelf barely visible from his chair, taking up residence in various places before it reached its final resting place. The longer he had the photograph, the more he felt like the image was taunting him, but he was never able to completely remove it from the office or even from view. For the first time in years, he touched the frame, felt its cold silver exterior. It had been a wedding gift from Jean's parents, but she never filled the frame with a wedding portrait because she said she hated the way the photographer had made her look, felt her figure looked too heavy because she wasn't photographed properly, from up on a ladder looking down as her friends' wedding photographers had done. But she approved of that new-house photo, said she liked the way the green jacket disguised her hips and stomach, said the photo was more about the house anyway, so what did it matter? Still, the photo never quite made it to a shelf in that house. It stayed in a box of possessions deemed too tacky for display, so Bert had rescued it and took it to the office. He wondered now if Jean ever knew it was missing, if she had meant to display it but simply forgotten, and now, twenty years later, he saw all the flaws of displaying such a photo. There she was—that old version of Jean with dark searching eyes and those generous hips that she hated but made him want her. Her black hair fell easily below her shoulders, a few strands caught in the breeze just as the picture was snapped, and her smile still held the possibility of a life that never quite happened for them.

"What am I doing?" he said aloud. Speaking his inner thoughts was a habit he still hadn't broken since childhood when he spent hours alone in the house while his parents dealt with their own disasters.

"About what?" yelled Patricia Thorn, the math professor across the hall.

"Sorry, just thinking aloud again ... trying to figure out my lecture for tomorrow."

"Isn't it the same one it's been every time you taught the class?"

"Nothing is ever the same," he said and placed the frame back on the shelf.

"That's the great thing about math," she said. "It really is."

*

Back in his dorm room, he thought about what Patricia had said. Math *was* always the same, and his life with Jean had been too – too predictable, too routine. They had dinner with her parents every Saturday night, she always asked him to rinse the dishes out before heading to bed, she vacuumed the living room every Tuesday after work (for reasons he never understood), baked the same cookies for Christmas every year, wore the same ratty nightgown with the coffee-stained collar every night, and always started the day by putting the cat's toys in the basket even though they would be removed within the hour. He wondered if he would have been better equipped to deal with the sameness at home had he not had to endure a similar fate at work, wondered if those facts had driven him to sign up for the FDD program.

He had grown to hate the way Jean rushed around the house, always searching for things to do, as though she were a prisoner who was not allowed beyond the confines of those five rooms. He hated the way he feared the new items she might add to his column on the chore list, that stupid raggedy piece of notebook paper clipped to the side of the refrigerator. Their life had somehow become the same as the once-funny comic strip about the dull married couple who mused about their mediocrity each week so that readers could chuckle at the figures on the page while sipping the day's first cup of coffee.

Jean hadn't really looked at him in years, and he couldn't even remember the last time they'd had sex, but Bert was surprised to find that the constant presence of sex, the way the idea of it loomed in the corners of the dorm building, was a comfort to him. It made him feel like there were still possibilities that existed in life, things long forgotten.

That night, when he heard the headboard of the neighboring bunkbed pounding against his wall, he felt alive for the first time in nearly a decade. He was glad he had come. He had made the right choice. Still, he found himself wondering how Jean would feel about this place. She had refused to accompany him on move-in day, said she couldn't encourage something she was so opposed to by helping him in the endeavor, chose to stay home and watch hours of Seinfeld reruns while he settled himself in to the new place, taping old posters of bands he used to enjoy to the walls and fitting the new twin sheets on the thin dorm mattress. He wondered if the sexual undercurrents of dorm life would strike something in Jean too or if she would be uncomfortable with the thrill of it all the way she was at home when the love-making scenes quickly passed on the late night TV they habitually watched together, the way she always filled in the moments of sexuality on screen by asking Bert what he wanted from the store the next day or making an exaggerated fuss over the cuteness of the cat sleeping in the blanket basket. Once, while she rushed to the kitchen to bang around some pots that needed to be unloaded from the dishwasher, he had even shouted out, "You're not fooling me. I know you think you are, but you're not. I know what you're doing. Don't think your attempts at distraction are working. I do remember what sex is. Hell, I even remember what sex was like with *you*." But it only made her bang the pots louder, and the next night, when George Costanza pulled off his pants and climbed onto Susan, Jean suddenly had a need to passionately discuss a new-found preference for ranch dressing over Italian that had hit her unexpectedly when the waiter brought the wrong kind at lunch earlier that day.

After the pounding bed stopped, he listened to the low murmurs of unrecognizable words spoken by the lovers beyond the wall, and he wondered what Jean was doing across town. He flipped on the small television he had purchased for the room and remembered he had forgotten to pack cokes and snacks to stave off hunger between dining hall hours. With more than enough quarters in his laundry stash, he headed down to the first-floor vending machine. As he turned the corner, he saw her – a young, beautiful girl wearing the kind of shorts that didn't quite cover her generous thighs and ass and a tiny tank top with braless breasts pushing against the fabric. It was Camille McCloskey, a student who had taken, and failed, Bert's introduction to algebra class twice. He was frozen in his steps and stumbled over his words. "Oh, hi. I bet you're wondering why I'm here. I'm not, like, creeping around the dorms as some creepy . . . I said that already ... professor. I'm here ... officially ... with the DDF, I mean, the FDD program. Have you heard of that?"

"No," she said while noticeably covering her breasts with her arms folded firmly against her so that he could no longer see the outline of nipples poking against the shirt.

"Faculty Dorm Dwellers. Some of the faculty are living in the dorms this semester, as a way to encourage you all, to help you with whatever you need."

"Oh."

"So I'm here ... if you need anything." He heard the sleazy insinuation his voice had unintentionally made, followed up with, "For school," and then felt guilty for that statement, deciding it might be taken as an attack on her intelligence, an attack she certainly hadn't asked for at eleven at night when she was just trying to brush her teeth in the communal bathroom.

"Okay," she said and rushed down the hall and into the bathroom, leaving him to watch her ass jiggle beneath the tight material of her pajama shorts.

He felt his dick pushing against the newly formed hole in his underwear, the underwear that Jean would have thrown out had he been home for her to do the wash, the way she always did, even after he put up such a protest that time she threw out the paint-stained boxers he had worn to paint the dining room that summer before they had the air conditioning installed. When he first broke the news to Jean that he was moving into the dorms, her first question was, "Will you at least come home so I can do your laundry?" She seemed unusually distraught when he explained that it would be easier and more in-line with the whole system, the whole purpose of this experiment, for him to do laundry in the common room alongside the students. The truth is he had missed doing his own chores, missed the separateness of it, the kind of separateness that marriage simply didn't allow. And there was a freedom, that night in the dorm hallway, in feeling that small hole forming, in realizing that he could just keep on wearing the underwear without Jean ever knowing.

Chapter Four

"Hey, Joy Toy," Juanita Jane yelled as Joy quickly rounded the last corner before the dorm exit. Trying to escape without Juanita Jane noticing had become a kind of game for Joy. While Joy preferred to spend her weekend afternoons alone, Juanita Jane loitered in the doorway, waiting to trap people in long, unwanted conversations. At only two weeks into the FDD program, Joy found herself devising plans to get outside without being stopped by Juanita Jane.

"Can't talk now. Gotta run. We'll talk soon," Joy yelled over her shoulder as she hurried past Juanita Jane.

"Where ya going?" Juanita Jane shouted in her direction.

"Errands. Appointments. Have a good afternoon."

"What kinds of errands? Let me come with you. I'm bored out of my freakin' skull here," she yelled while rushing after Joy in her stiletto sandals.

"Just boring stuff. We'll hang out later," Joy said with a tinge of desperation in her voice.

"Come on, Joy Toy. Let me come with you." Joy hated this nickname. From childhood on, it was a name that only the most irritating people in her life called her by, and she wished Juanita Jane would be a little more conscientious of the fact that student ears surrounded them. How could she maintain respect in her classes with a stupid nickname like that getting out?

"Next time. I promise. Today it's just better if I go alone."

"Oh, come on! Where ya going? Where ya going that I can't just ride along and keep you company? It's not like we have a sex shop in Marshall," she shouted. "Unless we're going to Sioux Falls. Are we going to Sioux Falls?"

"No, no. It's nothing like that."

"So?"

"I just have to look at a few ... possibilities ... for a wedding ceremony," Joy said as they reached her car, knowing she was defeated.

"Whose wedding?"

"My wedding."

"You're getting married? Let me see. Let me see the ring. I didn't even notice," she said and grabbed Joy's naked hand.

"He hasn't given it to me yet."

"Are you engaged?" Juanita Jane asked and pursed her lips so tightly that the lipstick from the lower lip smeared onto the skin above her upper lip, leaving a dark smudge well beyond the lip line.

"Well ... not technically, but it's definitely where things are going."

"Oh, this will be good," Juanita Jane said, leaning against Joy's blue hatchback, a smile starting to form in the creases of her eyes. "So let me get this straight. You're not even engaged yet, but we're going to search for a wedding location so that you'll be all ironed out and pressed and ready to jump into it all when he does propose? Is that what we're doing?" Joy wondered why she kept saying *we*.

"Something like that, but not really. No, not really at all."

"Oh, I'm in. I'm totally in. I've been looking for a scheme like this, almost praying for it. This is just right up my alley," Juanita Jane said and pulled hard on the locked car door. "Come on. Unlock this puppy. Let's do this. Juanita Jane is the person for the job when it comes to wedding planning."

"But you're not married, right?"

"Oh, no. God, no! I tried. Believe me, I tried. It's just not for me. Took me fifty years of my life to realize that. It simply is not for me," she said and ruffled the roots of her blonde hair in a failed attempt to mask the grays growing in. "But I sure as shit love a good scheme."

*

As they pulled up to Camden State Park, a wooded area five miles out of town, Joy wondered if maybe she *was* doing this all wrong. Shouldn't Miles be sitting in the passenger seat and not this loud woman she had just met a couple weeks ago? Maybe Juanita Jane was right, but how could she be? She didn't know anything about Joy and Miles. She hadn't been there that time he said he loved her while they waited in the Taco Bell drive-thru in the middle of the night after making love on his roommate's couch. She hadn't been there on their first date when he slipped his hand under her thigh and kept squeezing it all through the movie she couldn't concentrate on, didn't know the adorable way his dark hair fell in loose curls just above those sad eyes, even right after a haircut. She hadn't heard the way his voice sounded when he said, "How's my cute chick?" or the way his lips possessed the sweetness of whiskey and cokes when he came home after a long shift at The Steady Saloon.

"So what's the plan? Just walk around and case the joint to see if it's a good wedding spot?" Juanita Jane asked while stepping out of the car and onto the soggy dirt parking lot.

"Something like that, but I've been here before. I know what it looks like. I pretty much know the exact place I would want to do the ceremony. I just need to talk to someone in the office about the logistics."

"Logistics? Don't you just show up and do it? I was supposed to get married in a park once. Long story ... didn't end up happening ... but we were just going to have a few guests stand in a circle holding hands and get married in the middle of them."

"Oh, no. No, I had something a little more elaborate planned. I need to have rental chairs brought in and little tables with candles and flowers and maybe an aisle runner with rose petals – the whole works. I need to find out if all of that is allowed here and how much they charge for the use of their space, and I need to make sure it's open for winter events. I'm sure it would be, but I just need to check."

"Winter events?" Juanita Jane asked with a smirk on her face. "You want to do this shit in the winter?"

"Yeah, it's always been my dream—just picture it ... snow falling lightly in the background, me in one of those winter wedding coats ... you know—the ones with the big fur cuffs around the neck and wrists. And the photographer gets that perfect kiss shot with a light veil of snow streaking across the scene. It's just what I always pictured," she said with a faraway smile forming around her eyes.

"Seems like a lot of logistics for an assumed-engagement," Juanita Jane said with obvious judgement in her voice. "But I hear ya. Your life, your plan, your wedding. Let's do this."

The park ranger's office was a strange assortment of wood paneling, taxidermy, national park pamphlets, and bookshelves lined with dozens of pink beanie babies. When they entered, the woman inside immediately turned off the tiny television set, leaving Joy to wonder what program her wedding mission was cutting off.

"Park's open 'til eight today. You can park in any of the lots except the one by the pond today, and don't worry about it if you don't have a park sticker. I won't tell," the overweight ranger woman said.

"Thanks, but I actually have some questions about using the park for a wedding ceremony," Joy said and suddenly felt a tightness in her chest.

"Oh," the ranger said, perking up and turning to face Joy directly. "Man, we haven't had a wedding here in over ten years. This will be fun. What's the date?"

"We haven't really decided that yet," Joy said. "I'm just doing some preliminary—"

"Oh, sure. What time of year?"

"Winter," Juanita Jane said. "Some crazy shit, right? A winter wedding in Minnesota—crazy, crazy shit," she said and shook her head. "Hey, I'm gonna go walk a bit and have a smoke."

"You can't smoke in state parks," Joy said and gave her a dirty look.

"Don't bother me," the ranger said. "Go ahead and smoke. Just don't burn the place down."

"You're my kind of woman," Juanita Jane said and squinted to read the ranger's worn-out nametag. "Loretta."

Loretta winked at Juanita Jane as she left the office and turned to Joy. "When did you get engaged?"

Joy couldn't bring herself to go through another round of humiliation, and besides, what did it matter if this ranger woman knew the truth? "A few weeks ago."

"Where's your ring?"

"Oh, I don't have one. We don't believe in that stuff. You know, the whole blood diamond thing, and besides, they get in the way. My friend cut her hand really badly trying to garden with her ring on. It got stuck in a trellis." Joy couldn't believe what was happening. She had never been a particularly good liar before, was always caught when she tried to cheat in school and hadn't even made it a week before breaking down and confessing the one time she siphoned a little money out of her mother's coin box, and here she was – lying to this Loretta woman with the kind of ease she hadn't expected. Still, something swirled uneasily in her stomach as she watched Loretta's broad face nodding to her story.

"I hear ya. When we got married, my husband Dave and me, we couldn't afford a diamond, so he gave me this knockoff ruby ring. We always said we'd buy a real ring when we had more money someday, but now I love this thing so much I couldn't part with it," she said holding the ring out for Joy to see.

Seeing the woman's ring gave Joy a sudden sense of shame, a desire to run out of that tiny office, back to her car, and away from this woman, but instead she said, "So what do you charge for use of the park for a wedding?"

"I'd have to look that up. I have no earthly idea. My guess would be it's either free or about five-hundred. Probably no more than that," she said.

"And can I bring in items, like chairs and such?"

"Oh, sure."

"Candles?"

"I don't see why not, as long as they're contained in something. And, hell, if it's in the winter, what's really gonna happen anyway? You couldn't burn the place down, even if you tried."

"Is photography allowed?"

"Of course. This ain't a museum. The trees won't fade from a flash," she said.

"Of course. Yeah, of course." Joy could feel herself becoming noticeably nervous, could tell that her pale cheeks were shifting to that deep crimson color that always betrayed her inner feelings, could sense that she was pushing her chin-length locks behind her ears more than what was necessary to keep the hair out of her eyes, that she was shifting from foot to foot in such a way that the rhythmic clicking of heels on the wood floor called attention to her movement. She put her hands in her pockets and stiffened her feet in an attempt to regain poise, but she knew that she was losing.

"So why isn't your fiancé here with you today? Don't couples do this stuff together anymore?"

"He had to work, but he'll probably come next time," she said and wondered if Loretta knew.

*

"Do you think you've found a winner? Will it be a state park wedding for you?" Juanita Jane asked as they made the trek back to the car at a much slower pace than Joy would have chosen.

"How can you walk in those things?" she asked, gesturing to Juanita Jane's stilettos.

"It ain't easy, but it ain't hard, and you're not about to pull a subject switch like that on me. I'm onto you," she said and playfully punched the air in front of Joy's face with her cigarette-clad hand. "Are you really doing this? Planning this wedding on your own? Just waiting idly for him to choose what you've already chosen?"

"I think this place could work. It's a definite possibility, but I've got to see other options. People don't get married at the first place they look at."

"And are you going to look at those other places now or wait for him to be ready to come along?"

"I'm going to do it now."

"Hmph," Juanita Jane grunted and tossed her half-gone cigarette into a pile of dry leaves on the side of the path. Joy used the tip of her tennis shoe to relocate the cigarette to the path and covered it with a bit of damp soil. "Wait! Didn't you say ... at the orientation thing ... that he wanted space? Didn't you say something like that?"

"Oh, no. No, not really. That was just a summary. That's not really what he said."

"Well—what did he say?"

"He just explained ... that ... it might be better if we took a little time apart. You know, so that he could work on himself, like make himself the perfect husband ... before we get married."

"He said that?" Juanita Jane said, with obvious doubt and disgust in her voice. "He said, 'make himself the perfect husband'?"

"Well, no. I'm summarizing, of course."

"What did he say exactly?" Juanita Jane asked and stopped just short of the car. *Who did this Juanita Jane person think she was?* It wasn't like *she* had it all together. She couldn't even put her eyeliner on in a way that didn't make her look like a washed-up 80s stripper trying desperately to hold onto a time that had long passed her by. "Well?"

"I don't know. It's not like I have a tape recording of exactly what he said, but it was something to that effect. He wanted to spend some time apart so that he could work on himself. It sounds like a responsible thing to do, sounds like the sort of thing I would want my future husband to do."

"Trust me. He's not your future husband."

"How do you know?"

"What we have here is a classic example of pulling a me."

"Pulling a you?" Joy asked.

"Yeah. He's engaging in a textbook example of extraction."

"Extraction?" Joy asked and dug her hands deeper into the pockets of her jeans, waiting impatiently for the answer.

"Yes, yes, extraction. He's pulling himself out, removing himself from the situation, so to speak. I've done it a million times. He was just in too deep, didn't know where to go, had to make a bold move. Trust me, he's doing it. This is just the kind of thing *I* used to do," Juanita Jane said, still standing at that awkward length from the car where it wasn't quite socially acceptable for Joy to get in yet.

"No, no. He's not making that kind of a bold move. You've got it backwards. It's the opposite. Trust me. I was there. I had the conversation, not you."

"Oh, I had the conversation too. Trust me—way more times than I really care to admit to. And I was him. I was—" She paused.

"Miles."

"I was Miles. This is not going to bode well for you, Joy Toy."

"You don't know. You just don't know. Besides, even if he thinks that's what he's doing, I know better. Women always know better, right? Men never really want to get married. It's our job to push that issue along, to help them get there," Joy pleaded.

Juanita Jane felt the old kaleidoscope of past proposal images flash through her. Nearly a man every adult year of her life before forty-five had asked her in one way or another. There had been flowers and late-night walks and car rides to the Louisiana coast, phone calls and rooms filled with candles and poems and songs penned to tempt her. Some of them had been an act, a thing only done because the men knew she would turn them away sooner or later, but some had been real. Lives had been temporarily shoved off course, and, in the case of Edward Thompson, completely cut off when her rejection sent him into a rage of rash decisions leading to an army enlistment and death in a country he never would have seen had Juanita Jane just kept her promise.

"Maybe," Juanita Jane said with a shrug and moved toward the car.

"You see, the thing is ... I have a plan," Joy said, stepping into the car. "I saw this on a movie once. This girl was in love with her boyfriend, and he was in love with her too. He just didn't ... fully see it yet, and so, while he was deployed, she spent his time away planning a wedding, and when he got back, she surprised him with it."

"And what channel was this movie on?"

"I don't remember. That's not the point, though. You're missing the whole point. It was amazing." Her arms moved wildly while she spoke. "He came back, and she proposed in the airport, and he said yes, and then the next day she surprised him with this perfect wedding she had planned, and that was the end of the movie," Joy said and started the car.

"But your story is completely different. Don't you see? It's completely different. This guy was at war, for God's sake. Any fool would want to get married after being at war, and Miles isn't at war. Where is Miles, by the way? What the hell is he doing?"

"Right now he's working."

"Working where?"

"He's a bartender at The Steady Saloon."

"This boyfriend of yours is a day bartender at the shitty bar in Marshall, and you think he's going to fall into some Hallmark movie plot you saw. Not gonna happen."

"He works some nights too."

"Doesn't matter. Not the point. And what are you going to do if he doesn't propose?"

"That's the thing."

"What's the thing?"

"The plan's different from that."

"What do you mean, 'the plan's different from that?'" Joy hated the way her own statements sounded stupid when repeated in Juanita Jane's raspy voice.

"Weren't you paying attention? That's not the plan. The plan is not for *him* to propose. I'm going to do it, surprise him with it on his birthday, and I'll have the wedding all planned out, so he doesn't have to do a thing. It will be the most romantic birthday of his life."

"And when is this guy's birthday?" Juanita Jane asked. "How long do we have to plan this surprise birthday wedding?"

"December third."

"This oughta be good."

Chapter Five

At a little before ten, Lyla reluctantly answered the persistent knock on the door.

"Dr. Benson?"

"Yeah, that's me. Only, it's not Dr. It's actually Ms. Benson ... never got my doctorate. Long story. Anyway ... what's up?"

"The R.A. told me to come here."

"Okay—"

The girl standing in Lyla's door looked slightly terrified. She held a stack of books against her chest and wore a backpack so stuffed to the seams that it threatened to tip her over if she stood there much longer. This girl had a boyish haircut that made her thin nose and large black-liner-rimmed eyes more cartoonish and less beautiful than they would have been with longer hair to soften the effect. Her legs were noticeably shorter than her torso, and her hands were a bit lanky, like the hands of a high school boy. She, like so many others, was almost beautiful, but something was slightly off.

"What's up?" Lyla asked.

"You see ... I ... just got back from my night class, and I have a paper due in my eight o'clock class tomorrow, and I haven't even started it yet. It's not like me. It's really not like me, but I've just been so stressed out with everything, and my computer is trapped. It's trapped in my room." She flailed her arms wildly as she spoke, reminding Lyla of a rabid raccoon once trapped in her parents' front room.

"Trapped in your room?"

"Yeah. This is kind of awkward to say this to *you*. I mean ... someone so much older ... not old. I'm not saying you're old. Just—this is awkward."

"Just tell me," Lyla said, hoping they could settle the issue so she could go back to watching the *Top Ten Tornadoes of the Last Century* countdown on The Weather Channel.

"You see I just got back from my night class, and my roommate has a ... tie on the door."

Lyla laughed. "I'm assuming that means the same thing it meant twenty years ago, back when this old lady was in college."

"I'm sorry. I didn't mean you're old. It's just weird, you know, talking about my roommate's sex life. I mean, you're a *teacher*." She said the word like it was dirty. Lyla suddenly remembered being disgusted once when her high school English teacher chaperoned the prom and saw Lyla making out with her then-boyfriend in what she thought was an empty hallway.

"Don't worry about it. What d'ya need? If you're asking to use my computer, that's fine. I'm not really doing anything."

"Really? Seriously? Are you sure? I feel horrible asking *you*. I mean, I was trying to ask my R.A., but, truth be told, I think she might be smoking weed in her room right now. It smelled weird in there, and I could swear it took her a lot longer to answer the door than it should have. I'm Margie, by the way," she said and extended a clammy hand.

"Call me Lyla, and please think of me as a dorm mate, not a teacher. After all, you're not in my class."

*

The next night, Margie was back, but this time she didn't have a paper to write in a hurry. She just didn't have anywhere else to go.

"I can't believe they have so much sex," she said, making herself comfortable on the other end of Lyla's twin bed. "I honestly didn't realize people would be having sex in the dorms. I always thought that was just a movie thing. Did *you* have sex in college?"

Lyla didn't know how to answer this question. She remembered Mr. Administration saying that her job as an FDD was to assimilate into dorm life, to make herself just like the students. In theory, this seemed plausible enough, but in reality, sitting there on the green comforter she had picked up from Walmart the week before move-in across from this girl twenty years younger than her, she suddenly felt the awkwardness of everything she had stepped into. "I don't know if we should talk about that."

"Why not? We're both adults. I'm not a baby, you know. I just turned nineteen."

Nineteen. Lyla's mind flashed back to her own freshman year of college, to a boy named Anton who spent hours staring at her in the computer lab as she typed papers and emails home to her parents, to Nirvana posters she had put up, not because she liked the band but because she thought they looked cool, to late nights in the student center surrounded by male friends and assignments, to snowy afternoons in Anton's bed when classes had been cancelled due to white-out conditions.

"I know. The truth is I don't really remember. It was a long time ago," Lyla said.

"Oh," she said and leaned back against the concrete wall.

"Okay, that's not true. Of course I remember. It's just awkward to talk about, but yes, I did."

"Oh."

"But that doesn't mean that you should."

"Trust me. That's not an issue. My boyfriend is ... like ... ten hours away from here. I'll be lucky if I see him at his parents' house over Thanksgiving break."

"Long distance relationships are tough."

"Yeah," Margie said with a sigh. "So what was he like? The guy from when you were in college. Were you in love?"

"It's weird," Lyla started and shook her head.

"What?"

"I'm not really sure what happened. We dated most of college, were kind of the star couple on campus back then. Everyone assumed we'd get married, have a couple of kids. You know, the whole deal, but then, the week before finals senior year, he just cut it off out of nowhere, wouldn't give me an explanation, wouldn't even talk to me, stayed locked in his room in between taking finals, and skipped graduation. I never heard from him again."

"Really? That's crazy," Margie said and took a sip of her coke. "Is he on Instagram?"

"*Instagram? I'm* not even on Instagram."

"Oh, yeah. You're like my mom's age. No offense," Margie said. "Is he on Facebook?"

"I have no idea."

"Are *you* on Facebook?" she asked.

Lyla shot her a look of disbelief. "Really? I'm not *that* old. Of course I'm on Facebook."

"So how do you not know? You've never looked?"

Of course she had looked. She had looked about a thousand times. "No, of course not."

"Really? That's insane."

"I'm pretty sure Anton's not the kind of guy who uses Facebook. He's very hippy. He's more of a sit-and-read-a-book guy, or a skateboard-around-town kind of guy."

"I'm sure he's not skateboarding. Wouldn't he be almost forty now?" Margie asked.

Forty. Anton was almost forty. And for some reason, this realization slapped Lyla in the chest the same way her divorce had. Of course she knew Anton was older now, but she couldn't quite picture him as anything but what he was the last time she saw him, at twenty-two. Everything about their relationship had possessed that electricity of youth that can only exist the first time. There was the staying up until irresponsible hours playing board games in their underwear, the way he spontaneously scooped her body up and spun her around and around in snow-filled skies, the laughter that came so easily back then, his long hair in her fingers, the subdued tone of his voice, and the way she had to lean in hard to hear those last whispered sentences he spoke right before sleep. She had loved him, and it bothered her that this girl couldn't see the way it had all looked back then.

"He was your age, right?"

"Yeah, that's right."

"Come on! Let's look him up," she said, pulling out her phone.

"No. No, it seems like a bad idea."

"Why? What's the harm? If he is, wouldn't it be interesting? Wouldn't you like to know what your old flame is up to?"

Hearing Margie use the term *old flame* irritated Lyla. Anton was so much more than that. He had held her as she cried herself to sleep after her dad died sophomore year. They had attended weddings together and even took a trip to Las Vegas junior year, a trip where one night, while watching the fountains dance in front of the Bellagio, they suddenly decided to get married the next day but chickened out somewhere between midnight and morning. Anton wasn't a flame. He consumed her, first for those four years, and then for nearly a decade after, even the first two years of her failed marriage.

"Come on. Let's just look," Margie pleaded.

"Okay, but I really don't think he's on there."

Margie sat up on her knees and bounced on the bed like a child. "What's his name?" she asked.

"Anton."

"And last name?"

"Filmore."

"You were into a guy named Anton Filmore? Wow," Margie said with a snort. "Okay ... I'm looking. I'm looking. Huh." She rested the phone on her knee. "How do you spell it?"

Lyla grabbed the phone from her, and there it was—his name but no results found. He was still an unsearchable person, at least on the internet. "That's his name. I told you he wouldn't be there."

"Huh. Nothing. That's so weird. I just can't even imagine. I mean ... how could a person live in the world and not be using social media? It seems crazy, right? I read once that ninety-seven percent of people between the ages of thirty and fifty are on Facebook. I just can't believe he's not on there."

"Yeah, looks like he's not."

"So what's the next step?" Margie asked.

"What do you mean the *next step*?"

"I mean, come on, we gotta find this guy. It'll be fun, give us something to do, a project."

"I don't want a project. I have enough things to do. I have a stack of tests to grade, lesson plans to write, a lonely mother to visit. And, to tell you the truth, I'm not really that curious. Years ago, sure, but I've moved on."

"Are you seeing anyone now?" Margie asked.

"No, no. I'm not really ready for that. I just went through a divorce. I need time."

"Oh, sorry. I didn't know. How long were you married?"

"I'm barging in! I'm barging in," yelled Juanita Jane from the other side of the door before bursting in. "What the hell are you up to, Marg?"

"You guys know each other?" Lyla asked.

"I know everyone. It's like that administration dude said. You gotta socialize. You gotta make yourself known. I just got some wine from Walmart, and I'm looking to share. Who's in?" Juanita Jane asked and pulled two boxes of red wine out of a large yellow shoulder satchel.

"There's no alcohol allowed in the dorms," Lyla said.

"Oh, shoosh! Don't you get it? We're the authority here. For the first time in my god-damned life, I'm the fucking authority, and I plan to take full advantage of it," Juanita Jane declared. "But shit. I forgot the glasses. Whatcha got? A couple of plastic cups or anything, or do I have to run down to the dorm lounge?" she said and started walking back toward the door.

"No. Don't do that," Lyla shouted. "I'm sure I have something. Just stay here, but don't get drunk. Let's not get drunk. I'm pretty sure we're not allowed to even have that here, and Margie is underage."

"Just pretend we're in Wisconsin. The drinking age is eighteen there, and that's only a few hours away," Juanita Jane said and flapped her arms wildly in front of her.

"The drinking age is twenty-one in Wisconsin," Lyla said.

"No way. You shitting me?"

"Nope, has been for decades now."

"Well, fuck. Then let's all just pretend I'm still in college," Juanita Jane said. "That's kind of been the theme of this whole FDD role anyway. If they're going to give us the rules and ask us to act like everyone else who lives here, shouldn't we be breaking the rules? I mean, that's what the students would do, right Marg?"

"I don't think that's the—" Lyla started, but it suddenly struck her that the whole thing *was* ridiculous. Here she was, a middle-aged woman, and she wasn't allowed to drink a glass of wine in her room just because that room happened to be in close proximity to the rooms of minors? There had been students living in the studio apartment across the way before she came here, and they may have been underage, but she could drink there. Maybe Juanita Jane was right. Who did these administrators think they were, paying her less than two grand a month to teach a full schedule, forcing her to jump recklessly into this FDD program, making her share office space with the TA who habitually slept in a beanbag and often scolded her for waking him when she crept into the office before her first class, and then giving her a booklet of dorm rules she hadn't been subjected to since her own years in college? "Maybe you're right," she said.

"That's my girl. I knew you were in there. Just lock the door and make Marg sleep here tonight," Juanita Jane said. "Now, let's have some fun."

Chapter Six

In Juanita Jane's mind, the clunky chords coming from behind the door in room 17 could have been the most beautiful music being played anywhere on earth, so, on her way back to her own room, after a night of far too much wine, she lingered outside the door. And as the music swelled and folded over her, she steadied herself against the wall, moving her arms up over her head and back down to her sides, over and over again, like a child trying to make snow angels in hard-packed snow. "You're amazing," she shouted. "Don't stop. Don't stop. Don't stop. You were born to play. You kick so much ass," she shouted louder, pushing herself away from the wall and drumming her palms hard on the player's door. In her mind, the click of the door lock latch did not signify fear but rather the player's approval, so she drummed louder and started chanting, "Keep playing. Keep playing. We need your music. We need your music. Keep playing." This was what it was all about. She was one of them, one of the masses of college students living in dorms across the country. She had somehow, after decades away from it all, found her way back. She was free.

In the room across the way, Bert was startled awake by the commotion in the hall. He shrugged it off as an immature freshman getting home late from a party, until he heard that voice, a voice far too weathered to come out of the mouth of a young woman, a voice he recognized. Juanita Jane. *What the hell was she doing?* He hesitated before grabbing the gray Prairie State sweatshirt off the desk chair, clumsily pulled it on, and headed out.

"It's four in the morning. What are you doing?"

"Did you hear? Did you hear him?"

"Hear who?"

"Whom. It should be 'whom.' Hear 'whom.' What do you teach again? Ha! I may teach English, but I should be way too drunk to be correcting anyone's grammar. Ha!" she shouted and swayed back and forth to the sound of her voice echoing down the empty hallway.

"What are you talking about? Don't you know what time it is?" Bert asked.

"Time? Do you think anyone in the dorm gives a holy shit about time? Didn't you go to college? Weren't you ever young?" Bert took offense to this line of questioning, but Juanita Jane wasn't the one doing the offending. He was offended by himself. Even in his sleepy state, he realized she was right. He looked at his bare feet, pinched the now-wrinkled skin at the top of his nose, and wondered when he had gotten so old. Years ago, after first arriving at his new house in Marshall, he had thrown a party to celebrate the new place. Friends from back in Madison made the long drive thanks to the promise of beer and music and whiskey. They started drinking before sundown, and, as the evening wore on, the radio got louder, the dance moves more impressive, and the conversations grew and grew in intensity until they could no longer be contained behind the thin barrier of the stucco-sided walls. Around midnight, an older neighbor man with white sideburns and a belly that extended far beyond the bounds of his belted jeans, had come over to threaten a call to the cops if the party didn't settle down and fast. For years, Bert hated that guy, frequently calling him an "old shit bag" to Jean when they spotted the man shuffling around his perfectly kept yard or carrying groceries and mail into the house.

"You're right. I was just—" Bert started.

"Just criticizing me for enjoying the music."

"What music?"

"It stopped. I think you scared him off. There was a guy in there," she said, pointing to the door, her fingers formed in the shape of a handgun. "And he was playing mighty good. Oh yeah. He was good. I haven't heard anything like it in years. Damn. I wish he was still playing. Come on!" she shouted. "Play for us ... just a little more. We need your music."

Bert didn't want to be Old Shit Bag, but he didn't want to lose his job either. "Let's just call it a night. I'm sure there will be plenty of nights to listen to the music."

"And that's what they always tell you, isn't it? Your whole damn life, they tell you that—that there will *always* be another night to listen to the music, but guess what? They're wrong. This is it. This is the last night, and now it's over." As she spoke, Bert's eyes stared at the deep grooves carved through the skin around her lips, and he found himself trying to picture Juanita Jane's face younger. "Damn it!" she yelled and banged on the player's door one more time. "It's over."

"Just try to get some sleep," Bert urged. "You'll feel better in the morning."

"Sleep? Are you fucking kidding me? Ain't gonna happen. Let's go somewhere."

"Go somewhere? Where? Where would we go in the middle of the night?"

"Come on!" she shouted. "We're the same damn age, you and me, but you're so much older. Can't you just embrace this whole thing? We're living in the dorms again. Make it matter. Let's go somewhere. Do you even teach on Fridays?"

"Well, no, but I really should—"

"No. No. You really shouldn't ... anything. What you really *should* do is enjoy the moment for once in your life. Let's get some pancakes or something."

"Pancakes?"

"Yeah, pancakes," she said and slumped down in front of his door. "I need something solid to soak up all the wine, and I want pancakes. I'm not moving until you agree, so you might as well start walking."

"I left my wallet—"

"I have money. C'mon. Let's go."

*

The Happy Chef across from campus had that late-night diner glow that emanated from every surface and corner of the place, the kind of glow one desired at an afternoon birthday party for a two-year-old but hated during the last hours before dawn after a night of little sleep. Bert found himself blinking hard between quick glances at the laminated menu and bright orange surfaces of the walls. Juanita Jane smiled as she ordered an orange juice and short stack and excitedly ran her fingers over the turquois formica tabletop.

"Isn't this better?" she asked Bert.

"Better than what?"

"Sleep. Isn't this better than sleeping?"

He wasn't sure if it was or not. It was certainly one of the more interesting encounters he had had in years, and it reminded him of the early days with Jean when she still lived with her parents and they had to sneak time together in creative ways. Occasionally she told her parents she was going to a study group before her first class when she was really meeting Bert at an abandoned church parking lot to kiss and feel their bodies pressed together for an hour before school. Sometimes he had tried to slip his hand under her skirt or sneak his mouth down the wide neck of her sweater, but she always maneuvered out of his attempts and talked for a while before letting him kiss her again. She was a senior in high school, and he was twenty-three, a slightly-taboo fact about their relationship that he believed would ensure him a life of excitement, but he was wrong. "Yeah, I suppose so," he said. "It is better than sleeping."

*

It was nearly six a.m., and Bert found himself roaming the streets of Marshall with Juanita Jane. After the four cups of coffee administered such strong bursts of caffeine that he could feel his pulse beating behind his ears and between his toes, going for a walk before bed seemed like a good idea.

"Do you know what the problem is ... with normal, adult life?" Juanita Jane asked Bert.

"Marriage?"

"No ... well, I wouldn't know. I guess on some subconscious level I must think so because I've always avoided it, but no. That's not what I'm talking about."

"Well?" he asked.

"Well what?"

"What's the problem? You started to say something. What's the problem with normal adult life?"

"Oh, yeah. Yeah. Shit. I had way too much to drink tonight and way too few pancakes apparently. Clarity's a problem," she said.

"So you forgot?"

"Forgot?"

"Yeah, you forgot what you were going to tell me?"

"No. No, I didn't forget. Are you ready for this shit?" she said, stopped walking for a moment, stared straight into his eyes, and continued on.

"Lay it on me."

"The problem is that anything real in life happens after two a.m."

"Isn't the slogan 'everything happens after midnight'?" he asked.

"I don't know. I'm not talking about a fucking slogan. I'm talking truth here. Think about it. I mean really think about it. Think about the most inspiring moments of your life. When did they happen?"

Her question made him stand still for a moment. The day was just opening up, the navy sky above fading more and more with every step they took, darkness replaced with orange rimmed clouds intensifying in color every minute, the hurried movement of squirrels and birds that signified the approaching presence of the sun.

"Well?" she said. "I'm right, right?"

On the next block over stood Bert's house, a small drab gray one-story stucco home, a house that lacked a porch or a basketball hoop or one of those mailboxes that looked like a green tractor, a house that lacked anything to make it stand out from the others. As Juanita Jane spoke, it was hard to believe that the house was there, that they could easily pass it by while his wife slept soundly in the back bedroom. "I suppose so, but you're missing a piece of the puzzle. It's what we call faulty reasoning in my field."

"Everyone knows that term. What? What piece am I missing?"

"Adults can stay up late too."

"But they don't," she shouted and playfully punched his arm. "And you're proof of that. I bet this is the only time in at least ten years that you stayed up all night."

"Not true."

"Stomach flu doesn't count," she said.

"I've had airline flights that left at five, and I—"

"You know that's not what I'm talking about. I'm talking about the passionate hours of youth, the passionate hours that we just stop visiting at some point in life. I'm talking about those hours when you actually live poetry. I mean, look at that," she said, nodding at the forming sunrise. Her voice was accompanied by a level of enthusiasm in her face that looked more like pain than pleasure, and for a moment her tangled platinum hair, smudgy eye makeup, and over-tanned skin was almost attractive to him. Juanita Jane was a mess, but for a moment it thrilled him. He enjoyed not knowing what she was going to say or do next. "I mean, look at us," she said. "We're out here. We managed to stay up later than even the last people leaving the last house party in town. We're experiencing that moment when the night intersects with the day. Can't you feel it? Can't you feel that anything can happen in these hours? We're off the grid," she said and took a right down Elm Street, moving further away from Bert's house.

"What grid?"

"The schedule. Adults live for the schedule. They have to always be somewhere, stick to the times, the rules. We're off, baby ... way off, and doesn't it feel good?"

"I guess so."

"Think about it. We're right in the middle of those hours of total delirium, standing right in the center of it. We can do anything right now, and it's like it doesn't matter, like the consequences of tomorrow don't exist. That's why young people do so much crazy, fun shit – because they're up late enough to not give a shit." The morning breeze picked up, pushing piles of dead leaves across sidewalks and over empty roads, Juanita Jane's hair fell loosely over her eyes and back again, and the first sliver of sun snuck into view out in the fields beyond the last row of houses. Everything was suddenly beautiful.

"I haven't kissed my wife in over a year," he blurted out.

"This is what I'm talking about. We've been living together for a month now, and you're just now talking to me ... really talking to me."

"Living together? What are you talking about? We don't live together."

"Under the same roof—close enough," she said, took off her heels, looped the straps between her finger and thumb, shoved the shoes at Bert, saying, "Hold these for me, would ya?" and walked on ahead of him barefooted.

"Are you crazy? You might step on glass or something."

"Glass? This is Marshall, not Vegas. Besides, my feet are so calloused I might as well be wearing shoes right now." He couldn't remember the last time Jean had worn heels like that. All of Jean's shoes were constructed in what she called the practical-comfort style, and she only bought shoes in black or brown, declaring that they would then 'go with everything.' But Juanita Jane's clothes went with nothing. She seemed to choose patterns and colors that couldn't be paired up with any other items, seemed to purposely dress herself in a constant contradiction. He looked down at the heels in his hand; studied the red soles, yellow heels, and hot pink straps; noticed that the same colors were expanding in the sky above him; and wondered if he could convince Jean to wear a pair of shoes like that. "It's weird," she said, with the obvious inflection in her voice that people use when they are seeking follow-up questions, but he didn't respond. "We should probably head back," she said, squinting into the rising sun. "I mean, we all know what could happen. We all know the obvious course of things after my little live-in-the-moment speech. We all know how I could stare at you in an I-want-you kind of way, how we could make out in this lonely road and stumble back to my room and fuck like all those other kids in the dorms. We all know that you are sexually desperate enough to ruin your life over twenty minutes of excitement and that I'm probably the right kind of person to help you destroy everything, but then where would we be? I mean, we're not doing this FDD crap to do what's expected of us, right? It's about something more than that, right? No more clichés."

He shook his head yes, but more out of an attempt to end her speech than to agree with it. Everything was piling up within him—the pancakes and the lack of sleep and the raspy rhythms of Juanita Jane's voice and the sun in his eyes and the possibility of all the things his life was leading to. All of it was swirling inside of him and making him sick. She was right; he suddenly felt alive in ways he had not for years, but he didn't like the feeling and wished his legs were younger so he could sprint back to the safety of the empty dorm room.

*

"Daylight ruins everything," Juanita Jane said when they reached the dorm building. "Next time we need to leave earlier, have more time to stand in the night." *Next time?* Bert smiled and nodded and handed back her crazy shoes. She reached out her bony arms to embrace him, but he turned his body to the side, only allowing one of her arms to find his somewhat stocky waist. She squeezed the fabric of his pants, said, "Sweatpants are a good look for a guy with your build," winked at him with one eye first and then the other, and then she was gone, tracking dirt and grass down the hallway, up the stairs, and back to her own room.

Chapter Seven

"Hey! Let me ask you a question!" Juanita Jane yelled into the hallway as Joy attempted to dash past the open door unnoticed.

"I'm in a hurry to get to class. We'll talk later."

"You are not. Your class doesn't start until four. Just come in here for a minute. I'm chatting with this guy on the Facebook right now, and I need to ask you a few things."

"It's not called 'the Facebook.' Just 'Facebook.' You sound like my mother."

"The wrinkles across my ass and that cherub-looking thing you got going on say I could be, but seriously, I need to know why all these younger women are shaving their cooch these days. I mean, what's up with that? Because ... the thing is ... this guy I'm talking to is all about it, seems to think it's a requirement now, that sex won't even work without a naked cooch. And I tried it once. I did ... didn't tell him that, but I'm telling you, and I think he'd think differently if he saw the rash it gave me. Nothing sexy about that."

"You do realize your door's open, that we live next to our students, right?"

Juanita Jane sighed loudly and threw her head back in that dramatic way teenagers do when they believe their parents have stepped out of line. "You and Lyla are the worst. I need to hang out with Bert more. He gets me. He's not so uptight," she said and shot Joy a look of wide open eyes and raised brows. "So just shut the damn door then if it's gonna be a problem." Joy wished she could shut herself *out* of the room and wished she hadn't said anything, knowing that shutting herself in would only guarantee that she stayed at least an hour. "Can you talk now, or would you like me to put some weather stripping around the door and window to keep all the sound out?" Juanita Jane asked as Joy sat down on the unmade bed.

"It's fine."

"So? Do you shave yours?"

"Well ... Miles likes it."

"Is that a yes?"

She nodded.

"Damn it. The numbers don't seem to be on my side with this one. I did a little statistical research online on the issue, and it appears that seventy-seven percent of women under fifty either shave or wax the thing and that the numbers are rising every year. The thing is ... it's starting to get serious with this guy, and I'm probably going to have to make a few changes before I meet him over Thanksgiving break."

"I didn't even know you were talking to anyone," Joy said.

"Well, it just started, but you know how the online thing goes. Once you start in, it's a fast ride to the meet-up. He friended me a week ago, we did the Facebook chat nonstop the next couple of days, he told me he can feel himself falling for me, and he asked me to start looking at flights to come visit him in Billings over the break."

"So you've never met this guy in real life?"

"Nope. I commented on his second-cousin's post. She was this crazy bitch I used to know when I worked as a waitress at Rush's, this diner on the side of the highway down in Shreveport ... anyway ... he and I got into this long debate about what I said."

"What did you say?"

"Her post was some bullshit about how The Civil War was

about slavery."

"But The Civil War *was* about slavery."

"I really don't feel like arguing with a Yankee about this right now."

"You do know what I teach, right?" Joy asked.

"No idea."

"Seriously? How many times have we talked about this?"

"Probably not as many times as we've talked about that crazy relationship you got going."

"I teach political science. I once taught an entire course on the history of the political implications of The Civil War. Trust me. I think I know what I'm talking about."

"Okay, okay. Whatever. You're the expert. We're getting off track. What am I supposed to do when I meet this guy?"

"Just be yourself."

"Says the girl who is secretly planning a wedding to a guy who doesn't want it."

"That's your interpretation, but that's not the case. You'll see. Besides, if this guy is telling you you have to change things about yourself and you haven't even met him in person yet, that seems like a bad sign."

"He's not. He doesn't know what I've got going on down there."

"And why is he even talking to you about this kind of crap before meeting in person? Doesn't that seem a little weird to you?" Joy asked.

"It's different now ... with the online thing. People have entire relationships before they actually meet. I once knew a woman who met this guy on the Facebook and got engaged and everything before even meeting. They planned the whole wedding and met up a couple of days before."

"And you think what I'm doing is weird? At least I know the guy."

"She knew the guy too. You're assuming knowing someone has to do with being next to him, but that's not the case, not always," Juanita Jane said and suddenly heard a tinge of ridiculousness in her own argument.

"Whatever. Shave it. Don't shave it. I really have to get to my office to grade a little before class," Joy said and left abruptly.

On the walk to her office in Chambers Hall, Joy wondered why she had been so short with Juanita Jane. Sure, the woman came off as having an overbearing and obnoxious presence with her early 90s music-video-hair and her hot pink nails and handbags and the way she stalked the other FDD faculty as they tried desperately to escape her desire for companionship. Sure, she spent most of her day sitting in her red dorm chair moving her eyes back and forth between the open doorway and the window overlooking the dorm entrance below, waiting frantically for someone to talk to. But Joy was lonely too. The semester of more time apart that Miles had suggested was harder than she thought it would be, and they were only a few weeks in. Maybe it wouldn't be so bad to spend a little time with Juanita Jane. Maybe the administrative guy was wrong, that the point of the FDD program wasn't to help the students at all. Maybe they were really there to help each other.

*

At dinner the next day, Joy didn't avoid Juanita Jane but walked right over and sat with her at the table by the long row of windows overlooking the brick building next to the dining hall. "So now I understand why people hire wedding planners," Joy said as she slid the green tray to the empty end of the table after removing her plate and cup.

"Why?"

"Because no one wants to talk about this stuff, so you have to pay someone to pretend to care."

"But you've been talking to me about it."

"I know ... but I can't talk to my mom or my grandma or any of my friends ... I mean outside of you."

"But that's not because they don't care," Juanita Jane said. "It's because you're a little on the crazy side—no offense—and planning this wedding in secret to a guy who hasn't proposed."

"I know. I wasn't talking about my situation. It's just something I was thinking—"

"Wait!" Juanita Jane yelled. "Holy crap! Wait! I was too busy enjoying these lukewarm mashed potatoes with cheese whiz to really hear what you were saying. Did you hire a freakin' wedding planner?"

"I spoke to someone."

"What does that mean?"

"I'm considering it. I mean, with my course load this semester and all the stress of trying to do this on my own, I think it might be helpful."

"You realize this is veering very close to insane territory, right?" Juanita Jane asked and scratched her eyebrow, unintentionally wiping away some of the makeup she always used to fill in the gaps left behind from over-tweezing. As she unknowingly rubbed some of the residue onto her temple, Joy watched but said nothing. Mentioning makeup mishaps to Juanita Jane seemed hopeless since she was bound to just make another mistake soon after the first one had been corrected.

"I don't know. Sometimes I'm not so sure anymore, but I've always believed that once you decide to do something, you better just do it. Otherwise, you'll always question yourself, you know?"

Juanita Jane certainly did not know. She lived her life in the opposite direction of this kind of advice. Hell, she wasn't even sure if she could make it through the semester-long commitment to stay in the FDD program. Years before, she had purposefully published less than was suggested for tenure, almost hoping to be denied. In the weeks leading up to the final decision, she dreamed of starting over somewhere new, stayed awake late and spread maps out across the huge floral rug in her bedroom. She scribbled names of towns she had never heard of in notebooks: Paradise, Nevada; Green Castle, Indiana; Vananda, Montana; Presidio, Texas. She filled pages and pages of these unknown towns, planning to close her eyes, point to one, and pick up and move there. Getting tenure meant staying in Marshall forever, but failure meant freedom. "Not really," Juanita Jane said.

"Well, anyway, I'm doing this, and trust me—it's not gonna turn out the way you expect."

Chapter Eight

"Are you going to skip Saturday dinner again?" Jean asked Bert during a quick call to his office between classes. "They're beginning to be suspicious."

"They've always been suspicious. Don't act like this is anything new."

"Well, are you coming? My mom wants to know how many plates to set out."

These kinds of arguments always infuriated Bert. Why did it matter how many plates would be used? The plates were always clean and stacked in the cupboard when they arrived, and Jean's mother always waited until right before dinner to take the plates out, so why did she need three days' notice to find out how many damn plates would be taken out ten seconds before dinner? "I don't know."

"When will you know, Bert? We can't go on like this, you know – you living in a dorm room and me staying here alone all the time."

"It's just a semester."

"A lot can happen in a semester," she said.

"You said you were okay with this, that we could make it work."

"Let's be honest. Okay? Can we just be honest for a minute, here?"

"Sure," he said and rolled his eyes.

"Honestly, I thought you would be home in a week, that you wouldn't be able to stand being away from me, from the house, from your whole life here. I thought you'd call me crying and tell me how being away just made you miss me and realize how much you have *here*. At the very least, I thought you'd be over here all the time, maybe spending several nights here a week or at least coming over for dinners, but you seem to be going in the complete opposite direction. I don't know what to think. I—"

"I can't talk about this now," he interrupted. "I have a class starting in three minutes, and I still need to take a piss. We'll talk soon."

"Just promise me you'll be at dinner on Saturday. Just give me at least that," she said.

"Okay."

*

"Jesus," Bert said when he saw Jean standing in the doorway of her parents' two story house. "What'd you do to your hair?"

"It's a new style I'm trying out."

"It's shorter than mine," he said.

"The woman at the salon said it would emphasize my cheekbones. Do you like it?"

No, he did not like it. As the brisk fall breeze tried to nudge him into the house, he stood still on the stoop and tried to remember the way her hair used to look, those first months of dating, when she flipped it over her shoulders in the bowling alley right before throwing the ball. It always seemed like a trick, that way women started out with long, sexy hair but kept going a little shorter, a little shorter, until one day it's just gone, and there's nothing left but eyebrows and pale lips.

"Well?"

"Yeah, it's fine. I'm just not used to it yet."

"Where did you get those?" she asked, nodding in the direction of his dark wash jeans. "You didn't have those before."

"I went shopping. What? I'm not allowed to shop for myself anymore? I'm not allowed to make a simple decision like picking a pair of damn pants out for myself anymore? I'm not allowed to—"

"You haven't bought yourself any clothes in the last ten years. Why do you suddenly have the need to shop?"

"I just felt like shopping."

"Well, they look a little young for you, if I'm being honest," she said and headed into the house.

*

After Jean's fourth miscarriage, her parents packed up and moved to Marshall. Her father's transition from city doctor to working in the small rural clinic ten miles out of Marshall had been a difficult one. Every time he complained about the ridiculous conditions in his new job Bert felt like he blamed him, like there was something about Bert that wouldn't allow a fetus to fully form in Jean's body. Even after her father's retirement, conversations in which comparisons were made between the old and new job came up too frequently, a fact that Bert decided could only mean that her parents used this subject as a way to punish Bert for not making Jean happy enough. And every time the comments were made, he noticed the way Jean's parents both turned to look at him, no matter where he was in the room, as though they took a kind of pleasure in seeing him squirm a little.

Sitting there at dinner, after missing the last four weeks, Bert wondered what had been said about him in his absence.

The house possessed a feel of temporary occupancy. Even though Jean's parents had lived in Marshall for eight years, they never really bothered to unpack. The spare bedroom housed piles of unopened boxes. Pictures leaned against walls, never properly hung, and they never considered stripping the bright pink floral wallpaper from the hallway, despite the fact that it was peeling away from corners, exposing dark globs of glue that had long lost their utility. "We'll just stay for a year or two," her father had said. "Just until you're feeling better again." But she hadn't felt better, and after the last miscarriage, Bert's decision to stop trying brought with it a wrath that her parents could only express by terminating all discussions of moving back to Madison.

And years later, there he was again, sitting across from two angry Midwesterners who would never state it outright but instead phrased their questions in such a way that everyone in the room knew. "So ... Bert ... what are you doing over at that college exactly? What is this deal with living in the dorms at fifty?" his father-in-law asked.

He was not fifty yet, still had another seven months to go, and he did not appreciate the slip-up. "Didn't Jean tell you? She said she told you."

"I guess she said something, but I don't remember."

"It's actually an important program they're doing. It's actually likely to revolutionize the way academic institutions do things, maybe across the whole region, maybe even the whole country. Who knows—I could be in the first cohort of something that really works. I could be one of the academic pioneers they'll talk about years and years from now," he said with a smug smile on his face. "But I'll have to tell you more about it next time. You see, I've actually got to get going. I have stuff to grade before bed tonight."

"On a weekend?" Jean's father asked with obvious judgement in his tone.

"Yeah. If I don't get started now, I'll be in trouble come Monday."

"That's hard to believe. I mean, how much time could it take to grade math homework? Don't you just look at a number and make sure it's the right one?" he asked.

"It's a little more complicated than that. I have to check their work, make sure they understood the proper way to work the problem."

"And that's the trouble with school now. Teachers are too focused on the process and not the end result. I can tell you, as a doctor, the only thing the patient cares about is survival. If I lost someone, no one gave a damn about the process I took to get there. No—no one. It was all about—"

"Just let him go," Jean said, and Bert was surprised by the authoritative way her voice sounded and by the fact that she had come to his rescue after being the one to put him in the situation to begin with.

"Will we see you next Saturday?" her mother asked.

"Sure, I'll be here," Bert said, but he knew that was a lie.

*

Bert hoped that Jean wouldn't follow him out, that her parents would have more questions just for her and trap her in that stale living room a while longer so he could get away, but he was not so lucky. Just as he reached the cool metal of his car's door, he heard that familiar screen door squeak and knew he hadn't quite made it.

"I just don't get it," she yelled as she raced across the lawn to his car. "What *are* you doing down there?"

"I told you. I'm helping."

"Helping what? Helping who? Just tell me," she shouted.

"I'm helping these young kids find their way in the world of college."

"I just don't get it. Is this because *we* never had a kid? I mean, are you trying to fulfill something that I couldn't give you?" she asked in a voice that was starting to shake.

"No. No, it's nothing like that. I explained all of this before. I don't have any weird ulterior motives. I never volunteer to do anything. Every semester I turn down study abroad. Every semester I turn down that trip to DC where they honor all the National Math Award recipients. I turn it all down. It was my turn. I was up—simple as that."

"I just can't understand why a math student would need to go on a study abroad trip anyway. I mean, isn't math the same world-wide?"

"It's not about that, Jean. You don't understand academics. They want us to shuffle around. We're supposed to present at conferences in far-away states and other countries. We're not supposed to just stay in one place. Everything with you is so stagnant," he said and immediately wished he hadn't.

"So that's what it is then, right? It *is* about me. That's why you're living there. Stagnant Jean. You just had to get away," she said, and he noticed the way that even the strongest gust of wind couldn't budge her shortly sheared hair.

"No, it's not about you. What I'm doing is important ... not that you would understand that. It's important for them ... and, hell, it's important for me. I'm changing. Being around them is making me remember things."

"What do you mean? What kind of things?"

"It's making me remember how my life used to be and how much it changed over the years and how I got to a point where I just couldn't do it anymore."

"Do what?" she half-shouted.

"This," he said and gestured with both hands at the air in front of him. "Any of this."

"What? Dinners with my parents? Nobody said you had to come."

"No. No, not just that – all of it."

"All of what?" she shouted.

"Our life, our life. I couldn't do it anymore."

"What do you mean you couldn't do it anymore?"

"I mean you are *always* around, and *they* — they're always around."

"They who?"

"Your parents. You and your parents. It's all you and your parents. All the time. It's dinners. It's church services I don't want to attend. It's stupid weekend vacations your mom thinks we want, but we don't want them. I don't care what Northern Minnesota looks like in the winter. I don't care about going on cruises. I don't care about any of it. I'm sorry, but I don't," he

Chapter Eight

said.

"So it's our life that you have a problem with? So you were running away? You didn't go live in the dorms because of some ultimatum by your boss; it wasn't you taking your turn, as you always said. You were running away from your life, from *our* life?" The look on her face pained him. It was the same look she had had after the first miscarriage, the same face she wore as he held her waist while she stared at her reflection in the bathroom mirror right after it was over, the face he had tried to avoid the subsequent times when he left the house for hours afterward. It was there again. He hadn't meant to see it, but he had forgotten to look away.

"It isn't our life," he said.

"What do you mean?"

"I mean all of this. It isn't ours," and then something shifted in her, and she got angry again.

"This *is* our fucking life," she yelled loudly enough to noticeably rattle the old woman across the street who had come outside first to check the mail, then to remove a few small sticks from the bottom of the driveway, and finally to move a small pile of leaves from one side of the yard to another, clearly all in an attempt to get a better view of the scene playing out in the house across the way. "It's our life whether you want to admit it or not. This is it. It's your fucking job that I followed you for. It's our fucking marriage, and just because it isn't the perfect picture you had in your head doesn't mean it isn't real. I hate when you do this. You *always* do this."

"Do what?"

"You always put me in these situations. My parents right in there and Mrs. Williams—do you think I wanted them to hear this? I'm the one who's been covering for you."

"Covering what?"

"Covering your stupid fucking decisions. Do you think my parents know how much you used to drink? Do you think my parents know that I didn't want you to go live in the dorms? Do you think I told them that? I didn't tell them that. In their world, everything's fine. You're just being the provider. You're stepping up, and now you have to embarrass me because now they're gonna know everything," she said and let out a huff in his direction that made her look like a pouting child. "Maybe I should be the one to stop caring for once."

He had a sudden urge to tell her things, to tell her about the night he and Juanita Jane had walked so close to his own house, to tell her how beautiful the young women who lived on the floor above him were on mornings when the temperatures were getting colder and they rushed out of the building in hooded sweatshirts over tight leggings. He wanted to tell her things as though she were a friend, but he knew he couldn't, so instead he just stood there and let the surge of her sadness and anger consume him. "That's fine," he said and pulled the keys out of his pocket.

"Don't you even want to kiss me goodbye?"

"What's the point? It's not going to lead to anything."

"What do you mean?" she said

"I mean that I'm tired of doing things in my life that go nowhere. Kissing is supposed to be a gesture that precedes sex."

"What are you talking about? We used to kiss all the time, and it didn't lead to sex. When we were first dating, we'd kiss for hours without anything else happening, and it was wonderful. Don't you remember that?"

"Yes," he said. "But that was when everything in life was leading up to something. Kissing was leading up to sex. School was leading up to careers. Saving money was leading up to a house and trips, but we've already done it all. We've already been there. It's not the same anymore. There's nowhere else to go, as far as I can tell. It's like one of those problems they spend years trying to solve only to realize the numbers are never going to line up the way they want them to."

"I need to get back inside," she said with a dullness in her voice. "I'm sorry, but I can't have this conversation with you right now. I just can't do it. Not now – not with my parents right in there and the open ears of the whole damn street around us. I just can't do this," she said and walked away from him and back to the house. And then he was free, finally free to drive away from all the awkwardness waiting for her on the other side of her parents' front door.

Chapter Nine

On the way back to campus from Jean's parents' house, Bert suddenly had the urge to stop off at The Steady Saloon. He pulled the car over and hesitated a moment before going in, thinking about the fact that, in his old life, going alone for a drink would have been an act perceived as betrayal by his wife.

Inside, the darkness of the bar, a stark contrast to the brilliant sunset outside, had a calming influence on him. As he made his way to the only stool without a cracked cushion, down at the end of the bar, he noticed that the place seemed particularly slow that night, even though it was still too early for the stream of college students to come through the door. He had heard that Saturday nights at The Steady Saloon were the bread and butter of the bar, the time when they made up for the long, lazy afternoons when old farmers staggered in to play illegal games of poker and bitch about crop prices and all the ways Marshall had changed since they were young.

"What'll it be?" asked the man behind the bar.

"Just a Miller Light for now."

"Miller Light? Man, not to get too in your shit, you know, but you look like you could use something stronger."

"Just the Miller Light for now," Bert repeated.

"Oh. Okay," the bartender said and threw his hands up in mock surrender before reaching down to pull a bottle out of the ice chest behind the bar. "Man, it's slow as shit tonight, even for this early."

Bert nodded.

"Any plans later?" the bartender asked Bert.

"Nah. Probably just heading back to the dorms," he responded, too quickly to remember how ridiculous such a statement would sound to a stranger.

"Are you one of those teachers who live in the dorms, that faculty in the dorms experiment thing?"

Bert nodded.

"No shit! This girl I'm seeing ... well, seeing is putting it a bit strongly ... sleeping with anyway. Anyway, she does that. She lives there too. Crazy small world!" he exclaimed and seemed to lean in closer to Bert, a move that could only mean the conversation was just getting amped up and not likely to finish quickly, as Bert had wished it would.

"Are you the one who's dating Joy?"

"Like I said, dating is putting a bit of a spin on it."

"That's weird," Bert said.

"What?"

"For some reason, I thought you two were serious. I thought someone said you were engaged, but now that I'm thinking about it, I didn't hear it from Joy, so never mind."

"Engaged? Ha! It's just something fun to do, you know. I'm not planning on spending my whole life behind this bar, and she'll likely be in this town forever. You see, the thing is," he said and leaned in even closer, as though he were about to reveal the world's biggest secret. "To her, *this* is her land of opportunities," he said and spread his arms out in front of him. "But, to me, this is the shithole I'm trying to get out of. I think it's a matter of where you're raised."

"What do ya mean?" Bert asked.

"I mean I'm from this place, and no matter how many town festivals you attend as a kid or how many this-place-is-the-greatest slogans the local commercials throw at you, no matter how many friends you have here or how pretty your girlfriend is, it's always going to be the town you've got to make it out of to know you did something. You know what I mean?"

Bert nodded.

"My plan is three years—tops. That's what I'm giving it, and then I'm getting out."

"To where?"

"I'm not sure yet. It could be anywhere really, but it's got to be out, like really out, if you know what I mean. I'm not going to be one of those pathetic assholes who makes the move to Sioux Falls and acts like it's a big fucking thing."

"So what's really out?"

"Five hours or more. That's my rule."

"And what'll you do when you leave? Bartend somewhere else?" Bert asked.

"Dunno, but that's not the point really. It's not about what I'm doing. It's just that I did it, that I left."

"And do you really think it'll be that different, working at a bar—or whatever—in another town?"

"Shit. Do you teach psychology? I feel like I'm really getting the once-over, but don't get me wrong, I kind of like it, this kind of questioning. It's rare to get this from sober people, so getting it from a guy only half into a Miller Light who'll actually remember this conversation tomorrow, it's actually pretty fucking refreshing."

"I teach math."

"No shit? Really?"

Bert nodded.

"Never would've guessed it," Miles said, shook his head, and walked over to the other side of the bar as two middle-aged men took their seats.

*

The music across the hall from Bert's room mixed rhythmically with a muffled sound that Bert imagined was the steady beating of a headboard against the wall. Something about the song had caught his attention, so he muted the late night talk show and focused instead on visions of the long-haired-sophomore-whose-name-he-had-forgotten bedding another beautiful freshman from the second floor. He found himself filled with envy and hatred. But it was that song, the heaviness of the low male voice and the extended dissonance of the chords paired with the driving force of drums that made him feel awake in a way the past decade had denied him. And he realized he hadn't discovered a new song in several years, maybe longer. Maybe that was the problem with being an adult, this lack of discovery, this need to always tune the radio in to channels that promised only the familiar tunes. "I need to ask him the name of that song," Bert whispered to himself. "I need to know what it is. It's incredible. Just incredible."

The song played a few more times, and then there was silence in the hallway followed by a loud knock on Bert's door. It was Juanita Jane.

"Oh, my God," she said. "Oh, my God. I can't believe what I did. Oh, my God. Oh, my God. Oh, my God. Oh, my God," she repeated over and over again and then slumped to the floor in a way that seemed to defy the gravity of her age and the stiletto shoes she stood on.

"What happened? What's wrong?" he said.

"Oh, my God."

"What happened? What did you do?"

"What makes you assume *I* did something?"

"Didn't you?"

"Well, yeah, but what makes you assume that?" she asked.

"Just tell me what happened."

She pulled hard at the hair behind her ears, looked up at Bert, and said, in a voice barely loud enough to hear, "I slept with the guy across the hall."

"Are you serious? That was *you*?"

"What? What? There is *no way* that information got out already. It just happened like five minutes ago. I *just* fucking left.

What are you talking about?"

"Relax. It's not in the paper yet. I could hear it. I live like three feet away," he said and nodded toward the hallway.

"Oh, thank God!" she yelled and started laughing uncontrollably.

"How did this even happen? Isn't he like nineteen? How could this happen?" he asked and suddenly wondered what he could be doing if he didn't have that wedding band weighing him down.

"What does age have to do with it? What are you saying? I'm so old I can't attract guys anymore?"

"He's barely a guy. He's barely out of high school. How does this even happen?" he asked.

"It's a bit foggy, truth be told, but I remember having some wine in my room and then walking around the halls looking for Joy. Never found her, but he was smoking in his room, and I could smell it, and damn, that smell gets me every time. Every single time. It's like babies and avocados."

"What?"

"Never mind. Inside analogy. Back to the story—so he said I could smoke a bit if I didn't 'tell on him.' Then one thing led to another ... and it turns out weed and wine are a bad combination if you're trying to be the responsible adult in the room."

"And that's what you were trying to be?" Bert asked.

"Obviously not, but that's what I should be, right? Isn't that the whole point of this, to teach these kids some lessons, some shit like that, and all I taught this kid is that sex with an older woman is 'totally awesome.' His words, not mind, but come to think of it, maybe that is a good lesson for this kid to have, make him look at aging in a whole new light. Maybe I altered this kid's whole perception of the process of living tonight."

"Or maybe he's just the kind of kid who'll take it where he can get it."

She shook her head vigorously, pulled herself up off the floor, glanced at her face in the mirror, and said, "Do you know what this means, what this really means?"

"What does it mean?"

"For one thing it means I might get fired, but more importantly, it means my own perception of age might be totally wrong. I mean, think about it—a nineteen-year-old. This blows the possibilities way open again. Way open," she said and spread her arms out in front of her.

"As far as getting fired is concerned," Bert started and sat on the far side of his bed. "Not gonna happen. Those administrators would be staring at a pretty huge double standard if they tried that. Look at how many male faculty are married to former students, hell, some of them even married while the student was still in the damn class, and administrators too. The provost himself is on his third marriage, this time to a student thirty years younger than him. I think you've got nothin' to worry about there, but the age perception thing seems wrong too," he said while inwardly hoping it wasn't wrong. "Think about it. This doesn't really mean anything. It just means that a guy was willing to fuck a woman who's older than him. So what? It's not a relationship. It's not love. He's nineteen and trying to create a story for future drunken nights with guys at the bar. That's it. It's a basic item on the checklist. Cliché even."

"Checklist?" she asked.

"Yeah, a sexual checklist. All guys have them."

"Really? Is it like written down?"

"No, it's not written down. It's a mental checklist."

"And what's on this checklist?" she asked with a grin on her face.

"You know, all the different things we want to do sexually."

"I know. I meant what *specifically*?"

"Oh, no. It's not like that. It's different from guy to guy, but the teacher thing—that's pretty universal."

"What's on *your* checklist?" she asked.

He thought about it for a moment, considered avoiding the question, but decided that if she was brave enough to confide in him, he should do the same. "Just between us, right?"

"Of course."

"Do you want the current list or my life list?"

"What's the difference?"

"The current list is all the things I'd like to do now, assuming I wasn't married," he said and instinctively pulled his wedding ring up over the knuckle and pushed it back down again. "The life list is all the things I've wanted to do since I was old enough to think about sexual scenarios."

"I want the life list," she said.

He felt his palms sweat and the skin around his eyes go hot, and he realized he was nervous, a feeling that had grown harder and harder to conjure up as the experiences in his life accumulated. "It's weird talking about this."

"Who gives a shit? Life's weird. I'm fifty-one and just slept with a nineteen-year-old," she said and giggled like a teenager.

"True."

"So? Are you gonna tell me or what?"

"Okay, okay. Just give me a minute to think. It's not like I'm thinking about this all the time. I've been married a long time," he said, obviously stalling.

"That doesn't mean you don't think about sex."

He took a deep breath and started in. "Okay, let's see ... there's the prostitute, the stripper, the pastor's wife—"

"Really? The pastor's wife? That's a thing?" she said and started to laugh.

"Are you gonna be judgmental? If you're gonna be judgmental I'm gonna stop right here."

"No, no judgment. Just surprise."

"Sounded like judgment."

"Surprise and judgment are not the same thing."

"Okay, let's see ... you made me lose my train of thought," he said.

"You said 'stripper, prostitute, pastor's wife,'" she said and stifled a giggle. "Keep going."

"Okay. Teacher, which, as we've established, is fairly common."

"Kind of like pastor's wife," she said and chuckled.

"Shut up," he said playfully.

"Sorry. Keep going. Keep going. You've piqued my curiosity."

"There's the threesome."

"Of course."

"The woman with only a year left to live."

"Really? That's a thing?"

"It's a thing for me," he said.

"I guess it makes sense, the whole living-life-to-its-fullest thing?"

"Yeah, exactly."

"What else?"

"I've always wanted to sleep with a woman who didn't speak the same language as me, you know, hear her shouting things in a foreign language, not sure what she's saying but knowing what she means."

"That sounds a little romance-novely for a guy, don't you think?"

"If you're gonna make fun of me, I'm not gonna say anything else," he said.

"I'm not. I'm not. Just making conversation. What else?"

"Lesbians."

"What about a gay man?"

"Fuck no!"

"Just kidding. Continue."

"My mother's friend ... obviously not now. A gymnast, someone I hate, a student, a masseuse, an orgy, a virgin, a stewardess, a nurse, a woman whose name begins with the letter Z, a stranger."

"I like how you just sandwiched student in there like I wouldn't notice," she said.

"Come on. You have no room to talk," he said and chuckled.

"Didn't say I did. So how many of those have you crossed off the list?"

"Not many. I got married too young," he said and felt a pang of guilt for enjoying this conversation so much and for not calling

Jean that night as he had promised he would.

Chapter Ten

The buildings at Prairie State College were simple, bland bricks, weather beaten from years of hard winters filled with blizzards and strong winds and summers where the raw sun beat down over the harsh landscape. Instead of the brick-laid paths of colleges further east, the paths at Prairie State were basic concrete with nothing but the occasional tree and short grass in the warmer months and a stark canvas of white during the long winters. Every interior wall was painted white, and plain tables and chairs filled the library, dining hall, and classrooms. Professors often referred to the look of the campus by using the word *institutionalized*, a comment that was always followed by the kind of laughter reserved for jokes visited too often. But none of this mattered at nineteen. College students didn't need the stimuli of lush gardens, hilly cobblestone streets, historic buildings, columns inspired by European buildings, or those long sweeping avenues lined with statues of important figures. Prairie State College proved that, even on the desolate landscape of the prairie, the excitement of youth spilled life from the students' faces onto every bland surface.

"What're you doing? Why are you still in sweats, and why's your door cracked open?" Juanita Jane said, standing in Lyla's doorway. Juanita Jane looked even stranger than normal, with horses painted across her cheeks and her hair pulled high into pigtails. She wore a tie-dyed Prairie State College sweatshirt with the bottom cut off so that it just met the hem of her short jean skirt and knee-high wedge-heeled boots over purple fishnet stockings. When she turned to close the door behind her, Lyla noticed the horse's tail pinned to the back of her skirt.

"My mom's stopping by for lunch," Lyla said.

"What? You're meeting your mom for lunch? It's freakin' homecoming. Aren't you going to the parade?"

"Wasn't planning on it."

"Well, you better come to the game later. Margie and I are going all out this year," Juanita Jane said.

"I can see that. What look are you going for exactly?"

"Just the fun homecoming look. Such a great perk of living right here on campus, isn't it? I never even thought about going to this crap before."

"I'm not sure how long lunch will go, so I'll probably skip the game this year."

"Nope. Not an acceptable answer," Juanita Jane said, and started inspecting the sparse supply of makeup Lyla had sitting on her dresser. "Do you realize half your lipsticks have *nude* in the color title? I never understood the natural look. I mean, if I wanted to look natural, why would I pay money for the stuff? Makes no sense. And don't even get me started on clear mascara. What the hell's the point of that stuff? Who's the market for that, people who want the uncomfortable feel of mascara with absolutely no benefit?"

Lyla looked at the clock and imagined how it would go if her mother walked in and Juanita Jane was there. How would she explain the presence of a person like Juanita Jane to a person like her mother? How much of this explanation would dominate the lunch conversation, and what would her mother think of her choice to do the FDD program when she associated the experience with this woman dressed as a trashy hippie horse? "Okay, I'll meet you guys at the game later," Lyla said, knowing it was the only way to get rid of Juanita Jane.

Chapter Ten

*

Being at the homecoming game felt strange to Lyla. As a student of Prairie State she had never attended a football game and only experienced homecoming peripherally by participating in the weekday activities of homecoming week, like the portable hot tub soak, the ping pong tournament, and an ice cream eating contest where she came in fourth after eating nearly a gallon of mint chocolate chip ice cream in front of an audience of far fewer people than the number of contestants. She never even considered going to the actual game. That was an activity delegated to the kinds of students who cared about the outcome of a football game or the kinds of people who cared about running into old friends from their college days years ago. She wished to be neither, and yet there she was, looking around at the crowd of current students and alumni from years past, wondering if there was anyone there who graduated the year she did.

"I don't think I'd ever come back here after graduation," Margie said. "It seems kind of depressing, don't you think?"

"Are you kidding me?" Juanita Jane piped in. "I'd be all over that shit if I didn't have like twenty guys from my alma mater who would like to harm me. Otherwise, it'd be kind of fun to walk around now, not knowing who I'd see at any moment. It'd be fun to see some of my old girls. The thing is ... you don't know what you're going to want twenty years from now. You don't know who you'll be then. You think you know what looks depressing on the other side of where you're at now, but you just don't know."

"I guess so," Margie said and pulled out a geology textbook.

"Oh, no. Hell no! You're not doing that here. Didn't those guards look through your purse? How'd that one slip by?" Juanita Jane asked.

"They were looking for guns," Margie said, and Lyla wondered if she really failed to get the joke.

"They should've been looking for books. This is freakin' homecoming. No books allowed," Juanita Jane yelled over the roar of the crowd as Prairie State tied the game. "I can't believe that's what you're wearing," she said to Lyla and pulled on the material of Lyla's jeans that bunched up around the knee.

"I'm wearing my school sweatshirt."

"Yeah, but who isn't? You're in the FDD program. You're on both sides, so you've got to be twice as festive," Juanita Jane yelled.

"How drunk are you?" Lyla asked and laughed.

"Not too bad. They took my flask when we went through security. What kind of crap is that? At least most of it was gone after the parade."

"You're insane. I can't believe you tried to take that in here," Lyla said.

"Just trying to have a good time and relax. If I can have one in my office, why shouldn't I be able to have one at a game?"

"You have a flask in your office?" Margie said.

"She's joking," Lyla said. "You're joking, right?"

Juanita Jane smiled in a way that suggested she wasn't and said, "Doesn't Margie look cute? Couldn't put her hair in the pigtails because it's too short, but doesn't she look so festive? Half those clothes are mine, you know." Margie's makeup was slightly bolder than normal with dark eyeliner smudged across the lash line and pink glitter across the lids. Her cheeks had a similar horse design to Juanita Jane's, and she wore a bright yellow dress Lyla had seen Juanita Jane's body squeezed into the week before.

"She does. She looks—" Lyla started and suddenly went silent. Everything around her—the strong smell of Juanita Jane's floral perfume, Margie's steady cheering for the outcome of the game below, the sun streaming into her face, the feeling of chilly fall breeze against her cheeks, the band playing YMCA again, the coach yelling at a player as he ran back to the bench, the cheerleaders dancing to the chorus of the band, and the older women behind her chatting about the complications of cooking the perfect roast—disappeared. There he was. *Anton.* She watched for a moment as he tucked the still-long hair behind his ears, and then she got up, mumbled something to Margie, and ran away, down ten rows of stands, across the front row, out of the stadium, across the parking lot, and into the open grass field across the road.

What was he doing there? Anton wasn't even on Facebook. How could he be sitting at the homecoming football game? In college, he had ridiculed things like football. Calling most sporting events a gathering for the idiot masses, Anton preferred a more solitary existence, spending long afternoons in his dorm room playing the same songs over and over again on his guitar, reading novels with a strong philosophical slant, watching long documentaries about causes no one in Marshall had heard of, and scribbling lyrics to songs he would never sing to anyone in the margins of his school notebooks. *What events must have transpired to bring him to Marshall for homecoming?*

After only a few minutes alone in the field, Margie came into view. "What happened?" she yelled while walking briskly toward Lyla.

"I just had to get out of there."

"Why? What happened? All of a sudden you were just rushing down the stairs. Are you okay? Are you feeling sick?"

"I guess I just started feeling claustrophobic," Lyla said.

"Oh, that makes sense. My mom gets like that sometimes, has to take these special pills to fly, and once completely flipped out in an elevator when we were staying in this really tall hotel in Chicago. We figured you had to throw up or something. Juanita Jane was going to run out after you, but I was pretty sure she'd fall to her death on those stupid shoes."

Lyla would tell herself later that it must have been the way the sun scorched her eyes or a lack of sleep the night before or the depressing conversation her mother always made during their lunches, but it was the sight of Anton after all those years without any explanation that made her cry for the first time in over a year.

"What's going on? Are you having a panic attack? It's okay. We don't have to go back there. I'll text Juanita Jane and let her know we're going back to the dorms, and she can meet us there. Truth is, I don't think she was having much fun at the game anyway. She kept making snide remarks about the girl sitting with Mark for some reason."

"I can't believe I'm doing this," Lyla said, more to herself than Margie. "I'm not supposed to be doing this, talking to a kid about this, but I can't just go back to my room and act like that didn't happen."

"What happened? And I'm *not* a kid. What happened? What's going on? You can talk to me."

"You know that guy I told you about, the one we looked for on Facebook?"

"Your college boyfriend?"

"He's at the game," Lyla said.

"Oh, my God! Oh, my God! It's a classic RCTHTBF."

"A what?"

"A random coincidence that has to be fate."

"That's an acronym?"

"Not officially. My high school friends made it up because this kind of stuff just kept happening, and now it's happening again, to you," Margie said and squealed.

"It's not fate. It's weird. This isn't the kind of thing Anton would go to."

"Exactly."

"What do you mean 'exactly'?"

"We have to go back to the game. You can't run away from this. Trust me," Margie said and reached for Lyla's hand to pull her back to the stadium in a way only a very young woman would do. "Come on. Don't you want to know what happened? Don't you want to know the truth?" Margie asked, but Lyla didn't know the answer. All those years back, the week after he ended the relationship, Lyla had struggled to even shower, her final exams didn't go well, leaving her nearly flawless GPA permanently scarred with the mark of the two Cs those exams had produced, and the entire summer after graduation was spent in a state of severe depression. So many of Lyla's life decisions were an attempt to cut Anton's memory from her consciousness, and now he was literally a football field away from where she stood. Margie was aggressively trying to pull her back into her past, but she was afraid she still wasn't ready to hear the truth about what happened all those years ago.

"I just don't even know what I'd say," Lyla said and stopped walking.

"Just say hi and ask him to have a coffee with you. Just do that. Was he alone?" she asked.

"I have no idea. I didn't really look. It was so weird. I just saw his face and ran out of there as fast as I could."

"Come on. How are you going to feel in a week if you just run away from this? There's no real way to get ahold of him if you don't do this now. He's not even on Facebook," Margie pleaded, but the truth was that Lyla knew several ways to get ahold of him. A little light internet stalking about a year before had revealed that he still used the same email address, his parents still lived in the same house in Fargo and had the same phone number she had called Anton on during the long summers of separation in college, and the uniqueness of his name made a search for basic information easy if she ever decided to look for his location. A few months after Lyla's divorce, she had even typed out an email to Anton, put the address in and everything, but closed the window at the last second before hitting send, too afraid to open herself up to another rejection if he never wrote back. Still, maybe Margie was right; running into him at a homecoming game was a lot easier than forcefully initiating contact out of nowhere. "I promise I'll stand next to you the whole time," Margie said, and there was something about a girl the age Lyla was when she first met Anton standing next to the woman Lyla was now that made her change her mind.

"Okay, but I'm just going to say hi, not asking him to have coffee. I'm just going to hear his voice for a minute, and then we'll go."

"Okay," Margie said, grabbed Lyla's hand again, and started pulling her back toward the stadium.

Chapter Eleven

Back in the stadium, Lyla felt like every rush of excitement through the crowd, every drumbeat from the band, every unified fist pumping in the air, every brown and gold ribbon waving in the wind, every scream, every smile, every person hoping for a win, all of it was for her. This feeling that it was only her experience with the world that mattered was one that she had forgotten about, an old sensation that had fallen away somewhere in the years after she had lived at Prairie State with Anton. But, as the nearly tied game on the field gained intensity, she wondered if Margie's idea about random coincidences could have some validity.

Anton spotted her before she reached him, got out of his seat, and walked over to the small aisle between the stands. "I didn't suspect you for a homecoming kind of girl," he said with a tense smile on his face that suggested he might be more nervous than she was.

"I thought the same about you."

"What's it been, over ten years, huh?" he said and tucked his hair back behind his ears. It was strange. Anton's shoulder length hair that had been so sexy in college suddenly looked a little ridiculous with its gray strands by the temples and the way it surrounded a face that now had tiny wrinkles around the eyes and more prominent creases below the outer edges of his lip line. Still, his face held onto that glow, that dreamlike gaze that had always made her feel like he would say something life-altering if she only stood next to him long enough.

"Close to twenty."

"No. No way."

"Yeah, I'm thirty-eight. You're thirty-nine. I left at twenty-two, so—"

"Shit. Really? It's so weird," he said, and Lyla glanced down at his hands. No ring.

"Yeah, it was a long time ago."

"Yeah," he said, and then they just stood there silently while pretending to pay attention to the game.

"She wants to know if you'll have a coffee or drink or something with her," Margie suddenly blurted out.

"Oh, no," Lyla said, aggressively shaking her head. "No, I—"

"Sure. We could do that," he interrupted.

"Oh, oh okay."

"Truth is I'm not really watching this. You should know ... I'm just here because Jar wanted me to come," he said and did that signature squint-at-the-end-of-a-statement thing Lyla had once found so endearing. "He's been having a shitty time with the divorce and all, so I thought 'what the hell? Why not?' Didn't even cross my mind that you'd be here," and she wondered if he was saying he wouldn't have come if he had known.

*

An hour later Lyla was sitting at the coffee shop in downtown Marshall across from Anton. "It's kind of weird being here again," he said and looked around at the row of dusty potted plants sitting in the windowsill in front of their table. "I wonder if these were here before," he said and touched a dusty leaf.

"Yeah, maybe. Probably," she said and realized she might not be able to figure out anything else to talk about after the plant conversation concluded.

"I mean, they would have to be, right? How fast does a potted plant grow? Not fast, right?"

Chapter Eleven 93

"I don't think so. I'm not sure," she said and pretended to take a sip of her still-too-hot-to-drink coffee.

"Yeah, yeah, me either."

It wasn't going well, and Lyla wanted to kill Margie for putting her in such an awkward situation. *Why had she thought this was a good idea?* They had nothing to say to each other.

"I'm guessing by the look of that soil that those plants have been here a long time ... I mean a really long time. Look. Normally, when you buy the soil you use for potting plants, it has that white styrofoamy looking stuff in it. You know what I'm talking about?"

She nodded.

"And look at this," he said and lifted a pot up so she could peer inside. "This soil is totally trashed. It's weird, huh, that these very plants might have been here back when we were in college?"

It didn't seem that weird, but she nodded.

"And now here they are, and here we are. Remember the first time we came here?"

She did. Being college students with no money, they hadn't really gone on dates, a fact that never bothered her as she'd rather spend time in his single dorm room anyway. But one night, after a couple of weeks of established coupledom, Anton took her out for a coffee, an act that seemed to solidify more than just a passing interest in her. As a college student, spending three dollars on a frivolous beverage could only mean that he was truly invested in being with her. "Not really," she lied.

"Really? You don't remember?"

"I guess maybe ... kind of ... I don't know."

"We used to come here all the time. You don't remember?" he said.

"Yeah, I remember coming here. I just didn't remember the first time."

"Oh. Oh, okay. How's your ... what'd you get?" he said, gesturing toward her cup.

"French vanilla latte."

"How is it?"

"It's good."

"Good," he said. Lyla scanned the room and wished desperately that she was one of the young women studying in silence at the table across the way. She remembered what it used to be like sitting there with Anton, the ease of their interactions, the fun they used to have as they mocked the speaking styles of their professors and invented itineraries for trips they couldn't afford.

"How's your coffee?" she asked.

"It's good. I'm not really a coffee guy anyway. Remember?" She did. She remembered the way he used to order a hot chocolate, the way he'd tell the barista, "Not too hot, just warm – but not too warm. Sorry. I'm not trying to be a pest." She wondered why he hadn't gotten the warm chocolate this time. "So why'd you come to homecoming anyway?" he asked. "I mean, it doesn't really seem like your scene."

"Or yours." She took a long sip of her latte and said, "I work here. I work at Prairie State."

"You do? I'm sorry. I didn't know that. I'm sorry I didn't know, but I guess ... how would I know? There'd be no way to know, right?"

"Yeah, of course not. I teach here."

"What do you teach?"

"History. Don't you remember I majored in history?"

"I remember. Of course I remember. You used to help me study for exams when I had that horrible Western Civ class with ... what was his name? What was his name? Oh yeah, Dr. Krenshaw. Yeah, that was his name."

"So ... yeah," she said as she aggressively played with a loose thread forming on the knee of her jeans.

"I can't believe you work here. Doesn't it feel crazy? Doesn't it feel weird working where you went to school? I mean, are any of the same professors working here that were here when we were? I think that would be *crazy*."

"Yeah, it is weird. I remember one of my high school teachers said she had gone to school there. She always talked about it, brought it up like once a week, kept saying how weird it made her feel. I didn't understand what she was talking about at the time, but now I do. Sometimes I forget for a minute that I'm on the other side now. Sometimes I see a college guy and think he's looking at me, but of course he's not." *Why had she said that?*

"Yeah, that would be weird."

"But there's something a lot weirder than that," she said and felt her face go hot as she realized she didn't want to tell Anton that she was living in a dorm room again at thirty-eight. She shouldn't have said anything, should have just left it at that, made herself out to be a successful professor. She should have just let him imagine her going home that night to one of the big Victorian houses on 10th Street.

"Oh yeah. What's that?"

She tried to think of a lie, but nothing came. "I actually live on campus."

"Really? Why?" he asked, but instead of sensing judgment in his voice, Lyla thought he seemed amused.

"It's this thing the administration is trying. They have this idea that if faculty live with the students, the students will be more excited about college and do better in their classes and stay here and graduate. *Retention.* That's the buzz word of the year. You see, the school is now partially funded based on graduation rates. Some dumbass in the state legislature thought that was a brilliant idea, so schools like this, schools that basically let everybody in, get totally screwed, so the last few years the administrative people have been coming up with all these ridiculous ideas to get more students to stay and graduate."

"And they haven't figured out that some of the students are just stupid and shouldn't graduate in the first place? Remember that kid in the dorm—"

"Cory," she interrupted. "I remember."

"God, didn't he have down syndrome or something? Why the

hell was *he* there? Remember that time when he drank too much and was running up and down the halls naked screaming, 'Somebody fuck me. Somebody fuck me'?"

"Shhhhh!" she said and made that lower-your-voice motion with her hands. "My students could be in here," she whispered.

"Sorry. So let me get this straight—they think that you living in the dorms is going to make a bunch of dumb fucks stay and graduate, like having their mom there or something?"

"I don't know. To be honest with you, I don't really know what they're thinking, and not all my students are dumb. Some of them are actually really smart."

"I know. After all, we went there."

"Exactly."

"Man, what's it like?" he said. "What's it like living in the dorms again? What dorm are you in?"

"Homestead."

"Wow. Crazy. Lyla Benson is back in the dorms. It's like one of those shows where you go back in time."

"Except that I didn't. I'm still thirty-eight, just living like I did back then."

"Crazy," he said and leaned way back in his chair with a grin spreading across his face. "This honestly might be the most interesting thing I've heard in a long time."

Chapter Twelve

In the middle of the evening news, there was a knock on Lyla's door. She got up, looked through the peephole, and there he was. Anton. She pulled the elastic band out of her hair, placed half of it in front of her shoulders, did a quick glance in the mirror, straightened the waist of her pajama bottoms, and opened the door. "What are you doing here?"

"I got bored at Jar's," he said and shrugged. "Wanna go for a walk?"

"How'd you know which room was mine?"

"Your name's on the mailbox," he said and stepped into the room. "Well? You don't look like you were sleeping yet. It's nice out."

"It's like forty degrees."

"Come on. If it were forty in March, we'd be in shorts."

"Yeah, that's true," she said and hesitated a moment. "Okay. Why not? Let me grab a sweatshirt."

Outside the late October air formed beautiful clouds of condensation with every exhale. An unseen owl hooted repeatedly, and the last leaves of autumn crunched and shattered under their footsteps. Lyla had always hated this time of year, had always stayed inside to avoid it. She hated the way the cold seemed colder than even those January nights when the temperatures fell below zero, hated the way her skin was never ready for it when it first arrived. She hated the way winter stood in fall's doorway, waiting for the right moment to rush in, hated seeing those last remnants of summer slowly destroyed as the air grew colder and colder with each passing day.

"I'm sorry it was awkward ... you know ... at the coffee shop," he said.

"It wasn't that bad," she lied.

"It was. It was awkward."

"Is that why you came over tonight, to tell me that?" Talking to Anton in the dim light of sparsely illuminated streets somehow seemed easier. Lyla had always felt her bravest in the hours between sundown and sunrise. There was something about the anonymity of not being fully seen that made everything feel less terrifying.

"Let's just say I wanted a do-over." She wondered what he meant. A do-over of the awkward conversation that afternoon— or something more? Was he really saying he wanted to go back to that last week of college when he had left her with no explanation? Was that what he wanted to change now?

She wanted to ask him this but instead said, "Yeah, I understand."

In college, Anton wore army green cargo pants and old t-shirts. His long, dark hair made him stand out among the other, more clean-cut guys on campus. During his junior year, he got his left eyebrow pierced, and he occasionally filled in for the often-unreliable bass player in his friend Jar's band. The audience was always small, and the songs they wrote were terrible imitations of the bands they adored, but Lyla didn't care. She sat in smoky small-town bars and made sure to clap harder and yell louder than anyone else there. She was in love.

As they passed the little houses on 3rd Street, the kind of houses that young couples moved into for a few years before they built enough equity to upgrade, she imagined moving her stuff into one of them with Anton. She would put a big green pot with orange flowers on the front stoop in the summer, ask Anton to paint the interior rooms a light shade of yellow, place the floral vase collection that was boxed up at her parents' house on a long shelf across the dining room wall, and buy soft lilac colored sheets for their bed. These were things that other people did so easily but always felt out of reach for Lyla. But that night, as he spoke about the monotony of working as the events coordinator for the Fargo library system, when he said, "I think it's time to get out of the library jobs. I think it's time for some kind of a radical change," it all seemed possible.

"I can't believe they let you work in the library with that hippie hair," she said and chuckled.

"Everyone is always giving me shit about my hair. What's wrong with my hair? You used to like my hair, remember?"

"I know, but you're almost forty."

"So?"

"So long hair at twenty-two is hot, but long hair at forty is getting a little creepy."

"That's such bullshit." His voice sounded angry, but even in the relative darkness, she could see a smirk on his face.

"Think about it. Just think about it for a second. When we were in college, who did you know that had long hair at forty?" she asked.

"I'm not sure."

"Oh, come on! Yes, you are. Who was it?" she said and picked up the walking pace a bit to get out in front of him so that when they rounded the corner she could choose the rural road in the direction going away from town.

"Just tell me."

"Dr. Morgan, the philosophy professor."

"That guy was like sixty."

"Nope. He was exactly forty your senior year. He still teaches here."

"Really?"

"Yes, really, and he looked totally ridiculous."

"But that was different," he said.

"It was not. You just want it to be different. It was the exact same."

"Now you're just being mean."

"I know, but I'm mostly just giving you crap," she said.

"I don't like that. Remember?"

And she did remember. In college, she had once pinched a tiny bit of fat on his side and made a playful comment about how everyone talks about the freshman fifteen but ignores the junior three, and Anton reacted by spending hours in the campus gym every day. He became so obsessed with the rowing machine that people started calling him Rowboy. Students became frustrated that the rowing machine was never open, and the exercise psychologist had to be called in to chat with him about the dangers of exercise addiction. The fat-pinching incident was so blown out of proportion that Anton's younger sister had even called Lyla to warn her to "be nice to my brother, or he'll find another girlfriend."

"I'm sorry," she said and looked down at his hands. It was strange. Sixteen years earlier those hands had traveled all over her body, held her face between kisses, brushed her long hair as they stayed in bed late watching rented movies on weekends, and now there they were, the same hands with the broad fingers and the three freckles on the left thumb that she couldn't see that night but knew were there. She had heard once that a human's skin completely regenerates every seven years, and it hurt her to know that the skin which had once touched her was long gone. She wanted to hold his hand, to lock her cold fingers in his, but she knew she couldn't and shoved her hands into the pockets of her sweatshirt instead.

"That gas station on College and 3rd looks really different."

"Yeah, they took down the old one and rebuilt a few years back," she said.

"Ah. Hey, do you remember that crazy Native American history professor? What was his name ... something like Nohotmo? No ... that wasn't it. What was it? Does he still teach here?"

"No, he doesn't," she said and felt a sudden and unexpected surge of anger. *What the hell was Anton doing? Had he come by to take her on a walk to talk about a retired professor with rage issues? What was the point of that?* The wind was picking up, and she could feel its bite penetrating the thin socks she had only intended to wear for sleeping. She thought about Margie's theory of random coincidences that were really fate, the way Margie had forced her to go back to the football game, and she wondered what Margie would think about the timid way she was acting now.

"That's too bad. I was hoping you'd have some crazy new stories about that guy. Remember the time he totally flipped out on that guy in class for wearing the Redskins jersey?"

"Yeah."

"I mean, I see his point. I'd probably be pissed about that too if I were Native American, but I just don't think people think that deeply about it, you know? I mean, you're from somewhere, so you cheer for the team, and you wear the stuff. You're not wearing it to make some larger statement about your opinion of Native Americans, you know?"

"Yeah."

"And then that time when he passed out mirrors to the white students and made us tell our reflection why we were disgusted with our ancestors. What was that? I mean, like I said, I agree with the fact that whites were awful to the Native people and all, but the way he went about—"

He was still talking. She could hear that his voice was saying things, but she could no longer hear what he was saying. She became fixated on the way his feet hit the pavement, that same slightly unsteady pattern of walking that she had forgotten about somehow, the way he always seemed to struggle to keep up with her steps even though he was taller. She looked at his face, noticed the way his eyes squinted up at the streetlamp and the way his full crimson lips exhaled between sentences. She could no longer contribute to this conversation because all the questions she had inside her were pushing at her mouth, forcing her teeth to bite the inside of her lip in a strange attempt to keep them in. *Why had he suddenly ended their relationship senior year? Why had he never contacted her again to explain? Why had he acted like nothing between them really mattered that much to him? Why was he able to move on with his life so quickly? Why?*

"I mean, it's weird to think that people you used to talk about so much just disappear one day, and you never know what happened to them, right? And it's weird that I haven't been back here much ... just a few visits to see Jar here and there. He's the only one of the guys who ended up staying here. Not surprising, right? I mean, could you picture Billy living out his life in Marshall?"

"Why'd you do it?" she suddenly blurted out.

"Why didn't I come visit Jar much?"

"No, to me," she said and realized her voice sounded a bit hysterical and definitely out of place with the tone he had set for the conversation. "Why'd you do it? Why? I mean, just leaving like that, just ending it, no explanation. You have no idea what that did to me." She stopped walking, faced away from him and continued speaking to the barren field beside the road. "I'm sorry—I know—we're supposed to be having this nice evening, this pleasant walk where we just talk about bullshit surface subjects that don't matter to anybody, but I can't do it anymore. I'm going crazy over here. I mean, how can you just walk and talk about Jar and talk about how the gas station was renovated? Are you insane? We went to Las Vegas to get married. I thought we were waiting for something bigger, you know, like a real wedding with your family and my family and a church and all that crap. I couldn't eat for weeks. My mom had to force me to eat a couple of saltines just so I wouldn't die of starvation. That was the summer after I graduated—saltines and stupid reruns of sitcoms just trying to get myself not to think about it. What the hell happened? Why'd you do it? I just want to know why," she yelled to the empty dark field.

"I don't know," he said with clear frustration in his voice.

She took a few steps, stopped, turned toward him, and said, "Look, you at least owe me that ... after all these years ... after all this time of going over and over and over what could have possibly happened. You at least owe me the truth, and I don't care right now if I look pathetic. I don't care if I look fucked up. I don't care if I sound desperate because, you know what, after tonight, I'm never gonna see you again, so it doesn't really matter anyway, but I need to know because, honestly, I really don't think I've ever been able to move forward with my life because I never knew what the hell happened. I mean, what happened?"

"I don't know."

"But you have to know because you're *you*. You're the one who did this. You're the one who came over to my room, handed me that box with my stuff in it ... and that stupid letter you wrote. You're the one, and I'm the one who was just completely confused. I'm the one who hated myself for throwing that letter away because later on I needed it. I needed some evidence of what the hell happened, and even though I was pretty sure I remembered what you wrote, I needed it, needed it so I could study every bit of it and find some clue as to how we went from being the happiest couple on campus to nothing."

"It was complicated."

"No. You don't get to say, 'It's complicated.' We're at least two miles from the dorms right now, and I am *not* walking back accepting that as your explanation. I gave you years of my life. The least you can do is tell me the truth."

"Can we just go back? I don't want to do this here," he said.

"You don't want to do this anywhere," she shouted.

"You were right. It was awkward this afternoon. It was awkward seeing you at the homecoming game. All of it was awkward, and I wouldn't have come if I thought there was any chance of seeing you there. It just didn't occur to me that Lyla Benson would be there, that you'd still be in Marshall somehow, that you'd—"

"No, I know what you're going to say next, and you're wrong about that. I have moved on. It's not like I just waited around this campus, this place, after you left, like I just waited around for you to come back. I'm not an idiot. I'm not pathetic. I had a whole life out there. I moved on—way on—got a masters, got married, traveled all over. I've done things, big things," she shouted and gestured wildly with her hands. And there they were again – fighting like they had so frequently in college. "And you're the one who chose this, the one who came to my room tonight ... asking me to go on a walk ... what did you think would happen? Did you honestly think this wouldn't come up, that we'd just walk around and talk about nothing for a while? You *had* to know this would come up."

"It was a long time ago. I don't really remember. I just—"

"Just tell me," she shouted.

He grabbed fists of hair on the back of his head, pulled his face to the sky like if he stared hard enough he could find the answer, a move he had employed many times in college. He shook his head at the night sky, exhaled hard, and said, "I guess I just didn't see the point."

"See the point?" she asked in a small voice, hoping he would go on.

"It's hard to explain, but it came down to not thinking we could make it out there."

"Out there?"

"Yeah. Beyond all this. College. Marshall. Somehow it seemed impossible, seemed like we'd crumble in the transition, like trying to move a gingerbread house to a different table or something."

"What?"

"I just couldn't see us on the other side of what we had in college. It seemed like we had done everything, like there was no way we could top anything, but what I didn't realize back then is that all of life is like that."

"What do you mean?" she asked.

"I mean it's always impossible to transition somewhere, and what you try to hold onto, those feelings of the first weeks together, they always leave somehow, whether you think they will or not. I started to feel stale to you, like I couldn't give you anything new. I remember sitting on that lofted bed in my dorm room with you, eating the same pepperoni pizza and telling the same jokes, and the look on your face was just blank, just bored and blank."

"So you threw us away because I looked bored one night?"

"No, it was more than that. I looked at my parents, at their life, just driving around together on Saturdays from one errand to another, arguing about whether or not to buy the shampoo the coupon was for, listening to talk radio in the car because they had nothing left to say to each other."

"But we wouldn't have been like that."

"But we would ... we would ... because everyone is like that if they stay together long enough. That's the whole point I'm trying to make; that's why I ended it. I couldn't stomach it. I couldn't let the girl I ran through spring rainstorms with, my beautiful kaleidoscope, lose her colors. I couldn't do it." She had forgotten about the old nickname, forgotten that he once bought her a kaleidoscope wrapped in a letter that explained how the colors and patterns inside reminded him of her, forgotten the way she had stomped the colorful cardboard tube after the breakup just to make sure no one could ever see those colors again before she threw it in the trash. "The only way I could guarantee that you'd stay the same to me was to walk away. I know that sounds crazy, but I couldn't watch us go to shit."

"You're talking about it like it was a TV show, like you wanted to cancel before the storylines started repeating and ratings dropped,but we were in love," she said.

"And this is why I couldn't tell you. I knew you'd try to talk me out of it, and I probably would have let you. But it was more than that."

"What do you mean?" she asked.

"I guess I just thought maybe there would be something a little more, you know—a little better than what we had ... just thought that I couldn't stop the search at my first serious relationship, that

I had to keep looking to make sure," he said and tucked his hair behind his ears. "And it was all happening too fast, too soon ... getting married at twenty-two ... that's some shit our parents did, not something we were supposed to do."

"Why'd you come over tonight?" she asked.

"Honesty, I don't know. I saw you at that game, and it was surprising."

"I was surprised to see you too."

"But that's not what I mean," he said, kicked a rock into the ditch, stared hard at her shadowed face, and continued. "You're still that girl, you know. You still look like her."

"That was a long time ago."

"I know. I didn't expect it, didn't think I'd ever see you again, and then there you were, talking to me at Prairie State College again, and you're still beautiful. And seeing you again made me remember that I never really said goodbye before ... I guess I couldn't quite walk away from that."

"So that's what it was? You just wanted to see me one more time, to say goodbye?" she asked, hoping the answer was no.

"Yeah, I guess so."

*

Back in her bed that night, Lyla watched the way a flickering streetlamp outside danced across the walls and ceiling of her tiny room. She thought about how he had been there, just an hour before, how he had stood silently outside her dorm door and said goodbye without a hug or even a handshake, and then he was gone. She closed her eyes, and the light and shadows rhythmically shifting around the room became the old colors of her youth, the reds and oranges, blues and yellows and greens, and those brilliant purple edges filled with light that defined the shapes and pictures as they slowly changed before her.

Chapter Thirteen

"I can't believe it. I can't fucking believe it," Juanita Jane yelled as she rushed down the dorm hallway toward Joy.

"What? What's going on?" Joy asked.

"That fucking Chinese place."

"What happened?"

"So I called in to order takeout. I just couldn't eat at that dining hall again this week, just couldn't do it. A girl needs a little variety every now and again, you know. So anyway, I called in, and on the way there, this asshole rear-ends me, holding me up for over an hour while we have to wait for the cops and deal with the insurance exchanges, etcetera, etcetera. You get the point. So I rush over to that Chinese place right after to pick up my food, and the bitch won't give it to me, says it's a 'three-strikes-you're-out' situation."

"What do you mean a 'three-strikes-you're-out' situation?"

"I mean the third time you don't go to pick up your food, you're done. It's like you're blacklisted or something, and this is the only Chinese place in Marshall. What the hell am I supposed to do now if I want Chinese food? God knows I'm not driving to Sioux Falls. That's an hour and a half," she shouted.

"What happened the other two times?"

"What?"

"You said it was three strikes. What happened the other two times?" Joy asked.

"Oh, hell, I don't know. I think one time I realized I didn't have enough money in my wallet and just said forget it. The other time ... I don't remember. Maybe I decided I wanted something else ... I don't know, but that's not the point. I got *rear-ended.*"

"So the other times—did you call and let them know you weren't coming, you know, before they made the food and all?"

"I don't know. I don't remember. That's not the point. I seriously feel like this is just one more example of karma biting me in the ass for leaving Kyle at the altar. My mom said, you know, that karma would kick me in the ass."

"I'm pretty sure leaving someone at the altar has larger karmic implications than not being able to order Chinese food," Joy said.

"I don't know. I wouldn't be so sure."

*

The harsh sound of Juanita Jane's heels on the hard tile of her classroom helped to instill a hint of fear in the minds of her students as she passed out exams quickly, reminding students to please put their cell phones, notes, and books away before starting the exam. It was the Monday after homecoming, a day when many students fought with exhaustion after a weekend of partying and little sleep, a fact that hadn't occurred to Juanita Jane while she had made the syllabus for this course. Maybe this was another benefit of the FDD program, a reminder of what students' lives were really like outside of the confines of the classroom. In the past, the habitual yawns seen so often during a Monday morning lecture had enraged her, making her feel like students lacked respect, that they should at least have the simple discipline of stifling the appearance of boredom, but something was different now. And when she saw Trevor Bridgeworth, the shy student with a crooked hairline who always sat in the front row, struggling to stay alert as he scribbled answers across the page, she found herself wishing he had stayed up all night, wishing his weekend had been too exciting to study, wishing he would fail the test but that he had found something better. She imagined him drunk and cartwheeling down the empty hallways of late-night dorm buildings, imagined him stumbling back to his room with a doe-eyed sophomore, imagined him wrapped up with her all night, a smile spread across his face in a way Juanita Jane would never see.

"Dr. Ruckler?" Matthew, the worst student in class said, interrupting Juanita Jane from her exam day fantasies. "Can I go to the bathroom?"

"Sure. Just leave me your phone, so I know you're not cheating," she said.

He paused for a moment, scratched the pimpled skin above his eyebrow, and said, "Oh. Oh, that's okay. I guess I can wait" before sitting back down.

*

"So he didn't even pretend to go to the bathroom, you know, to cover up the fact that he was trying to look up answers on his phone?" Margie asked before taking another sip of wine.

"No. Crazy, huh? Dumb bastard! I mean, if you're gonna try to cheat, go ahead and try, but at least be a little sneaky about it. At least give me that," Juanita Jane said.

"And this is why I couldn't be a teacher. I hate being lied to," Margie said.

"So what are you going to do?"

"Dental school. I mean, think about it, it's really hard to lie to a dentist. People try, but the teeth don't lie."

"Trust me, I know. You can't get away with *anything*. I remember this time in my twenties when I went in after a summer of nothing but sex and drinking, didn't want to go, but my mother made the appointment and gave me the guilt trip really bad that time, kept saying she'd still have to pay even if I didn't show up, preaching about how it would embarrass her so much to have a daughter who couldn't even keep an appointment, so

I went. I went, and it was *awful*. Those dentists are worse than psychiatrists. In therapy, you can at least hide things by staying silent, but at the dentist it's like your whole god-damned life is out there on display, and it was bad. I was bleeding even before he took the floss out. 'Do you even own a toothbrush?' he said. Well, yeah, I did, but I barely ever slept at my own place and probably passed out most of the nights I did, and maybe I *didn't* own one. Who knows? Truth be told, even if I did, I was more of a dab-a-little-toothpaste-on-your-finger-just-to-get-rid-of-morning-breath kind of girl back then anyway," Juanita Jane said and laughed.

"That's crazy! I feel guilty if I go a day without flossing," Margie said and shook her head.

"And that's why you're hanging out with a professor and not having an orgy with the rugby team."

"Chad would kill me."

"Chad would never know, and, speaking of Chad, a long-distance relationship sure seems like an odd choice for a girl who can't stand the thought of being lied to."

"Are you kidding? No, he's not like that. He's very chaste. Trust me, he goes to church twice a week."

"Ha! Believe me, church has nothing to do with it."

"Well, it does with him, and you're in a long-distance relationship too, right? Aren't you talking to that guy on Facebook?"

"Yeah, we're talking, but it's different with me."

"What do you mean, it's different?" Margie asked with a furrowed brow.

"Just different. I'm not looking to marry this guy, not even looking to fall in love. It's all just a fun flirtation leading to a long weekend in Billings with him over Thanksgiving and not necessarily anything more," she said.

"Okay," Margie said with the kind of exaggerated nodding that always accompanies a lack of understanding.

Juanita Jane turned on the TV, flipped through a few channels before settling on an MTV Unplugged concert featuring a band she hadn't heard of playing the kind of music her younger self would have gotten high to. She thought of Donny, the guy who referred to himself as her Facebook beau, the fifty-five-year-old truck driver with the receding hairline and stocky frame, the guy who was probably waiting by his computer for her to respond to his latest message. She watched the way the singer on TV cradled his guitar like a lover, the way he seemed to search the air in front of him for words before he sang them, the way his body rocked to the beat of the bass behind him. She studied it all and thought of Mark, the nineteen-year-old she had slept with the week before, the boy with the guitar who lived in a room just two stories beneath her.

*

Late that night, Juanita Jane finally signed into Facebook, noticed the red number 10 above the message inbox, and clicked to read the messages:

Hey baby, I hope you had a great day teaching today.

Just thought I'd check in to see how everything's going over there in Minnesota.

I had a killer of a day out on the road, got 2 speeding tickets trying to rush an order of blinds over to Home Depot in Tacoma, got there 5 minutes before my deadline but still caught hell from my supervisor for the tickets.

Thought it might be nice to have a little sex talk before I go to sleep in this dumpy Motel 6 room.

Are you ok baby? You haven't signed in all day.

Busy day?

Crazy students?

Please write back babe. I'm going crazy missing you.

I keep scrolling through your pics over and over again, especially that tits shot you sent me last week. Love that one!

So here's a thought. Maybe we should move this Facebook chat along a little bit, talk on the phone or something. My cell's on my page if you want to talk. Would love to finally hear that voice baby.

She started typing but stopped. Maybe hearing his voice *would* be a good idea, maybe it was just what she needed to break up the monotony of a Monday night. She stared at the stack of composition papers, thought seriously of grading them, but decided to call Donny instead.

"Hello?" His voice was dull and distant, the kind of voice that was hard to assign to a particular region, the kind of lifeless voice that might be chosen to read names at a graduation ceremony. Juanita Jane was not excited.

"Hi, it's me, Juanita Jane. I thought I'd take your advice and do this phone thing."

"What you up to, pretty lady?"

"Just got home from work."

"And what does home look like to you?" he asked.

She looked around—the cinder block walls, the small student desk, the twin bed with its metal frame and the colorful but oversized bedspread she had to fold over so that it wouldn't touch the dusty tile floor. She considered telling him the truth but instead said, "You'd really like it. It's an old farmhouse, about a half mile out of town. I rent out the acreage, make a little side money from that endeavor, but the house itself is fabulous. I have this great reading room with all these great paintings done by artists I met while I was studying in Slovenia, you know, the kinds of paintings that are more about the colors than the images, lots of deep blues and oranges. It's really something, and my bedroom ... that's where I am now."

"What's *that* like?" he asked and made a clicking sound with his mouth into the phone.

"It has these great original hard wood floors. I had to have a guy in here to redo them after I bought the place. They were in awful shape, but you should see it now. I kept the wallpaper, almost had to. It'd be a crime to take this stuff out ... so ornate with its black and gold pattern. I bought this amazing plush gold comforter just to bring out the pattern. And the kitchen—don't even get me started on that. It's so cool and retro, hasn't been

redone since the sixties. I found this red fridge from the era to really emphasize the charm. Hell, I've even started incorporating more of those old recipes into my repertoire, you know, meat pies and stuff with gravy and real bread. I'm not talking about that grocery store crap with forty calories a slice. I'm talking butter. I'm talking *real* eggs, none of that egg-whites-in-a-carton crap."
She wondered why she was lying but couldn't stop herself. Why be an aging woman living in a tiny dorm room when she could be sitting on a big bed in a quirky but stylish farmhouse bought and paid for?

"That's great. I'm still shacked up in a one-bedroom apartment over the movie theater. Maybe I should come to see you over Thanksgiving instead of the other way around."

"Oh, no. No. I've never been to Billings, always wanted to go but never been. I'm looking forward to the change of scenery."

"Speaking of change of scenery, when you gonna send me the pic to match the tit shot? Know what I mean?" She looked out the window and saw Mark entering the dorm building alone. "Well?" he urged.

She didn't want to talk about this, didn't want to imagine this man getting off to carefully posed shots of her aging body, and she didn't want to continue this conversation with the man who didn't even look attractive in his profile pictures.

"You could always send me an ass shot, if you're not ready to give me the full view yet," he said.

"You know what, I see my mother pulling up the drive right now."

"At one in the morning?"

"Yeah, the woman knows no bounds when it comes to time. I blame her old career as an overnight waitress. She could never switch back to a normal schedule after that. She's coming up to the door now. Gotta go. We'll chat soon."

She hung up the phone and rushed downstairs to stage an accidental run-in with Mark before he got to his room. There he was, coming down the hall with a guitar strapped on his back and the kind of dirty blond hair that only existed in those years right between childhood and maturity. He was beautiful.

"Where you coming from, stranger?" she asked him and suddenly realized that she had forgotten to put shoes on before rushing down to see him.

"Had a gig at The Steady Saloon. Good gig. Paid fifty bucks."

There they were—a teenager with a guitar and a woman in her fifties who wasn't wearing any shoes. Still, she had been in his bed a week before—proof that anything was possible. "Cool. Cool. Want to hang out for a little while?" she asked and blinked at him in that slow way that had always intrigued men when she was younger.

"I'm really tired, got a test tomorrow ... probably shouldn't."

"I've got beer in my room," she said and pointed up.

"I don't know. I'm not sure," he said and scratched the barely-there stubble on his chin. "Okay, yeah, I guess so, but just for a little bit."

Chapter Fourteen

There were a lot of ways for a woman to start a day – the blaring and unwelcome sound of an obnoxious alarm, a gentle nudge from a sweet lover waiting for morning kisses, the slow waking of a lazy Saturday with no obligations, the steady and cheerful chirping of birds beyond the window, or a loud knock on a dorm door that couldn't be answered because there was a nineteen-year-old guy still sleeping on the bed beside her.

"Shit," Juanita Jane whispered to herself, looked over at Mark's nearly hairless thigh poking out of the hot pink sheet that covered the rest of his body, pulled the sheet back over him, and whispered, "shit" again.

She held her breath, used her bottom teeth to peel the last layer of yesterday's lipstick off her lips, and waited a moment. Just as she started to stand up, the knock was there again. "No, no, no," she whispered. "No, no, no."

"You don't want to miss the meeting," Joy's voice yelled through the door. "It starts in three minutes."

"I'll meet you down there," Juanita Jane yelled.

"What the fuck?" Mark yelled while sitting up so quickly he almost shoved Juanita Jane off the bed as he shifted his body's position on the tiny mattress. "What time is it? Why didn't you wake me up?"

"Shh!" Juanita Jane urged, but it was too late.

"Who is that? Do you have Sean in there?" Joy yelled through the door again.

"Yes. I'll meet you down there. Just go down, and tell them I'm on my way."

"Who's Sean?" Mark asked.

"Shh," Juanita Jane said again and looked at him with eyes wide with fear and layers of smudged liner.

"Come on," Joy yelled. "I can hear everything in there. Who is that?"

"It's Sean. I'll meet you at the meeting. Just go on without me."

"But I heard him say he isn't Sean," Joy said.

"Can you please cut me a God-damned break? I'll tell you after the meeting," Juanita Jane said, and because Joy couldn't stand the thought of being late to anything, she agreed and went away.

"What time is it?" Mark asked. "Is it Wednesday?" Juanita Jane studied his morning face, the way the skin looked more radiant around the eyes than it had the night before, the way his lips were fuller, and the beautiful way his tousled hair caught the late autumn sun. She knew he was staring at a very different picture, knew that her morning face had long lost the light of its once youthful glow, that she had to now rely on low lighting and the magic of makeup, that the strong sun of morning only emphasized everything she didn't want him to see.

"It's Tuesday, and you better get out of here before anyone else comes by looking for me."

"I thought there weren't rules about co-ed visits in the dorms here, and you're the one in charge anyway, so what's the difference?" he asked.

"First of all, I am not *in charge*. I just live here, same as you, and second of all, look—I like you, kid. Obviously. I mean, who wouldn't, right? The sex is great. You're about as sexy as a person can be, and the way you play that guitar, I mean, holy shit—so good, but the thing is ... the thing I'm worried about is that other people might not understand. People don't really get me, don't really get the fact that I'm more like you than like them. I might be a little older than you, but come on, we're really the same, right?"

"Shit. It's after nine?" he said, squinting at his phone. "I gotta go. Unless you can talk to my math prof about his dumb-ass attendance policy."

She watched him get dressed, watched the way he bent all the way down to pick up his socks instead of retrieving them with his toes and sitting down to pull them on as middle-aged men so often did. She watched the way his strong legs lunged into tight jeans and the aggressive way he pulled on his sweater. She watched his face as he did a quick glance in the copper colored mirror sitting on her desk, and she wondered what would go through his head that morning as he rushed to make his first class.

"See ya," he said over his shoulder while heading for the door.

"Don't I get a goodbye kiss?"

He turned to look at her, this woman he had now slept with twice. She puffed up her lips and leaned forward on the bed, wearing that see-through yellow nightshirt with the purple and orange flowers lining the low-cut neckline. Her toenails with the chipped purple polish were in desperate need of a pedicure, and her makeup had somehow shifted sideways in the night. "I gotta run. I'm really late," he said, grabbed his keys off the shelf by the door, and then he was gone.

*

"So we're at the halfway point now," Mr. Administration said. "What I really want to do today is just have a conversation about how this is working – what you're learning – and I'd like to discuss any data you've collected the past few weeks." *Data*? Juanita Jane wasn't aware that they were supposed to be collecting data. Hell, she wasn't sure if this guy in the gray suit would care to know about her data anyway. And what would she tell this guy anyway, how she'd learned that living in a tiny room did have its benefits, that it was a hell of a lot easier to clean a ten by ten box than an entire apartment? Would she tell him how she discovered that nineteen-year-old girls who were having a hard time socially were actually fun to drink with, that nineteen-year-old guys weren't off-limits sexually to a woman in her fifties? Would she tell this guy that the idea of moving *out* of the dorms seemed as painful now as it had back when she was twenty-three, back when she stood sobbing in front of the white-columned building wishing she could stay just one more year?

"Well, I, for one, think it's working," Bert said.

"Can you elaborate?" Mr. Administration asked.

"Sure. Sure, I can. The thing is ... I've never felt so connected to my students before ... well, at least not since that first couple of years teaching. You know the years, those early days in the classroom where you learn everyone's names and you talk about your weekends with them, find out who has a baby blue 1970 Beetle, who went to Maui over spring break with their rich grandpa, who doesn't give a shit about the football team, who has a crush on the hot history teacher ... you know, that kind of shit. But then, at some point, you just stop seeing them. They're just kind of there, but they might as well not be. You're writing math problems on the board, and every now and then you look out, but it's just a sea of faceless bodies sitting there, at least that's what it was like for me. But then I moved here, and they were here again, I mean really here. I could see them again. And the really surprising thing is that this actually made me remember what it was like to *be* them," he said and shook his head. "Crazy shit."

"But how do you think this is affecting retention efforts?" Mr. Administration asked.

"But that's just facts and figures," Juanita Jane said, sitting awkwardly on the sofa arm next to Joy. "I think what Bert is getting at is that this is so much more than that."

"But we're here for retention, to try to get students to feel more connected to Prairie State, to make sure we get these guys through in four years, five tops. That's the whole point of the FDD program. Bert, you're a math guy. You know what I'm talking about," Mr. Administration said.

"I understand that that's the intention here, but what if that's not the real benefit of the program, what if it's more than that?" Bert asked.

"What do you mean?"

"What if this program isn't making the students care more, but it *is* making us care more?"

"But how does that help retention?"

As they spoke, Lyla thought about Anton, remembered the way he used to shake out his snow-filled coat in college when he got to her dorm room after a late night of studying in the library, remembered the way his long hair was speckled with snowflakes when he first arrived, remembered the way his skin felt cold against hers after he first got in bed, remembered how it felt to touch his hot skin until the early hours of dawn. When she first got the job at Prairie State, she worried it would be too painful to be there again, immersed in the places where she and Anton had fallen in love, but it was easy. While teaching, she was safely on the other end of things, firmly positioned on the professional side of campus, but it was different back in the dorms. The tiny bed, the small closets where Anton hung his army green coat, the desk chair where she leaned back against the wall and spent long afternoons talking to her friends back home, the small shower stalls where she had washed Anton's hair one night when everyone around them was sleeping—all of it was the same. She was back in it again, and she didn't want to be there anymore.

"Maybe it doesn't help," she said. "Maybe this whole thing was a bad idea."

"Let's not get ahead of ourselves," Mr. Administration said. "We have the funding for this until the end of the semester, so let's not come to those kinds of conclusions yet."

"Maybe you could ask the students," Joy said.

"How would we do that?" Mr. Administration said.

"Just talk to them," Joy said.

"Do you mean an open-ended survey or a closed-question survey?" he asked.

"What the hell does that mean?" Juanita Jane said.

"The open-ended survey would consist of a collection of interview questions where students could speak more freely and answer questions about the program. The closed-question survey uses a series of questions where respondents select answers based on a scale," he said.

"Like how much do you like sex—one to five? Like that kind of shit?" Juanita Jane asked.

"We would never ask students a question like that. That has absolutely nothing to do with the retention issue."

"I was joking."

"Do you think *you* could write and administer some kind of survey?" he asked and looked at Bert.

"I'll see what I can come up with."

*

"It's weird how hard it is to decide on a cake," Joy told Juanita Jane. "I mean, do I want a rustic looking cake, like this one?" she said and pointed to the picture of the two-layer round cake in earth tones with only a few white frosting flowers poking out here and there. "Or do I want something a little more elegant, like this?" she asked, pointing to a three-layer square cake with black and white icing in a chessboard design. "I mean, if I choose this elegant one then I'd have to totally rethink the dresses I've been looking at and go with something in satin."

"You haven't bought a dress yet?" Juanita Jane asked. "Don't you know it takes months to get those things altered and ready to go?"

"Oh, I know. I'm not getting anything too crazy ... probably just going to buy something in white off the rack. I really need to get going on that, maybe head over to Sioux Falls some Saturday and see what they have at the Bridal Mart by the mall. What do

Chapter Fourteen

you think of *this* cake?" she asked and pointed to a cake in the shape of a star with layers of rainbow icing down the sides.

"I think my niece had that at her birthday party the year she turned two."

"I really think I like this," Joy said.

"Don't you think the whole rainbow star thing is a little weird, a little too this-wedding-is-the-brain-child-of-an-insane-woman?"

"No," Joy said and play-kicked Juanita Jane in the ankle. "Unique wedding cakes are totally a thing now. I was reading an article about it. People plan the whole wedding around the cake now. It used to be all about the dress, but things have shifted. Now it's all about the cake. And those rainbow colors open up a whole world of possibilities. Suddenly the bridesmaids don't have to match, the flowers can literally be anything. I think it's really cool, and think of all the great things rainbows symbolize—like hope."

"Hope that the groom shows up."

"Oh, he'll show up. You should have heard all the things he said to me last night. It was amazing."

"Like what? What did he say?"

"He had this crazy shift yesterday. They got totally slammed, every table in the place packed. That band from Fargo, the one with the really old guy who raps, was playing, and Miles was the only bartender working because Chelsea called in sick again, so he was in way over his head all night. He called me around two for a ride home, and it was amazing. I've honestly never seen him like that. He wouldn't get out of my car when we got to his place. He just kept saying he doesn't know what he'd do without me, that he's so into me. And there was something in his eyes last night, like maybe he really wasn't in love with me before, but I know he is now. He had this brightness in his eyes. I've never seen that before." As she spoke, Joy's legs danced up and down off the edge of the dorm bed, and her body rocked back and forth like she heard music in the story she told.

"So he had you pick him up because he drank too much at

work last night?"

"No, it was more than that."

"Did he drink last night?"

"He always drinks at work. He's a bartender. It's just kind of part of his job."

"Look, I don't want to be the killer of dreams here. Hell, I'm actually really enjoying this crazy project, and everyone wants to know." Joy wondered who *everyone* referred to. "We're all curious about where this plot is headed. We all want to know if the guy shows up or not, but you haven't really done anything yet, right? You haven't really put any money into this yet, right?"

"Just the deposit on the wedding coordinator and the preliminary deposit on the community center."

"I thought we were doing a whole winter wedding at the state park thing," Juanita Jane said.

"We are, but that's just the ceremony part. Shelly thought it would be too cold to expect people to stay after the ceremony, even with coats on."

"I have to admit I agree with Shelly. Outdoor winter wedding seems a little nuts."

"Yeah, she thinks I should do the whole thing at the community center and just skip the outside part, but she's from Florida. She can't possibly understand how not-a-big-deal an outdoor winter wedding is to my North Dakota relatives. You'd think she'd have come around to the idea a bit after working in the wedding industry here for so long."

"Look, I really think you should call the whole thing off," Juanita Jane said. "And trust me; it's hard for me to say this because, honestly, I live for the craziness, and this is so far up my alley I can feel it pressing against every inch of my skin, but you can't do this to yourself. Look, this Miles guy got drunk last night, called you for a ride because he knows you'll always come running, so you picked him up, he spouted off a bunch of stupid drunk talk, and that's it. That's all you have here. If he wanted to marry you, he'd marry you on his own watch." *Who did this*

Chapter Fourteen

Juanita Jane woman think she was, Joy wondered. She wasn't in the car when Miles had said all those wildly romantic things the night before. She was just an aging woman with no life left of her own who felt the need to stomp all over Joy's plans with her stupid stiletto heels.

"No, it's so much more than that. I know. I was there. This isn't like your Sean situation at all," Joy said.

"I'll have you know—there isn't any Sean situation anymore. It's over. Finito. Haven't seen the guy in two months."

"So who was in your room this morning before the FDD meeting?"

Juanita Jane took a long swig of white wine out of the plastic Prairie State cup and said, "Mark. It was Mark."

"Mark? Who's Mark?"

"You know, Mark ... from downstairs."

"His name is Bert. You slept with Bert?"

"No, not Bert—the guy across the hall from Bert."

"A student? You slept with a student?" Joy half shouted.

"Shh. The whole god-damned building will hear that. Do you want me yelling your personal business to everyone? Guess what, everyone?" Juanita Jane yelled and leaned in closer to the wall. "Professor McPherson is planning a surprise wedding for a guy who barely even knows they're dating."

"He *knows* we're dating. You just don't understand my situation because you can't understand."

"What's that supposed to mean?"

"You just can't understand how it feels to be in love because you've never had that. You've spent your whole life running away from it, and now you're too old, and it's too late," Joy said. She noticed the way Juanita Jane's dull skin poked out underneath the day's fading makeup and immediately wished she could swallow back the words.

"You're wrong," Juanita Jane said and stood up. "I have too many options, actually ... don't even have time to keep them all going at the minute. It doesn't even matter that Sean stopped calling. I was about to break that shit off anyway. Donny wants to talk on the Facebook *all the time*, Mark has completely lost interest in those girls his own age who've got no idea what to do with a pork sword, and I've no idea how I'm going to let this kid down, will have to do it gently because God knows these modern college guys never learned how to handle rejection. The point is, I'm not out of options—not by a long shot, so don't sit there and try to tell me what *you* think you know about my life, about my situation, because you don't. You just don't know."

"I think we drank too much tonight," Joy said and slumped her shoulders against the wall.

"Maybe *you* did, but this is just me, and I'm fine," Juanita Jane said before slipping her feet into the gold slingback shoes. Because she was too tired to deal with the ankle strap, she moved awkwardly down the hall, keeping her balance with arms stretched out in front of her, straining and stumbling with each step, like a child struggling to move gracefully while wearing her mother's shoes.

Chapter Fifteen

"Alright, guys. We'll stop off there for today," Bert announced at the end of another college algebra lecture. He packed his books and dry erase markers quickly and averted eye contact with students as they rushed out of the room, a tactic he had perfected long ago to make a quick escape from those long classes right before the lunch hour. Unfortunately, the tactic failed miserably that day.

"Dr. Rojas," Heather Stowe said meekly as she approached the podium.

"What can I do for you?" he asked.

"I need to talk to you ... you see ... the thing is—"

"Yes—"

"I don't know if you noticed or not, probably not I'm guessing, but maybe you did. The thing is ... I kind of missed the test last week. I was going to come up with an excuse, say I was sick or something, but the truth is ... I wasn't sick. This is so embarrassing," she said, stumbling over each word as she kicked the toe of her tennis shoe into the podium, a nervous habit he had noticed while she took the first test of the semester, the test she had failed spectacularly, not even bothering to fill out the last ten questions. "The thing is ... I kind of slept through the test, and I know that's so ridiculous when the class starts at eleven, but it's what happened, and I—" As she spoke, Bert wondered what kind of underwear a nervous girl like this would wear, wondered if her body shook the first time a man undressed her, wondered why she hid her young figure under boxy sweaters that fell far below her waistline. "I was just wondering if there was any way that I could somehow make up the test sometime. I mean, I totally understand if I get a lower grade and all, but I would really appreciate—"

"That's fine," he said. *What was he doing?* Bert *never* veered from the policies on his syllabus, and the makeup test clause clearly stated that an exam could only be taken outside of the scheduled exam period if a student made arrangements ahead of time or in cases where a student had a documented medical emergency. These were the rules, and Bert *always* followed the rules, but somehow it didn't seem to matter as much anymore.

"Oh, my gosh. Really? Thank you so much. I'm so relieved. You have no idea," she said and smiled without making eye contact.

"Just send me an email, and we'll schedule something."

"Thank you so much. Seriously," she said. He pretended to fasten a buckle on the front of his bag as he watched her walk away, shoulder length blonde curls bouncing out of the room and the kind of ass that was just on the cusp of being too wide but not quite there yet swaying back and forth beneath her bulky blue sweater.

*

Later that afternoon Bert's office phone startled him out of his post-lunch exhaustion. The food in the dining hall was tailored to students who could handle the heavy cream sauces over mountains of noodles, the melted cheese over baked potatoes, the alternating array of full-fat ice cream flavors and fruit pies, the silos of soda, and grilled cheese sandwiches with extra butter. But Bert's middle-aged body was used to bland meals at home with Jean—a small salad with a dollop of fat free dressing often accompanied by a small fillet of grilled fish or a dry chicken breast. His stomach could no longer handle the flavors of youth without experiencing the consequence of severe sleepiness shortly after eating.

"Hello, Dr. Rojas here," he said.

"Seriously? That's how you answer your phone? It so doesn't fit you. Way too serious." He recognized Juanita Jane's voice instantly, but somehow it seemed softer over the phone, like she wasn't quite real when her crazy clothing choices and gaudy makeup pallet couldn't be seen.

"What should I say?"

"That's yet to be determined, but we need to think of something more snappy than that."

"Are you calling to remind me of the meeting later today? It's already on my calendar," he said.

"Does the pope shit in Germany? No, I'm not calling about a meeting—totally forgot about it myself, truth be told. No, I'm calling because you left too early."

"Left what too early?" he asked and searched his cluttered office for the desk clock he knew was there somewhere.

"Lunch. You totally missed it."

"Missed what?"

"Brynn and Will broke up again, and it was spectacular. I'm talking full-out scene. I'm talking orange juice thrown in his face and an accusation of cheating followed by him screaming, 'I wouldn't have to sleep with other girls if you'd quit being such a controlling bitch all the time.' And there we were, Joy and me, just sitting there, and you know the guy is in Joy's class this semester. Crazy. You really missed a show today. It was *spectacular*." The way she said *spectacular* made Bert sit up a little in his chair. He didn't have a mirror in his office but could feel his face smiling.

"What do you think the chances are that these two actually graduate?" he asked.

"Oh, not good, not good. Joy said he's barely passing her intro class, and you'd have to be basically brain-dead to fail that one."

"So what did he do after the orange juice? Was that at the end or—" and before he could finish, Jean was standing at the door. "Can I call you back in a bit? I have someone at the door."

"You can try, but don't count on it. It's not like I'm just sitting in my room waiting for the hot math professor to ring me up," she said and laughed so loudly that Jean could hear it from across the office.

"Will do," he said and hung up the phone.

"Who was *that*?" Jean asked with the unmistakable tone that had once been reserved only for bad tasting foods and annoying acquaintances. A few years into their marriage, the tone occasionally transferred to subjects related to him, and, as time passed on, he noticed it lingered in her words during almost every conversation he had with Jean.

"Just a colleague," he said and slumped back in the chair a bit.

"Which colleague?"

"You wouldn't know her. She teaches in the English department."

"And why do *you* know her? Why do you know someone who teaches in the English department? And why are you talking to her on the phone? Why was she laughing like that?"

"She's just a friend. I met her through the FDD program."

"Just a friend? Why'd you have to jump to that? If she's 'just a friend' then why'd you have to make a point of saying it?"

"Look, I'm at my job right now. Can we please not do this ridiculousness here? We're in my office, for God's sake. There are open ears all over the place, and you want to bring this crap up here?" he whisper-shouted at her.

"Fine," she said and crossed her arms across her tan pea coat. It struck him how dull this woman was, and he wondered how he could have been so fooled by it all as a young man, how he could have looked at that youthful version of Jean and not seen where it was all heading to, that the road would take a sharp curve to this short-haired woman with thin lips standing stiffly in a colorless coat.

Chapter Fifteen 129

"So what's going on? Why are you here?" he asked.

"So that's how it is now? I need to have a specific reason to visit my husband? I can't just come by to say hello and see how you're doing? That's where we are now?"

"So you just came by to say hello?"

"Well, not exactly. The thing is—I was thinking about the winter break, thinking it might be fun to go somewhere for a few days. I looked at flights, and we could fly into Florida and go on a seven-day cruise. With you eating in the dining hall for free every day, we could actually do a longer one this time, if you want," she said before moving the stack of ungraded tests from the spare chair to the desk so she could sit down.

"I don't want to go on a cruise."

"But we had so much fun the last time," she said through pursed lips.

"No, *we* didn't. *You* did, and, hell, I'm not even sure you did. I mean, think about vacations, the way people do all the expected things they're supposed to do when they're supposed to have a good time. You have to, right? You don't drop that kind of cash on one week to not at least pretend you're having fun. But was it fun? Was it actually fun, or did the pictures just trick you into thinking we had fun? Because, to be honest, that's not my memory of it. My memory is that fight we had in Jamaica when everyone on our pineapple plantation excursion was shuttled back to the ship. Remember that?"

"Yes, but you were being ridiculous."

"I was not being ridiculous. We spent a whole day in Jamaica and didn't even see Jamaica, didn't even step foot on the beaches."

"But we didn't choose the beach excursion."

"And that's the problem with cruises. You go all these places without really being there. You see one tiny aspect of each place and then get shuffled somewhere else. It's not a way to experience something. It's all very unsatisfying, so I've decided that the next time I fly somewhere, I want to just stay there for a while."

"So where do you want to go?" she asked. The truth is that on cold nights when the wind howled rhythmically outside Bert's dorm window, his mind compiled lists of places he wanted to go. He imagined walking through the cobbled streets of urban Lithuania, drinking huge margaritas in the French Quarter of New Orleans, photographing dilapidated lighthouses on the Maine coastline, and driving through the tiny impoverished towns of Appalachia. And in none of these imagined trips was Jean there. In his dorm room at night, he forgot about her completely.

"I don't know," he said and slumped back a bit further in his chair.

"Well, think about it, okay? It's already the middle of October. If we wait too long, the options won't be good. If we wait too long, we'll end up going somewhere horrible. We'll end up vacationing somewhere like St. Louis." As she spoke, Bert heard a familiar hammering of heels rushing down the hallway. A flash of fear ran through him.

"Hey," Juanita Jane said, slightly out of breath, standing in his office doorway. "I forgot to tell you the best part." Jean whipped her body around and stared straight at Juanita Jane. "Oh, my God! It's you!" she said to Jean. "Well, shit. I thought I'd never actually lay eyes on you. It's good to meet you," she said and thrust out her hand with the long turquoise nails to shake Jean's tiny hand. "I'm Juanita Jane. Some people call me JJ, but lately I've been back to the full deal, back to my roots. How perfect is that? Living in the dorms again and going back to my first name? I guess life has a way of putting us where we belong, huh?"

Jean just sat there stunned, and Bert wondered what she thought of this woman with the purple lipstick and platinum hair piled haphazardly on her head. "Juanita Jane is in the FDD program too," Bert said.

"Oh," Jean said.

"Yeah, those of us in the program have made fast friends. Crazy, huh? I've been teaching here for years, and so has he, and I wouldn't know the guy on the street before this crazy shit.

Don't you just love how that works out? So I had to rush over here because I forgot to tell Bert the best part. You see, we've been in on a developing saga between two students. A couple of times a week they get into a huge fight at the dining hall ... must be something about shitty dining hall food that makes these people just flip out ... so they keep breaking up, over and over again. Sadly, we never get to see the other side of the story—the makeup part. But I can only imagine. Know what I mean? So today it seems to kind of come to a head. Like I told Bert earlier, she threw a fucking glass of orange juice in the guy's face. Can you imagine doing something like that ... I mean ... without alcohol? This shit happened at noon on a weekday. Crazy."

"Wow," Jean said.

"Yeah, but the best part was after he left. She waits a few minutes, just sitting there finishing her lunch, and then she stands up but doesn't leave yet. She claps her hands a few times to get everyone's attention and says, 'I just want everyone here to know that Will Stevenson is an asshole and that he's addicted to porn,' and then she wipes up the orange juice from his side of the table, and walks out with a huge smile on her face. God, I love eating in the dining hall."

"Does this kind of thing happen often?" Jean asked.

"No. Oh, God, no. These Upper Midwestern kids tend to be pretty tight-lipped, but once in a while it does, and isn't that what really matters? Isn't it all about the possibility that it could? Isn't that what makes life worth something?" Juanita Jane asked, but she wasn't looking at Jean. She was staring straight at Bert.

Bert felt a sudden rush of guilt, and he didn't know why. All he knew is that he didn't want these two women in the same room together. It was hard to see Jean with Juanita Jane standing there, like trying to stare at a rock when a waterfall rushed wildly behind it. He tried to imagine Jean in the bright green dress Juanita Jane was wearing, tried to picture the bright strands of hot pink beads circling Jean's neck, the orange lace-up boots on Jean's feet, the bright purple belt looped around Jean's waist.

He found himself involuntarily smiling at Juanita Jane. There was something about her—the way she still made wild choices at this stage in life. There was something that made him feel like anything could happen, something that finally made him see the bright blazes of life again.

"Okay, kids. I gotta run. Class in ten minutes, but I just had to tell you about Brynn's announcement, couldn't risk forgetting about it when I see you later," she said, and then she was gone, heels echoing down the empty hallway.

Chapter Sixteen

One of the unexpected benefits of the FDD program was that weekends managed to regain the leisurely quality the participants hadn't seen since they themselves were in college. Without a house or apartment to clean, with no grocery shopping to be done, with fewer possessions around them, life took on a simpler nature, and free time expanded.

Lyla loved the feeling of living in a small space again. Seven weeks into the program she found herself bragging on the phone to her mother, "I forgot how amazing dorm living is. I can clean my whole room in fifteen minutes, and that includes sweeping."

"Don't you miss having the space, though?"

"You'd think so, but actually I don't. I don't miss it at all. There's something peaceful about being back in a small space. Something about it makes me feel lighter."

"I just can't imagine it – at your age. You know, when I was your age, I had three kids, three-thousand square feet, a three-car garage, two dogs, and a cat."

"But were you *happy*? Did all that stuff make you feel good?"

"Who knows? I didn't have time to think about nonsense like that. That's your problem, you know, you think too much ... always did. Everyone else is just trying to move forward, but you're always trying to analyze everything to death."

"That's not true," Lyla said. She didn't understand why this always happened, why conversations with her mother always took a bad turn so quickly.

"Oh, it's true. Look at you. You've made a whole career out of analyzing things that are long dead. Isn't that the whole point of history, to keep talking about stuff that no one else cares about anymore?"

"No, that's not—"

"Just look at everyone else in the family. Someone has a broken tooth, your dad fixes it. Someone has a broken car, Dave fixes it. And Jessica ... Jessica has four kids. We're all just living our lives right *now*, but your whole focus is on the past."

"So what would you have me do?" Lyla asked. "Change my whole career?"

"Are we calling it a career? Isn't that the whole reason you're living in a dorm room right now ... right next to your students, at this point in your life? Isn't it because this isn't really a career ... because they barely pay you enough to feed yourself?"

Lyla wanted to scream into the phone that her mother was wrong. She wanted to defend the choices she had made, but how could she? Working as an adjunct was, in fact, one of the worst jobs at the university. Even the groundskeepers and dining hall cooks had health insurance and a retirement plan. Lyla's job had no visible benefits and could be cut at any moment for any reason. As a college student, she had wondered why her intro to sociology professor worked the overnight shift at Walmart, but now she understood it. He was probably an adjunct. Even the word itself was demeaning. *Adjunct.* It meant something added on the side, something not really necessary. But in the classroom, she still had those occasional moments where her ideas seemed to soar far beyond the white walls and dusty blackboard, where she believed her words would settle deep in the minds of those few who were actually hearing what she had to say, where she still believed that it all meant something.

"I'm sorry," her mother started. "I don't mean to do this to you. I know it's been hard ... since the divorce. I just want you to see what I can see. You have no idea how fast your life is going to go. I just don't want you to be fifty and living in a dorm room, you know?"

"I know. I just—" she started and then heard a muffled knocking on the door. She got up to see who it was and could barely believe who was standing there on the other side of the tiny peephole. *Anton.* "Mom, I'm gonna have to call you back. Someone's at the door."

"Call me tomorrow," she said with a sigh.

Lyla looked down at her green fuzzy pajama pants, the ones always reserved for days right before the pile of laundry was finally washed, the ones that were so comfortable but made her thighs appear much thicker than they actually were. She quickly pulled her uncombed hair back into a ponytail and licked her thumb in a pointless attempt to get the pizza stain from lunch off her light blue sweatshirt. There was nothing she could do. He would have heard her talking on the phone. She couldn't pretend she wasn't there. She shrugged to herself and opened the door. "Hey, you. What's up?" she asked with a voice that barely worked.

"I just wanted to see you." And there he was, standing in her dorm door in an old pair of jeans and a green army jacket with scattered patches of bands he used to like sewn on the sleeves and across the front. It was so similar to the one he wore in college that she wondered if maybe it was the same one.

"Are you in Marshall to see Jar?"

"No, I came to see you. I just kept thinking about it, about the last time I was here, and I felt weird about it."

"Yeah."

"You look cute," he said and bent down to touch the knee of her fuzzy pants. "Soft," he said and smiled.

"Yeah, well, it's Saturday, and I was just grading some tests today ... nowhere really to go today, so I just did the lounge pants thing."

"Yeah, I remember, but the ones you used to have had those smiling clouds and stars all over them. These are a little more mature." Something about the fact that he remembered the old pajama pants that had been donated to the church rummage sale over a decade ago made her whole body go hot, and she felt like she might be dizzy if she didn't sit down immediately.

"Do you want to come in?" she asked and instantly regretted it. Having Anton back in a tiny dorm room with her felt uncomfortable, like they were middle-aged actors unsuccessfully playing the roles of much younger characters.

"Sure." He started to unbutton his coat but stopped midway through, as though he wasn't convinced yet that he wanted to stay long. With only a pushed-in desk chair and unmade bed for seating choices, he leaned awkwardly against the white wall.

Lyla quickly spread the yellow comforter across the bed, sat down on the side with the pillow and motioned for him to sit down at the other end.

"It's so strange," he started. "Being back in a dorm room. You know, I remember moving out and how I just assumed the next time I'd be back in one of these things would be moving my kid into college someday. Never thought I'd be back here visiting you in twenty years."

"Yeah, I know what you mean. Me too."

"It's crazy how similar it all is, how it even smells the same. I'd forgotten about that smell ... like the whole building smells like dryer sheets for some reason. Why is that? Does someone sneak in here and rub dryer sheets all over the walls, or do the janitors spray something? Is there a Febreze scent of college dorms they use? I just don't get it. Laundromats never smell like this," he said and shook his head in such a way that his long hair fell into his eyes. He pushed the hair out of his face and looked straight at Lyla. "It's just so weird being back here."

"I know what you mean. The first day I was back, I had to keep looking at my wrists to remind myself that I wasn't her anymore, that I wasn't the twenty-year-old version of myself."

"Your wrists?"

"Yeah, see the tiny wrinkles?" she said and held out her wrist for him to inspect it.

"No, no," he said and shook his head. "You always had those."

"What?"

"Yeah, don't you remember? I used to feel so bad for you ... and I thought it was so cute how you somehow had old lady hands at nineteen. Remember how dry they got in the winter?" he said, and suddenly she did remember. She caught a flash of the younger him rubbing thick lotion into her cracked knuckles, the way he massaged the lotion into every dry spot, the way he joked that she should be banned from handwashing during the months when daytime temperatures dipped below zero.

"Oh, my God. You're right. My hands are exactly the same as they were back then," she said and smiled. "Sadly, my weight is a different story."

"I like you with a little more meat on you," he said and leaned back against the cool wall. "Do you have anything to listen to?"

"Of course, but I'm guessing my iPod's selection is a little different from yours."

"It would be entirely different from mine because I don't have one of those things. When they switched from CDs to that crap, I decided I wasn't doing it. I'm done buying the new stuff. CDs were okay, but tapes were way cooler, so I decided to stage my own little personal rebellion and went back to those."

"Back to tapes? You went back to tapes?"

"Yeah. Hell yeah," he said and nodded his head in the exaggerated way he used to when he was really excited about something. "I went and bought a couple tape players at the used music store, and they sell tapes for less than a buck each."

"I can't believe you went back to tapes. Tapes were the worst. You had to keep rewinding and fast-forwarding to try to find where the song you want starts."

"No, that's the whole point. That's why tapes were the best. They force you to actually listen to the album. That's the whole trouble with CDs—it's too easy to just skip over stuff, and don't even get me started on the stupid system now. Now people don't even care about the album. They just buy one crappy song. It takes all the artistry out of the music world. But the thing I realized, after the CDs died, is that it's not even the iPod's fault."

"It's not?" she asked with a smirk on her face.

"No. Think about it. The CDs are really the ones to blame. They're the format that made skipping so easy, you know. People got used to it, started to see the non-radio tracks as just some crap around the songs they paid for, but most of the time, those non-radio songs were actually the best ones. Those were the ones that took real chances, the ones that weren't confined to the length and harmonic requirements the radio industry pushes," he said. "And that's why I decided to go back, back to tapes."

"Well, luckily for you, I'm old enough that most of the stuff on my iPod is just albums I transferred from CDs anyway, so I won't torture you with a bunch of one-hit wonders. And, just so you know, people younger than us don't listen to iPods anymore anyway," she said and started up the beginning of David Gray's album, *White Ladder.*

"Ah, I remember this," he said. "I think I hated it when we were in college, but now I kind of like it. It's like that, you know, with a lot of the old stuff. Hell, even a shitty Britney Spears song can put me in a good mood now."

"I know what you mean. A couple years ago, I was in the grocery store, and that horrible Macarena song was playing, and it actually made me happy. I hated myself a little for that, but it was comforting somehow, like part of me was back in the 90s again." She smiled and wondered if the middle-aged version of Anton and her could still comfortably fit in a single bed.

"I forgot how easy it is to talk to you," he said. "It's rare, you know, to be able to talk to someone and not feel slightly miserable the whole time. I didn't know that in college. I thought there'd be lots of people like that, but it's hard to find this."

"And no one tells you that. Maybe they try to, but they don't ever come right out with it. No one tells you that things won't get easier, that conversations won't get better, that everything in life just gets dimmer and dimmer, that it all starts to feel like this weird thing they made us do when I was in elementary school."

"What weird thing was that?" he asked.

"I was thinking about this the other day, how our teacher made us do this science project so we would know what moles see. We had to wear these glasses with this dark blurred film over them and walk around the hallways. We had to awkwardly find our way back to the classroom, squinting and bumping into each other as we went," she said.

"Man, this is exactly what I hated about elementary school. Remember dioramas?"

"Yeah, yeah, I remember those, but that's not the point of the story. The point's not that I hated elementary school. I mean, of course I did. Everybody did, and those dioramas were a complete waste of time. I mean, when are you ever going to use that skill in real life? But, no, that's not my point. My point is that my teacher was supposedly teaching us to empathize with moles for some reason, but I've realized lately that that's my life now."

"What do you mean?"

"I mean I feel like I'm walking around with that film on my glasses, like I'm only partially experiencing the world now, and I don't know when that happened, but it did. At some point, I just stopped feeling life completely. You know, like when you're driving around in your twenties, and you're singing along to the radio at the top of your lungs, and you're feeling every bit of the music, and you're completely alive?" she asked. "I don't feel that anymore, and I think I'd have to turn the radio up to levels that would destroy me just to feel the same level I felt so easily before."

He nodded.

"I just don't see things the same. I'm just kind of numb," she said. "But then I saw you. I saw you sitting at that game, and it suddenly didn't feel like there was a film over my glasses anymore. I didn't feel numb anymore. I felt free again. I guess what I'm trying to say ... is ... maybe you're right. Maybe if we had stayed together back then, if we had gotten married, had kids, bought a house, the whole deal ... maybe it would've been the same. Maybe that routine would've taken something out of life, maybe we'd be so bored with each other by now that we'd both feel trapped it in."

"Maybe so," he said.

"But I guess I'm just glad to know that I can still have that feeling of freedom again, that I can still be surprised by my own life," she said and instantly felt nervous with him again, like she had shared too much.

"Let's try it then," he said.

"What?"

"Let's drive around in my truck with the music turned up. I have a couple tapes you used to like. We can roll down the windows and pump *Joshua Tree* and see what it feels like," he said and stood up.

"Okay, sure. I'm in. Why not? Let's try it."

*

He waited until they were out of Marshall to put the tape in, waited another five miles to push play, and as the first series of guitar arpeggios steadily increased in volume, Lyla could feel it all again. She wasn't thirty-eight anymore. She was just a college kid in a car sitting next to a guy she was somehow falling in love with all over again, and, just like before, she didn't know if she could stop it.

Highway 23 wasn't quite the nameless street Bono was singing about, but with nothing beyond the car but empty cornfields and the occasional lonely farmhouse, Lyla felt like the rest of the world had somehow dropped away as they sped down the rural highway with windows open wide and the coolness of late October air waking up all the dead places within her. Suddenly Anton's long hair didn't look so out of place on his middle-aged body anymore as it whipped wildly in the wind, the same way it had all those years ago. And when the song reached its highest peak with guitars and drums crashing into every surface of the old truck, and Bono's voice mirrored the broken chords pounding behind him, Lyla understood that she was somehow living again in the beautiful uncertainty of not knowing what would happen next.

Chapter Seventeen

"What the hell is going on with your clothes?" Juanita Jane asked Margie as they met in the dorm hallway on the way to Monday morning classes.

"What do you mean?"

"They look weird," Juanita Jane said and scrunched up her over-powdered nose.

"Oh, yeah," Margie said and looked down at her jeans. "They feel kind of weird too. I tried this thing ... you know ... a different way of doing laundry, to save money."

"What'd you do?"

"Well, I got tired of paying all those quarters all the time, so I decided to just hand wash everything and hang it to dry ... works fine for swimsuits," Margie said with a shrug.

"You hand washed everything? You can't do that."

"People used to."

"Yeah, people also used to take a shit in the woods, but I ain't doing that either," Juanita Jane said.

"I know, and the truth is it doesn't seem like it worked anyway. Everything is really stiff, and I couldn't figure out how to get all the soap out. I just kept rinsing the clothes out, but the soap wouldn't completely go away, and now my room smells really musty from the wet clothes drying, and my roommate's kind of pissed, which is totally unfair because her boyfriend being over all the time is way more annoying than me just trying to do some laundry for free. It was a huge pain and took forever just to wash a few things, but it's just so expensive. At two bucks a load, I'm spending like twenty bucks a month just on laundry."

"Huh," Juanita Jane said and stopped walking for a minute. "Well, holy shit, I totally forgot about that. I can't believe I forgot about that," she said with a smile.

"That laundry's two bucks a load?"

"No, I can't believe I totally forgot about the poverty thing. You might be younger and have better legs and tits that still sit up straight without a bra, but I have something you won't have for a while yet. I have the money," Juanita Jane said. "Tell you what, kid—come by tonight for a chat and wine, and I'll give you the twenty bucks."

*

Prairie towns like Marshall didn't have a high-end beauty salon. With a population mostly filled with farmers and those who worked at the ice cream factory, there wouldn't be enough business to support one, so those rare women who desired a fifty dollar haircut had to make the drive west to Sioux Falls to get one. Juanita Jane was one of those women.

Juanita Jane rushed in an hour before closing and hobbled quickly over to the receptionist's desk in heels that were a little too high, even for her. "Didn't make an appointment. Who's got time for that, right? But I just drove in from Marshall, and I'll tip everyone in this salon if I can just get a trim," she said.

"You know we're always slow on Mondays, but we'll take the tips," the receptionist said and winked at Juanita Jane.

"Thanks, Stacey."

Of all the things Juanita Jane's mother had taught her, overpriced self-care was the one that stuck. After a couple months of the simplicity of dorm living, it felt good to be back in the Sioux Falls salon with its hot pink zebra print chairs, glittery glass bottles of styling products, framed photos of cafes in Paris, and the kind of lightbulbs seen in black and white movies in the dressing rooms of Hollywood starlets. As her stylist draped the black silk cape around her neck and leaned the chair back, Juanita Jane felt like she was right where she belonged.

"Have you ever thought of going a little shorter?" the young stylist asked her. "I think it would make you look a lot younger, really frame your face."

"Are you kidding me? You sound like my mother. If anything, I look a little *too* young," she said and caught a flash of herself in bed with Mark the week before.

"You know what would look really cute? You could bring it up a little over your shoulders and go a little darker, or maybe even a lot darker. I'm thinking something like chestnut. It would really soften up your look." *Who the hell did this girl think she was?* Juanita Jane wasn't interested in this girl's misguided advice. *Soft* was not a look she was going for.

"Trust me. This look is working for me just fine," she said and folded her arms tightly across her chest under the salon cape.

*

On the long, dark drive back to Marshall, Juanita Jane couldn't shake the conversation she had had back at the salon. She had *always* had long blonde hair, and what did *that* girl know about style anyway, with her short and spiky hair with purple colored tips? Who made *her* the ultimate judge of appearances?

She thought about Bert and how disappointed he was with Jean's newly short hair, thought about how so many women just discarded the old pieces of themselves too easily as the years ticked on. She had made a promise to herself as a younger woman that she wouldn't fall into that trap, and she wasn't about to let some stranger with scissors change her plans so easily. Still, she wondered why so few women past the age of fifty let their hair grow below their shoulders. Was it societal pressure, or was it possible that the stylist was right?

Juanita Jane had seen the box at Walmart on the shelf right below her sexy shade of blonde – Classy Chestnut. But was she *Classy Chestnut*? She had always been *Golden Goddess*. To the stylist, the change was easy, but Juanita Jane knew it was more complicated than a color change. To cut her hair and cover the goddess with something classy was to erase a painting she had spent her whole life creating and start over with someone new, and she wasn't ready to do that just yet.

*

As the semester wore on, Margie found herself spending more and more time in the dorm rooms of faculty members, a fact that didn't bother her but somewhat horrified her roommate. On the rare occasions when the roommate didn't have her boyfriend over, she wouldn't let Margie leave the room without first asking an unwelcome serious of questions. "How are you going to get a boyfriend when you're spending all your time with old people?"

"Don't you remember? I already have a boyfriend," Margie said while lacing up her gray tennis shoes.

"Oh, that doesn't count. That guy's not even here. If he's not here, you're in the clear," she half whispered and winked at Margie. "You're completely missing out on college by spending all your time studying with teachers. How are you supposed to make real college memories if you're just skipping all the good stuff?"

Margie thought about the night before, how Juanita Jane had convinced her to accompany her to Pipestone, a town forty-five miles south of Marshall, to eat a late dinner in a diner there because they "had the best damn chocolate chip pancakes you ever had." She thought about how they ate until they were almost sick, about the forkfuls of homemade whipped cream and those chips that melted a bit as soon as she cut into the pancakes, thought about the way they giggled about nothing all the way home after they stayed well past closing to play cards in a back room with the people who owned the restaurant. "It's only my first semester," Margie said. "There's lots of time to meet other people."

"Just be careful. This is a small campus. Once word gets out that you're hanging out with weird professors, you can kiss goodbye to any chance of being invited to Magnuson's parties."

*

With the last of the wine gone and the remaining red licorice spread out across the bright floral print bedspread, Margie and Juanita Jane searched the desk drawers for the cookies they swore they'd bought at some point. "I just can't eat any more of that licorice," Margie said as she pulled papers out of the bottom drawer. "They have to be in here, right? I mean ... is it possible we ate all the cookies last weekend? I totally don't remember anymore."

"If my ass is still connected to my legs, I swear they're in here somewhere," Juanita Jane said, but the truth was that she wasn't so sure anymore, that it was entirely possible that she'd eaten them with Mark on Sunday after they got stoned.

"How do you have so much stuff in here?" Margie asked and pulled out a tiny stuffed unicorn that was shoved to the back of the bottom drawer. "We've only lived here a couple of months."

"Who knows? Just keep looking. If I don't get one of those damn ginger cookies in the next five minutes, I might kill someone." They searched the rest of the desk drawers, rifled through the photo boxes at the top of the closet, pulled out all the shoes from under the bed, dug through the mountain of lacy underwear in the dresser, and even checked all the compartments of the red suitcase that hadn't been used since the day Juanita Jane moved in. "Look—they're not here. Those cookies are *not here*. They're not anywhere. We could search this place all night, pull up the floors and yank the stuffing out of that bedspread, but they're never going to be here," Juanita Jane shouted and spread her arms out to the room in surrender. "And, let's be honest. Let's just be real honest about the situation. I'm a little too fucked up to drive, and you're probably more fucked up than I am, so we're probably stuck with the shitty licorice."

"I guess it's better anyway. God knows how many calories are in those things," Margie said, grabbed a rope of licorice, and sat back down on the bed.

"Oh, no. No, no, no, no, no. You're not pulling that calorie crap on me. Do you have any idea how offensive that is? You're not even twenty yet, not even close to the day when your metabolism closes up shop, not even close to that moment when even the sight of pasta will make your hips spread. What the hell are you talking about? These are the years to use it ... use it before you lose it. If I were under thirty again, I'd be eating everything I could find. I'd be camped out in front of the Ho Ho store shoving those things down my throat as fast as I could chew 'em. I'd be eating for five just because I could. Let me show you something," she said and unzipped the back of her orange sweater dress. Before Margie could process what was happening, Juanita Jane was standing in front of her in a black balconette bra and see-through black mesh underwear.

"What are you doing?" Margie asked and sat back on the bed a bit.

"You need to see this. This is your future."

"I don't even wear underwear like that *now*," Margie said with a nervous giggle. "There is no way my future looks like that."

"This isn't about the underwear, kid. This is about the body. Look at this," she said, turned around, and grabbed the roll of fat just under her bra strap. "Do you see this? And look at this," she said and pointed to the dimpled skin that extended below her underwear. "And this," she said, showing Margie the way her skin was no longer tight around her belly button. "And look at this," she said and grabbed the sagging skin around her knees. "What the hell is up with this? Who knew this would happen? Who could predict this? And here's the thing ... the crazy thing. You're in college right now, but no class is ever going to teach you this. No teacher is ever going to say, 'look at this shit. Look at what will happen to you.'"

"Well, apparently that's not true because you're a teacher, and you're saying it right now."

"Yeah, and you better thank God that I am because ... here's the thing—no one ever said this to me. No one ever warned me, so I had no idea, and there is no time in your life when you'll feel more alone than that day you're in the shower soaping up saggy knee skin for the first time, and you suddenly realize what's happening, suddenly realize that you're all alone staring death right in the face, and you're supposed to somehow remember to clean the hair out of the drain before your clueless boyfriend takes his turn in the shower," Juanita Jane said and sat down on the opposite side of the bed, still undressed. "Life is so strange," she said.

"I know," Margie said.

"But that's the whole thing. You don't know. You're saying you do, but it's a lie. It's what you say at nineteen when you're trying to placate an older person you assume is spouting nonsense. You literally still have baby fat on your thighs. What the hell could *you* know?"

"Just because I haven't gotten there yet doesn't mean I can't imagine it," Margie said and took a large bite of licorice. "I know how aging works."

"But it's more than aging. That's the thing. It's the whole structure of life. The whole structure is fucked," Juanita Jane said. Just then there was a knock on the door, and Juanita Jane shouted, "Come back in an hour. I'm half naked and half drunk. Not a good time for visitors."

"What do you mean 'the whole thing is fucked'?" It was awkward for Margie to swear in front of a woman who was a little older than her mother. It went against all the rules of etiquette her family had drilled into her since early childhood, but Juanita Jane seemed so far outside of these rules, and everything about the way Juanita Jane presented herself challenged Margie's upbringing.

"Here's the thing ... I should be telling all of this to Bert, someone who actually gets it, but maybe it's good for you to hear this. Maybe it's some kind of fate that you're the one sitting here right now. Who knows?" Juanita Jane stood up, put her dress back on, went to the mini refrigerator to search for the wine she knew wasn't there, came back to the bed, and said, "The thing is ... you get to a certain point in your life where you realize you're still moving forward, but there's nothing in front of you anymore. You see what I mean? There's nothing to look forward to."

Margie squinted in that way the very young do, that always-failed attempt to look invested in a conversation that isn't quite compelling. "You mean because you're in your fifties?" she asked.

"No, Marg. No ... and this is why this conversation isn't for you. You're too young to understand that it's more than that."

"So tell me."

"It's not about being fifty, but the thing is ... at fifty you're smart enough to finally see the shit ahead of you. You're closer to seventy than twenty," she said and momentarily grabbed Margie's knee. "That's why the whole structure of life is fucked up. Think about it," she said and pulled a loose orange thread out of her dress. "In other parts of life, there's something good at the end—some reward. You finish your grilled chicken and broccoli, you get a piece of pecan pie. You finish all your grading for the semester, you get a week of binge drinking. But you get to the end of your life, and you don't get shit. You just get further and further from feeling like yourself."

"Not true," Margie said.

"What do you mean 'not true'?"

"Retirement. You get retirement."

"Wow, I can't believe I'm sitting next to someone who is actually young enough to believe that bullshit retirement fantasy, that sitting-in-a-rocking-chair-looking-at-some-mythical-mountains-from-the-porch-of-some-perfectly-rustic-cabin-somewhere fantasy. That's not real life, Marg. That's not what it really looks like for most of us. My grandmother was the most beautiful woman in Lafayette when she was young, spent the last decade of her life in a shitty apartment eating tuna fish out of the can, died with eighty bucks in her checking account."

"But that won't be you. You'll have more money than that, right?" Margie asked.

"Money? What's money even got to do with it? This isn't about money. This shit is way bigger than money."

"Then what is it about?"

"The thing is ... I figured out a way better life system than the one our sorry asses are stuck with now."

"What is it?" Margie asked and leaned forward a bit.

"So you get old, right? I don't even want to totally interfere with that. Getting old is fine—up to a point."

"Up to a point?"

"Yeah, you need all of that to learn all the lessons you're never going to learn if you look like *that* your whole life," Juanita Jane said and nodded in Margie's direction. "So in my system, you still get old, but two years before the end you get to go back."

"Back? Back to what?"

"Back to the version of yourself that felt most authentic, that version that felt most like the real you."

"So, when you reach a couple years before death, you become twenty again?" Margie asked.

"Twenty? Oh, God, no. No, not twenty, not for me. It wouldn't be twenty for me. God, Marg—you're so young you haven't even hit your high point yet."

"So what's your high point?"

"Thirty-four. For me, it's thirty-four. You should've seen my ass at thirty-four, Marg."

"So this is about beauty? I thought the desire to be beautiful goes away at forty."

"Who the hell told you that?"

"I think my grandma said something like that once."

"First of all, your grandma is a liar. Second of all, it's not just beauty. I'd love to get out of bed without my leg hurting for the first hour of the day just one more time."

"Or for two more years," Margie said and smiled.

"Exactly—and think about it ... think about how different eighty would feel if you knew you were just getting closer to being thirty-four again. Yeah, I think my system is far superior to the crap we've got now."

As Juanita Jane spoke, the first few snowflakes of the season swirled outside her window. As was typical for a southern Minnesota October, it would still be a couple weeks before daytime temperatures would stay cold enough to allow for any real accumulation, but they all knew what was coming—the white-out blizzards that would close down highways leaving town, the feel of arctic wind rushing through layers of clothing to sting the skin beneath, the ice-covered parking lots that became death-traps for the elderly, and the sludge of snow and ice that clung to their boots and tracked the gunk of the season into every room they entered. Winter was coming, and there was no way to stop it.

Chapter Eighteen

Joy sat in a booth alone waiting for Miles' late shift to end on another Thursday night at the Steady Saloon. It wasn't easy to watch him as he leaned way over the bar to hear the drink orders of pretty women while the local band filled the dark atmosphere with the steady beat of tired tunes and drunk couples swayed by the wooden stage, yelling, "Play something slow. C'mon, please play something slow." It wasn't easy to see the same women every week, those women who seemed to linger a little too long when Miles handed them a drink, the women who seemed completely uninterested in the band or the other men who populated the busy bar.

Joy looked at her watch: 12:28—two minutes until the band would abruptly stop playing and the bright lights would get turned on, two minutes until Miles would shout out "last call," and the people would swarm around the bar one last time to pay for their final drink. She could feel the rush of expectation as the singer motioned for everyone to sing along to the end of "Every Rose Has Its Thorn," could almost feel the fresh air beyond the bar where her cold car waited for Miles to sit in the passenger seat.

When they had first started dating, she hated when he asked for rides home from the bar, hated not knowing how long it would take for him to get rid of the last customer and clean up the place enough for the daytime servers to not complain about the night staff. Somewhere along the way, though, her feelings shifted, and she found herself enjoying the waiting. There was a certain pleasure in the anticipation of the hours after closing when Miles usually invited her in and sometimes let her stay all night.

After the band packed up and the last customer left and the front door was double locked, Miles called out to Carl and Josh, "You guys can take off, if you want. We've got it from here." Joy didn't mind that she wasn't being paid to wipe down sticky tables, empty out restroom trashcans overflowing with paper towels, vacuum up pieces of popcorn that had fallen behind booths, and wash the lipstick off wine glasses left on pool tables and bar stools. Having the other workers go home just meant she got to spend more time alone with Miles.

"You don't have to do this, you know," he said.

"I don't mind cleaning up a little. I actually kind of miss it, living in the dorms. I haven't cleaned a bathroom in months."

"I meant driving me home. You don't have to do that every time I work," he said, wiped down the bar, and threw the wet washcloth into the bucket by the sink.

"I don't mind," she said and tucked her chin-length hair behind her ears in an attempt to be flirtatious that seemed to go completely unnoticed as he emptied the cash from his pockets and counted out the night's tips.

"It just feels a little weird, you know, having you sitting there watching me all night, watching me work. Josh is married, and his wife doesn't ever even come to the bar." She couldn't believe it. There he was, talking about marriage, comparing their relationship to Josh, comparing the two of them to two people who had been married for almost a decade. "I just don't think it's a good idea anymore," he said.

"I understand," she said and couldn't contain the smile that was aggressively spreading across her face. Miles didn't want a woman to give him a ride home from work and sleep in his bed once in a while. He wanted more. He wanted what Josh had. He wanted a wife.

Chapter Eighteen 155

*

Back at Miles' apartment, Joy had a hard time concentrating as he stripped his black t-shirt and jeans off and pulled her onto the mattress on the floor where he slept. She wanted to tell him about Shelly, wanted to know his opinions on veil length and tea light candles, wanted to know if he thought an outdoor ceremony in December was crazy or romantic, wanted to know if he preferred traditional vows or quirky contemporary ones, wanted to know how he felt about weddings that didn't close with a dance. As he unhooked her bra and bit the flesh of her soft breast, she wondered where they would live after the wedding. His tiny apartment with the second-hand furniture and stained carpet was okay for dating, but if they pooled her faculty salary and his bartending cash, they could probably get a decent three bedroom house in one of the neighborhoods by the golf course. As he pulled off her pink cotton underwear and entered her, she wondered where they'd go to buy a bed frame. There were better options in Sioux Falls, but then they'd have to pay the extra fee for an out of town delivery. Still, it might be worth it if they could find a brass bed frame like the one she'd seen in *Midwest Home Magazine*.

As sweat dripped from his face to hers and stung the corners of her open eyes, she reminded herself to check the size of his jeans and jacket after he fell asleep. She wanted to order him some new clothes for after the wedding, clothes that looked like what a husband would wear, clothes with collars and crisp cuffs, clothes that would look good in vacation photos and Sunday afternoons at the nice restaurants in Sioux Falls. She tried to match the rhythm of his breathing as he increased the pace, and she wondered if Juanita Jane was right. Shouldn't she just tell him about the wedding plans? Wouldn't it be more fun to include him in picking out the food and the decorations and the music playlist? Wouldn't it be better to send out actual wedding invitations instead of telling the guests they were coming to just another run-of-the-mill birthday party? But wasn't the story of a surprise wedding a much better tale to tell their future children on those long winter nights before bedtime? Wasn't it more romantic to give him the gift of a lifetime of love in such an unexpected way, and didn't all guys secretly hate the process of wedding planning and wish they could just skip all the months of headaches leading up to the wedding and go straight to the good part?

As he finished and rolled back over to the far end of the mattress, she studied the long line that started between his shoulder blades and ran straight down the center of his muscular back. "Thanks for letting me stay over tonight," she said and ran her hand through his damp hair.

"Uh, huh," he said and started scrolling through something on his phone.

"I still can't believe I met you," she said.

"This is a pretty small town. Everybody meets everybody at some point," he said.

"I know, but that's my point. I can't believe that, out of everybody in the whole world, you're here, and I'm here," she said and wrapped her body around his.

"You think too much," he said, flipped on the light, and went to the kitchen for a cigarette.

It was perfect. He always sat on the folding chair right by the open kitchen window when he smoked, and it always took at least ten minutes for him to finish his bedtime cigarette. She'd have plenty of time to look in the closet for his measurements and be back in bed long before he returned.

*

Friday afternoons were an ideal time for meetings with Mr. Administration. Classes ended at two, but faculty were expected to be available until five, so believable reasons to miss a meeting were hard to invent. Because the weekend was just hours away, the FDD members showed up to the meeting in casual clothes that were a stark contrast to Mr. Administration's black suit with a tiny prairie dog pinned to the lapel as a subtle show of support for the school's athletic program. Joy, Bert, and Lyla wore jeans, and Juanita Jane wore a dress that violated her teaching wardrobe rule of having no more than two inches of visible cleavage.

"As you know, we administered the survey last week," Mr. Administration started.

"The survey about how the students feel about having us in the dorms?" Juanita Jane asked.

"It's a little more complicated than that," Mr. Administration said and dimmed the lights so they could see the numbers projected on the screen behind him. "It's not really about how the students *feel*. It's about the outcomes of having faculty in the dorms with them. It's about seeing how your presence might lead to better retention efforts."

"Can you say that in English?" Juanita Jane said.

"We need to know if having faculty living in the dorms is having any influence on the study habits of students, on the likelihood that they will attend classes regularly, on the sense of connectedness they feel to the university as a whole, and, more importantly, on the connnectedness they feel to the academic experience of the university."

"But how the hell would you know that? Isn't it all pretty random? Aren't there just some students who give a shit and some who don't?" Juanita Jane asked.

"We can't think that way anymore. Moreover, we don't have the *luxury* to think that way," Mr. Administration said. The way he said *luxury* reminded Joy of the year her dad lost his job and her mother sat the family down to explain that luxuries like name brand cookies and new clothes were about to end in their household.

"But it doesn't really matter what we think. It's just the truth," Juanita Jane said. "If anything, living in the dorms has just made it abundantly clear that some students are just here to smoke weed and get laid. Some of them don't give a shit about the D they're getting in Biology so long as their financial aid keeps bankrolling the college lifestyle a little longer. Some of them have no plans to graduate."

"But the state says they have to," Mr. Administration said.

"So what did the survey say?" Bert asked. "Because it seems to me that the students *are* having a positive response to the program."

"Of the 352 survey participants, only forty-seven of them even knew the program existed, and of those forty-seven, only nineteen stated that they had any interaction with the FDD members," Mr. Administration said.

"How did you administer the survey?" Bert asked.

"We had a booth set up at the football game last week and gave participants free t-shirts for taking the survey."

"Are you sure all the people who took the survey were even students at Prairie State?" Bert asked. "Because it they weren't then what you have is a non-representative sample, and any statistician knows that that automatically ruins the credibility of the survey results."

"It is something we considered, but with a survey cost of over two-thousand, it's going to be hard to get the provost to approve a re-do," he said.

"Two thousand dollars?" Lyla blurted out, suddenly engaged in the conversation. "Why would a survey cost two-thousand dollars?"

"We had to pay for the t-shirts," Mr. Administration said.

Lyla nodded silently and thought about the kind of vacation she could take for two-thousand dollars.

"So we may just have to go with the little information we do have," he said and nodded in the direction of the screen. "As you can see, the nineteen students who did have interactions with the FDD members were not entirely pleased with the experience. If we just look at the numbers, they're discouraging at best, but if we look at the additional comments, that's when things really start to unravel."

"But how many people live in the dorms?" Bert asked. "Even

in this dorm alone, it has to be at least a hundred students, right? And how many people filled out the comment section of the survey?"

"Of the nineteen who answered that they had some interaction with the FDD members, three filled out the comment section. There were actually eleven responses to the comment section, but the other ones commented on the perceived quality of the free t-shirts or the attractiveness of the woman administering the survey."

"So three people had something to say about the program, and you want to kill the whole thing over three people?" Bert asked.

"One of the respondents said that the presence of faculty in the dorms was creepy, that there were rumors of sexual involvement between one of the members and a student."

"That's crazy," Juanita Jane yelled out and shook her head aggressively.

"The administration understands that there is a margin of error with surveys like this, but even the perception of inappropriate conduct could be detrimental to the program," he said.

"So what's the bottom line?" Bert asked.

"The president and provost will meet in two weeks to determine whether or not they want to give the program another semester or just cut their losses. We just don't have the funding to go forward if we're not seeing a noticeable improvement in retention."

"But wouldn't retention be unknown until after the semester?" Joy asked. "Wouldn't we have to see the enrollment numbers for next semester first?"

"Yeah, God knows our students wait until the last second to register for classes. Hell, sometimes they don't get around to it until after the semester starts," Juanita Jane said.

"We're just going to have to see how early registration goes and make an estimate," he said. "And besides, I'm sure you guys are ready to pass the baton to someone else after the semester is over anyway, right? Don't worry. No one expects you four to bear the brunt of this all year. No one expects you to be trapped in the dorms past this semester."

Bert nodded, but the truth was that he did hope to stay with the program another semester. He thought about the house across town and how Jean usually used weekends for cleaning rituals that didn't need to happen. Suddenly the memory of mopping behind the dryer on Saturdays filled him with rage, and he could feel his face go hot as Mr. Administration turned off the projector and wrapped up the meeting. He could hear Jean's voice telling him to make sure he got the mop way back in the corner, the corner that no guest would ever see as it existed in the back of the laundry room, down in the basement, hidden behind the dryer. He could hear her saying, "Make sure you wring the mop out this time, and don't let the mop water splatter again when you pour it down the sink. If it splatters then we'll just have to mop the floor again, and we don't want to do that, do we?" She was always using that word *we* when it didn't apply to Bert at all.

Mr. Administration talked about the FDD program the way one would talk about being a prisoner locked in a cell or a chubby kid forced to spend a summer at fat camp, but he had it all wrong. It wasn't that way at all. At the house across town, Jean made him rinse out his beer bottles before throwing them in recycling, called him into the bathroom an hour after he fell asleep to point out the dirty underwear he forgot to put in the hamper, refused to ride in his car until he threw away the candy wrappers in the center console, and reported most of his mistakes to her mother during early morning phone calls when she thought he was still sleeping. In the dorm room he could sleep on the same sheets for weeks on end, keep the TV turned on way past midnight, leave stacks of ungraded tests spread out across the desk and floor, and feel the pulse of new music beating above and below him.

He suddenly realized the problem. In the house across town, he was still a child with a chore list and a schedule closely monitored by a wife he didn't know anymore. But in the dorm room, he was free. And even though Mr. Administration thought the end of the program was near, Bert knew he wasn't ready to give it all up just yet.

Chapter Nineteen

After the meeting, the FDD participants decided to continue the discussion, without Mr. Administration, over drinks and free popcorn at The Steady Saloon. In typical late Friday afternoon fashion, the bar was mostly empty, so they were able to claim one of the roomier booths tucked away in the back corner.

"I thought Miles didn't want you coming in here anymore," Juanita Jane said to Joy.

"No, that's not what he said. That's not it at all. He's fine with me coming in here. He just doesn't want me to feel like I have to pick him up from work every night, doesn't want me to feel like I'm his slave. I told you this. He doesn't want *less*. He wants *more*. And, besides, he's not even working today anyway."

"I just think you should seriously rethink this whole plan you've got going. I think you should seriously consider back-pedaling the whole thing because, if there's one thing I know, one thing I have some level of real experience with, it's that once a guy—Miles, in this case—once a guy starts limiting your access to him, well, that's pretty much the beginning of the end," Juanita Jane said and took a long sip of her white wine.

"I told you, he's not limiting my access to him. He's trying to change the relationship. He's trying to make it into a more long-term situation."

"What do you think, Bert? Should she be planning a wedding for a guy who hasn't even said 'I love you' yet? Should she be picking out a dress for a guy who asked her to stop showing up during his night shift?" Juanita Jane asked, surprising both Joy and herself with how easily she was willing to let the huge secret slip.

"I'm not planning a wedding. She means that figuratively. She means I've *thought* about planning a wedding, but what woman hasn't, right? What woman doesn't flash forward to the wedding dress and flowers the second she meets a guy she likes, right? What woman doesn't want everything to end that way, right?" Joy asked and shifted uncomfortably back and forth on the barely-padded booth bench.

"Fine," Juanita Jean said with an eye roll that was so pronounced it could be detected by the couple at the table across the bar. "You're not planning a wedding, but you're still completely deluding yourself if you think this guy isn't desperately trying to slow shit down because that's what he's doing. Right, Bert?"

"It's hard to say. I just don't think I can accurately assess the situation without having all the data."

"Now you sound like Mr. Administration. This isn't about data. This is a cut and dry case of a guy who wants a season pass to her cooch but doesn't want to pay the price of admission," Juanita Jane said.

Lyla tried unsuccessfully to stifle a laugh.

"If all he wanted was sex, then why doesn't he just sleep with the women who are all over him every night at the bar? Trust me—he could have sex with a different woman every night of the week if he wanted to, so what's that about? Why doesn't he just go that route?" Joy asked.

"Maybe he's trying to, and that's why he's so insistent on you not coming in here during his shifts," Juanita Jane said and slammed her palm down on the table to emphasize the point.

"Can we just talk about something else?" Joy asked.

"Fine," Juanita Jane said with a hand movement that was a strange mixture of jazz hands and the spastic signal of a startled person.

Chapter Nineteen

"So do you think the FDD program's really going to end after this semester?" Lyla asked in an attempt to neutralize the awkward situation.

"Probably. They always do this shit, you know. This semester it's all about improving retention by having us living in the dorms. Next semester they'll be offering that bullshit college prep class to incoming freshmen again, and the semester after that they'll go back to those motivational posters. Remember that shit?" Juanita Jane said.

"Oh, yeah. The ones they put up in my department had a spelling error," Lyla said. "It was supposed to say *your fate is in your hands*, but instead it said, *your fat is in your hands*. I heard they relocated it to the Health Sciences Department and tried to pass it off as a weight-loss slogan. My friend who teaches over there said students were mostly just confused."

"See, this is what I'm talking about. These people just reek of incompetence. And who the hell are these people that come up with this shit? Who's sitting in an office somewhere thinking that some dipshit is going to say to himself, 'I was going to go to that party and get shit-faced on Jäger tonight, but you know what? I remember how I saw this poster in the hallway outside my English class, so I'm going to stay in and study instead'? Who are these people who think this shit is going to work?" Juanita Jane asked.

"But you're missing the whole point," Bert said. "The point isn't for it to work. That's not the job of the person being paid to come up with these crazy ideas."

"Then what's his job?" Juanita Jane asked and raised her overly plucked eyebrows.

"His job is just to come up with the ideas. He gets paid either way. Doesn't really matter to him if it works or not," Bert said.

"So the possibility of me saving enough money to finally take a real vacation is in the hands of some guy who doesn't even care if the idea has results or not?" Lyla asked and looked across the table at Bert.

"Yep, pretty much," he said.

"Well, I hope they decide to give it another semester. I can't believe how much money I'm saving by not paying for food or rent," Lyla said. "Plus, isn't it kind of fun?"

"We all know why *you* think it's fun," Juanita Jane said. "Who wouldn't want to be shacked up with her college boyfriend in a tiny dorm room again? Who wouldn't want to go right back to the beginning with some guy who's almost as hot as he was at nineteen?"

"It's weird," Lyla said and took a sip of her rum and coke. "He keeps coming back, but we haven't even kissed, barely hugged even. He just seems to want to be around me for some reason. Most of the time our conversations aren't even interesting. He talks to me about how depressing it was when they had to throw all those index cards from the old card catalogs away when they switched to digital, how he kept a few for himself as a way of trying to preserve a piece of the past. He talks about his dad's mustache and how it always gets food in it, how his mom is still too polite to say anything even though they've been married for decades. It all just feels barely above small talk. But then there are these moments where he says something that almost seems like it's verging on romance, or he looks at me, and I feel like something's about to happen, but it never does. I just don't get it."

"He's in love with you," Joy said with a smile spreading across her face.

"I know, but I don't think it matters. It didn't matter in college, and I don't think it matters now. I think he just wants to make sure again that he made the right choice back then, and I don't know why I'm letting him do this," Lyla said.

"You see that guy over there," Juanita Jane said and nodded in the direction of a tall twentysomething with an exaggerated smile entering the bar. "If he wasn't in my class, I could totally fuck him."

Bert chuckled and shook his head to outwardly show his disapproval to Lyla and Joy, to make it seem like Juanita Jane herself was joking, though they all knew she wasn't. He wondered if Lyla and Joy knew about Mark, wondered if they too had been at first disgusted with the idea of Juanita Jane and a nineteen-year-old but later excited by it, wondered if they too had entertained their own visions of sex with the much-younger residents who lived around them. He looked down at Juanita Jane's legs in the booth beside him, noticed the way they were freshly shaved and kind of shimmery from that floral-scented lotion she was always slathering on when he visited her in her dorm room late at night, noticed the way her smooth knees kind of glowed in the low lighting of the bar. Yes, she often looked ridiculous when she walked across campus in high heels and those huge red sunglasses rimmed with rows of rhinestones, but at least she was trying. And there was something comforting to Bert about the way Juanita Jane was always fighting aging, the way she refused to just fall down in defeat to it all.

"You could not," Joy said.

"Wanna make a bet?" Juanita Jane said.

"I'm gonna go take a piss," Bert said and got up. He headed toward the back room where the bathrooms were, and, just as he turned the corner, he spotted her. Jean. His wife. She was sitting at a table right by the men's room with a man Bert had never seen before.

She saw him right away and smiled in that way people do when they don't want to be in a particular situation but have to feign pleasantness in the name of social conventions. "What are you doing here?" she asked as he approached her table.

"I'm having drinks with some coworkers, talking about the FDD program, just killing some time before heading to the house."

"Oh, okay. Well, it's nice to see you," she said. *Nice to see him?* He wondered why she spoke to him like *he* was the stranger, like she was trying to make the conversation end quickly so she could get back to the man at her table. He felt his face go hot and grabbed the table in front of him to steady his balance, almost tipping over her glass of wine in the process.

"I thought you were having dinner with your parents tonight."

"Don't you remember? They're in Wisconsin this weekend." Of course he didn't remember. If he had, he wouldn't have asked the question.

"Are we still on for dinner with your parents next week?" he asked.

"I'll have to check my schedule," she said and seemed to be staring at him with please-leave-me-alone-now eyes.

"Check your schedule? What the hell are you talking about?" he asked. "You always want me to have dinner with your parents. What has suddenly changed? What could you possibly have going on that would make you too busy to do what we've been doing for years?" He could feel his voice getting louder, could feel the eyes of the retired farmers playing cards at the other side of the room boring into him, but he didn't care. "Why don't you introduce me to your *friend*? If that's what he is," he half shouted at her. The stranger looked at Bert. He was a short, plump pale man with features so muted they almost disappeared in his round face. Something about the stranger being there made Jean's face stand out again, and it occurred to Bert that maybe she was still attractive, that maybe he just couldn't see it anymore. As he stared hard at the stranger for a moment, he felt a rush of nausea thinking about this man groping Jean's breasts, running his chubby hands through her short hair, putting his mouth on her neck, thrusting himself inside of her, and rubbing the thick places on her outer thighs before she fell asleep. Suddenly, without any warning, he wanted to kill this stranger.

"I'm Owen," the guy said and extended his hand to Bert.

"Owen?" Bert yelled at him. "What the hell kind of name is Owen? What the hell's going on, Jean? Who is this guy?"

"He's just a friend."

"Friend from where?"

"He's just a guy my parents know. My dad bought some sod from him," she said, and Owen nodded.

"Sod? He's a sod salesman? Are you fucking kidding me? I leave for a couple months to do something for the university, to do something for my job, and your parents set you up with a fat fucking sod salesman?" he yelled.

"I think I better go," Owen said and stood up. "And for the record, we're just friends. Trust me, I'm not interested in screwing up someone's marriage." *Trust him? This guy wanted Bert to trust him?* Owen pulled out his wallet, set a twenty down on the table, and said, "That oughta cover it. Thanks for the visit, Jean. I really enjoyed it," and then he was gone, heading quickly across the bar and toward the door to safety.

"I can't believe this," Bert yelled. "I can't believe your parents are this desperate to get me out of the picture. I can't believe they set you up with this Owen guy."

"You're not listening. You never listen to me. My parents didn't set me up. The guy is new in town, doesn't know anyone his age yet, so my dad thought he might like someone to hang out with. That's it. That's all it is, and now the poor guy has to get accosted by my husband who doesn't even bother to drive the two miles to see me most of the time. You probably scared him half to death," she said and started putting her coat on.

"Scared *him* half to death? How do you think *I* feel? I come here to relax after a crappy week at work, and my wife is here on a fucking date."

"I told you. It's not a date, and it's not like you're so innocent. It's not like you don't have a whole life I don't know anything about anymore. I had to catch you at work with that Jerry Jane woman to even know she existed, and we both know that doesn't exactly look innocent ... you in the dorms a few rooms away from that woman ... like I don't know what's probably going on there."

"First of all, her name is Juanita Jane, and second of all, I can't believe you'd think something's going on. Why the hell would you think that?"

"Are you kidding me? Are you really that stupid?" she shouted. Bert couldn't believe what was happening. Before the FDD program, Jean never raised her voice in public. She was the kind of woman who went to great lengths to create the appearance of stability when others were around, a tactic that had once made her pretend she didn't know Bert as he yelled at the incompetent paint guy at the hardware store while she casually made her way out to the parking lot. But here she was, just like that night in her parents' yard, yelling at him in front of the onlookers in the bar.

"I'm not the stupid one. I'm not the one who hasn't so much as looked at her husband in over a year, and that's not to say anything about the fact that neither of us can remember the last time we had sex," he yelled. Just then the country music coming from the overhead speakers increased in volume, probably the bartender's attempt to cover up the shouting match happening in the back room of the bar.

"So you're admitting it then? Your wife won't give you any, so you have to get it from the crazy woman down the hall," she shouted over the music. "And that's how it is then?"

"No, that is not how it is, not even close. This isn't even about sex anymore. I just had to get out of there, just had to get out of that house with the same soup for dinner every Monday night. I mean, who the hell eats clam chowder for dinner every Monday night at five? Who the hell does that? I swear to God, if I ever see another bowl of clam chowder, I might snap. I just couldn't take it anymore."

"So now you're trashing my family's traditions? Now you're attacking my childhood? You're sick of clam chowder, so you move out of the house, leave me high and dry to wonder what the hell is going on ... all because you want something different for dinner. Why didn't you just say something?"

"This is ridiculous. It's not about the soup. It's the whole thing, like I said before. It's the whole routine of our lives. It's all just blending together now. Every week, I know that Monday night is going to be the exact same as it was the week before. I know we're going to eat clam chowder at five, do the dishes at six, watch those stupid sitcoms from seven to nine, read for an hour, put the trash can out on the curb, watch the weather portion of the news, check to make sure the porch lightbulb didn't burn out, and get ready for bed. What kind of life is that?"

"Why do you think I cut my hair?"

"What?"

"Why do you think I cut all my hair off? Don't you think I might want to change things once in a while too, take a risk, do something crazy? Do you think you're the only one who's bored? I'm supposed to be taking kids to baseball practice, but I don't have that. Do I? And how do you think that feels? Everyone else has that, but I'm just standing alone in a house with nothing to do," she said, her voice suddenly softer.

He looked at her face, noticed the way her big eyes were still a dramatic contrast to the thin peach lips, noticed the wrinkle lines around her eyes, more pronounced than they had once been, but still barely noticeable next to those dark eyes. For a moment, the haircut looked different. Maybe instead of taking something away, it enhanced something. Like the simple frame they purchased to display the perfect photo of a Florida sunset, maybe the short haircut made her eyes shine.

"I need to go," she said and retrieved her purse from the chair next to her.

"I'm coming with you," he said and suddenly remembered that he needed to pay for his beer. "Just give me a second to pay out."

"No, I don't want to do this with you tonight. Just go back to your friends. We'll talk tomorrow," she said and stared at him with pleading, wide open eyes.

"Fine," he said and watched helplessly as she made her way toward the exit.

He went to the bathroom and walked back to the table. "I just ran into Jean," he said as he sat down.

"I know. We heard," Juanita Jane said with a smirk on her face. "What the hell happened?"

"She was here with some guy. I got pissed. What can I say?"

As his friends talked about the way the quality of campus dining hall food declined as the semester wore on, Bert couldn't concentrate. Undercooked slices of pizza and burned grilled cheese sandwiches seemed unimportant as he pictured his wife driving across town to meet up with Owen again. Would she join him at a different bar? Would they go get pancakes at The Happy Chef? Would she meet him at Marshall Bowl and teach him how to put a good spin on the ball the way she had taught Bert when they first met? And afterwards, would they just part ways and head back to their own houses alone? Or would she invite him back to Bert's house and strip off her clothes in front of him, explaining, with a sexy smile on her face, that she hated smelling like a bowling alley? Was it possible that it would all be the same as the way she initiated sex with Bert all those years ago?

He couldn't stand it. He had to get out of there.

Chapter Twenty

Bert tried to drive the two miles back to the dorms but couldn't do it. He found himself scanning every parking lot from downtown Marshall to East College Drive for Jean's car, found himself getting angrier and angrier with each failed attempt to find out where she was, found himself almost veering off the road and into the Redwood River as he spotted a woman in a camel colored coat walking toward the amphitheater, a woman who he quickly realized couldn't be Jean because this woman had long blonde hair that fell far below her shoulders, the kind of hair that bounced against her back with each step. And when he got to the last turn before his building, he couldn't bring his hands to turn the wheel. Instead he kept driving, past the University, out onto the highway, and back toward his house across town.

Before he knew what he was doing, he pulled up to the house, and there it was – Jean's white Buick in the driveway. He parked beside her car, pushed the garage door opener button, got out of his car, and rushed inside. "Where is he?" he yelled across the house, standing alone in the yellow kitchen as the white cat rubbed up against his legs. "Jean? Where are you?"

And then she was there, standing in the doorway of the kitchen, wearing a new red nightgown and her old purple-rimmed glasses. The fact that the nightgown was new both enraged and excited him.

"Why are you in pajamas?" he asked.

"What are you doing here? What are you trying to do?"

"Did he go home? Did he leave already?"

"He went home after the bar. He didn't—" she started.

"He didn't come over? You didn't keep hanging out? I just assumed—"

"What are you doing here?" she asked again, and he felt a rush of relief race through him. Maybe it wasn't a date after all because what kind of date involves two people driving their own cars to a central location? What kind of date ends after the first sign of trouble? What kind of date is over before the sun goes down on a Friday night? "Well?" she said.

"I'm still your husband, you know. Just because I'm living in the dorms ... we're still married, you know."

"I know," she said and scooped the cat up, cradling him just above her breasts and kissing him on the nose as he purred in her embrace.

"So I don't need a reason to be here. This is still my house too, you know."

"I know," she said and set the cat down on the kitchen table, a habit that usually irritated Bert but somehow relaxed him because of its familiarity.

"Do you want to watch something?" he asked.

"I just want you to go, just want you to go back to the dorms and leave me be. The thing is ... when it first started, when you first moved out, it was really hard. I couldn't even sleep more than an hour here or there because it was so scary, the idea of being alone again, the fact that you might be gone for good ... really gone. But now, now after I got past all that, it's almost the opposite."

"What do you mean?"

"I mean, and don't go into a rage over this ... because I can't handle that after everything we've been through tonight, but I guess what I'm trying to say, what I realized a couple of weeks ago, is that maybe I don't mind so much, that maybe this is okay. I'm just used to it now, used to you not being around, and I'm okay now. I got over the shock of it somehow. I've come out on the other end of it," she said and pulled on the bottom of her nightgown, trying unsuccessfully to cover her knees with the fabric.

"You look beautiful," he said, surprising even himself.

"What are you doing?"

"I'm telling my wife that she looks beautiful. I haven't seen that nightgown before. I like it. It's shorter than what you normally wear."

"You're just saying this because you saw me with a guy tonight ... because you totally misread the situation and freaked out ... because I just told you I'm okay now with you gone. You're just saying it because you can't handle losing anything, even if it's something you didn't want anymore."

"No," he said and stepped toward her. "No, that's not it. Maybe the whole damn thing is my fault. Maybe it is. Maybe I let the thing run off the tracks. I don't know anymore, but I'm here, and you're here, and you look beautiful, and I can't stand it. I can't keep doing this anymore, can't keep living with us just looking past each other. I want to be with you again," he said and started kissing her. For a moment, she just stood there frozen as he smooshed his lips against hers, licking her bottom lip like a dog desperate for attention, but then it all changed. She started kissing him back, and, before either of them knew what was happening, the red nightgown was on the kitchen floor, and they were racing toward the bedroom to try to somehow reclaim everything they had lost.

*

"I slept with Jean last night," Bert told Juanita Jane while sitting on the unmade bed in her messy dorm room.

"Really? Holy shit. So you guys are good then? Everything's worked out between you now?" she asked and took a sip of what she called 'afternoon whiskey.'

"No, everything is not good. Honestly, everything is horrible. I'm such an idiot. I can't believe I did this. I can't believe I let this happen."

"So she initiated it?"

"No, it was all me. She was all ready to slam the book of our marriage shut, and, like an idiot, I said, 'No, let's not end it all just yet. Let's keep it going. Let's have sex again like the last five years never happened. Let's just start all over again.' What the hell was I thinking? How can I be this stupid? I'm a math professor, for God's sakes."

"What's math got to do with it?" she asked.

"Are you kidding? Math has *everything* to do with it. I'm like those idiots who just keep working the same equation and are always shocked when the answer comes out the same. What the hell was I thinking?" he said and slumped back on the bed.

"Was it good?" she asked.

"What?"

"The sex. Was the sex good?"

"Oh," he said and paused a moment. "No, no it wasn't good. Well—it wasn't bad, but it wasn't good. But it's not even about the sex—don't you see? It's about what comes *after* the sex. It's about the outcome of the sex."

"So you're having some next-day regrets?"

"Next day? *Next day?* It didn't even last that long. Any excitement there was vanished immediately after. I mean, *immediately*. As soon as we were finished, she made me get up out of bed so she could strip the sheets off. God forbid that woman ever slept a night in sweat stained sex sheets. She can't do it. I'd forgotten about that somehow. It's like she put on the red nightgown—still not a sexy nightgown by anyone's standards—but seeing her in something different, seeing her out at the bar with a stranger, it was like all the facts seemed to converge just at the right moment to make me forget everything. How could that be? But I did. I forgot all of it, but now it's all the same. I woke up this morning, and she was sitting at the kitchen table, and she wasn't wearing the red nightgown anymore. No, she was wearing one of those old ratty ones again. How crazy is that? It's like that crazy symbol crap you literature people are always talking about," he said, and Juanita Jane smiled. "And she was sitting there drinking that same weak coffee, and the chore list was somehow back on the fridge. Hell, maybe it was the night before, and I just didn't notice it, but the point is—I didn't notice it, but the next morning, it was there again, waiting for me."

"Please tell me you didn't have to do chores this morning. Please tell me that didn't happen," she said and burst into laughter.

"Oh, it happened. After the weak coffee and the horrible conversation about the Canadian geese pooping all over the driveway and the toast with low fat butter, she handed me the list. Can you believe that? She just handed it to me without saying anything, like the last three months never happened, and I spent the next two hours cleaning the grout on the tile countertop in the hallway bathroom and dusting the mini blinds in the living room. It's like she gave me the two worst cleaning jobs on purpose, and all the while, she's walking around the house whistling Fourth of July songs out of tune while I'm desperately wishing I could take my decision to drive over there last night back. God, I'm such an idiot. And now what am I gonna do? Now I'm really trapped. You can't sleep with your wife after years without and then leave her. Everyone knows that's not an option," he said.

"So you're just gonna stay in a situation you hate?"

"I don't see any way around it," he said and looked across the twin bed at her, as though searching for an answer to an unsolvable equation.

"Don't look at me. I didn't put you in this shit," she said.

"But I know your history. I know you've managed to get out of these things dozens of times. How do you do it? Tell me how you do it."

"First of all, dozens might be a bit of an exaggeration. Might," she said and winked at him. "Second of all, there's always a mess

... I mean, sometimes a real mess ... I mean, sometimes a huge fucking mess. Third of all, I've never been married. I can't speak to this with any certainty of what I'm saying, but I'm pretty sure it's not the same thing."

"So what? I'm just stuck then? There's nothing I can do?"

"Oh, there are things you can do, but there's gonna be a mess," she said and took another sip of whiskey. "There's gonna be a huge fucking mess. No way around that, my friend."

Chapter Twenty-one

Lyla looked out her dorm room window, killing time before meeting Margie and Juanita Jane in the dining hall for dinner. The forecasted snowstorm was just starting to swirl outside her window, covering the last of autumn's leaves in a thin sheet of whiteness. For the moment, grass shoots still poked through the snow, a final reminder of the previous summer before it fully sank into the forgotten shadows of the past.

Three stories below, students rushed in and out of the building in sweatshirts and light coats. In Marshall, a snowstorm meant that it wasn't cold enough for a thick jacket yet. Instead, the locals reserved their fleece-lined coats for the real winter days, the kind of days where temperatures dipped down below zero and stayed there even in the presence of midday sunshine. Lyla smiled at the students below and felt a rush of gratitude that these weren't the college students of movies and pop songs. These students didn't know where to buy designer jeans or trendy tennis shoes and wouldn't have the means to do so even if they did know where to get them. Instead, they shopped for clothes at the Shopko out on the edge of Marshall and in Ricky's Farm and Supply Store which stocked only the basics in apparel. These students were always a year or two behind on the music that ruled the airwaves in the more densely populated areas across the country. Instead, they listened to songs that had already slid to the backside of billboard chart success and gave their real devotion to live bands that drove in from Sioux Falls and Fargo to play to appreciative crowds in The Steady Saloon and Prairie State's gymnasium. These students didn't dream of starring in Broadway plays or being the head chef in a five-star restaurant in London. Instead, they majored in things like accounting or agricultural business, imagining a life in a tiny bank office somewhere or hoping to somehow hold onto the struggling family farm.

Before moving into the dorms, Lyla saw her relationship to the students as merely transactional. She stood at the front of a room and told them about the major events of American History, they took tests to show how much of the information they retained, she ran the tests through the Scantron machine, and each student got a grade to reflect his/her performance. There was no reason for it to be anything more than that. But something about living there was changing everything. Something about sleeping and eating in the same spaces that they were in had shifted her perception of the whole thing, and she found herself doing things she had never done in class before. The week before, while passing out a test to an early morning class full of exhausted students, she announced the answers to three of the questions for no reason at all. Two of the students still got the questions wrong, either out of sheer laziness or because they didn't trust Lyla's out-of-character behavior, but the rest of the class seemed thrilled by the free points and didn't even notice the fact that it only shifted the curve a bit and had no real impact on their test grades. In another class, she spent the last five minutes of the lecture critiquing the unhygienic way bread was prepared in colonial times—a subject that had nothing to do with the scheduled lecture for the day—but veering off course seemed to entertain the students far more than what she had originally planned.

Was it possible that Mr. Administration was right? Was the program having a positive effect on both her and the students she taught? Was she starting to form a more authentic connection to the people in her classes? Or was the reality of living in the dorms making her regress? Was sleeping in the twin bed between cinder block walls and working at the same small desk of her own college days slowly putting her back there? Was she relating more to the students now simply because she was forgetting that she wasn't actually one of them? Was she losing the role she had spent years carefully carving out, the role of fair but authoritative instructor? It was hard to know.

"I'm barging in. I'm barging in," she heard Juanita Jane yelling outside her dorm door.

Walking to dinner with Juanita Jane and Margie on Monday nights was becoming more than just a routine. It was an expectation. As the three of them descended the steps toward the dorm exit, Lyla wondered what life would feel like next semester, wondered if she would still have dinners with her newly-formed FDD friends or if the absence of the program would make it all just fade away.

"Hey, Professor Ruckler," a male student sporting a bad goatee shouted at Juanita Jane as she walked past him in the dorm lounge. "I heard you give blow jobs to students."

"Hey, dip shit," Juanita Jane shouted back. "I heard you're failing biology."

"Good one," Margie said and high-fived Juanita Jane so hard that Juanita Jane almost couldn't keep her balance.

"He really is failing biology. Dr. Heiser told me," she announced to a lounge scattered with students, ignoring the fact that such an announcement was an obvious violation of the Student Privacy Act training she had completed just the week before.

As they stepped outside, Margie spread her hands out to catch a bit of the snowfall on her fingertips.

"Don't you just love this?" Juanita Jane said. "I know everyone always says *spring* is the time of love, the time of passion, the time of sexual awakening. But don't you think they have it all wrong? Look at this," she said and tipped her head up toward the maple tree with its leafless branches already buried in snow. "Look at this shit," she said and threw her arms up to the snow-filled skies. "You don't get this shit living in Louisiana. I can tell you that right now."

"It is beautiful," Lyla said.

"I heard we might not have school tomorrow," Margie said. "I heard we might be out half the week ... supposed to be a big one this time ... like total white-out conditions for days."

"God, wouldn't it be great? Imagine the fun we could have," Juanita Jane said. "I mean, it was always fun before, but not like this, not like it will be this time. Last year it happened when my mom was visiting, and let me tell you—that's not as great as you're imagining. I mean, the first day was fine ... just a lot of drinking and crazy movies, but the second day ... oh, the second day is when shit really started to decline. Trust me, ladies, there are just some conversations you don't want to have in a snowed-in situation. Believe me. It can go bad. It can go really bad."

"I heard they're closing the roads leaving town at seven tonight," Margie said. "It's definitely a good sign. They never close the highways if the forecast isn't really bad."

"Here's hoping," Juanita Jane shouted and raised up her empty hand to the sky, like she was making a toast to all the snowflakes that hadn't fallen yet.

*

When Lyla turned the last corner heading to her room, she couldn't believe what she saw. Seated outside her door with an army-patterned duffle bag beside him was Anton. "What are you doing here?" she asked. "Are you crazy? How did you even get here? Some guy at the dining hall just said the highway visibility is down to zero. I couldn't even see that well walking back here from the dining hall. I couldn't even—"

"The last few miles weren't great. I'm not gonna lie, but I got lucky. They were just getting ready to close the road gates when I pulled into town," he said and stood up.

"Didn't you look at the forecast before you left?" she asked.

"Yeah, but I figured I'd make it. I was hoping to have a little time here before it really started blowing, but that's not gonna happen, so I just wanted to say hi quick before heading to Jar's."

"You just came here to say hi quick?" she asked with a shrug. Maybe it was just as well. The logistics of Anton staying for a visit were tricky. Her jeans and socks were soaked through from the aggressive snowfall happening outside, and she wanted to take a hot shower to warm up before changing into dry clothes.

"I'll try to come visit tomorrow, if the roads are plowed," he said. She wondered why he was visiting Jar on a Monday night, wondered if she was his real reason for risking death on the road to get there, but she couldn't bring herself to ask.

"Okay," she said and forced a smile.

Back in her room, she threw a new shampoo in her shower basket and grabbed the oversized white robe she always wore after showers so as not to be seen in a towel during the quick walk back to her room. Just like in her own college days, she was often surprised at the lack of modesty some of the students possessed. Margie's roommate sometimes lingered in the hallway after showers, wearing a tiny towel that barely covered her ample backside, making conversation with anyone who passed by, an obvious attempt to be seen by male residents. A student at the end of Lyla's hall always walked to the bathroom topless if she had to pee after midnight, a fact that was mostly deemed unexciting by male residents due to the almost nonexistent nature of her small breasts. And Bert said many of the male residents didn't even bother shutting their doors while getting dressed after morning showers, a fact that Juanita Jane found intriguing as she sometimes took the long way out of the building in order to sneak a peek at those undressed boyish bodies.

After a quick shower, Lyla was shocked to see Anton in front of her door again, standing there with the duffle bag slung over his shoulder. She pulled on the robe's collar to make sure her cleavage was covered and just stared at him with raised eyebrows.

"It's bad out there. There was no way," he said. "Look, I know this is awkward, but I'm gonna have to stay here tonight ... no way around it. I'll sleep on the floor. I could barely see two feet in front of the truck. The snow's blowing so hard. I just couldn't risk it."

"Okay," she said. "Just wait out there, and I'll put some clothes on."

She couldn't believe it. After all the years that stood between her and her college self, she was right back there, back having sleepovers with Anton in a college dorm room. Her hair was a little thinner and her body a little heavier, but the feelings were the same.

Alone in her room, she combed her wet hair quickly, hung the damp robe on the hook by the closet, and put on tight black lounge pants with an old gray oversized Prairie State t-shirt. She looked in the mirror for a moment, in an attempt to steady herself, before opening the door.

"I had this idea that I had to run by you," Anton said as he stepped into the room. "It's why I had to come here." She looked at him—his long hair wet from the snowstorm outside, just like so many times all those years ago.

"I thought you came to see Jar."

"No, I came to see you. I was going to stay at Jar's place tonight, but I had to talk to you about something."

"So you drove all the way here from Fargo in a snowstorm to talk to me about an idea?"

"I told you. It wasn't snowing until the last few miles," he said with a frustrated smile.

"I just don't get it. You have my phone number. You could've just called me."

"I had to see you while I said it. I don't know why, but it didn't seem like a phone conversation," he said.

"Okay. What's up?"

"I was at work today, and I just kept thinking about how if I were just plopped down somewhere in my past, in my own life but a different part of it, I kept thinking about how I wouldn't know how to exist there anymore. You know what I mean?" he asked, standing in the middle of her room.

"No."

"Okay—think about it. Let's say you wake up, and suddenly you're in your junior year of college," he said. "Imagine that."

She looked around her room—the plastic cup full of brightly colored pens sitting on the dorm desk, the stack of political biographies leaning against the wall by the bed, the half-eaten package of Double-Stuffed Oreos sitting on the mini fridge, and the postcards of snowy owls tacked to the gray pin board above the bed. "Yeah, I think I can imagine it," she said and smiled.

"No, but I don't mean symbolically. I mean literally. I mean, think about it—you wake up, and it's your junior year of college, and you don't know what your classes are. You don't remember *where* they are. You don't remember how to do your math homework. Maybe you don't even remember the names of some of the people you pass in the hallways. Think about *that* for a minute," he said and nodded at her. "It's like you're totally shut off from entire pieces of your life ... huge pieces ... like you're somehow a stranger to something you used to know so intimately. That's what it is, right? I'd never thought about that before, but something about coming here made it all so clear, made me understand that, at some point, we just lose all the pieces of our own lives, and how can that be? It's crazy, right?"

"So that's why you're here then?" she asked. "You're trying to remember something, to feel a part of your life that you lost? You think sitting in a dorm room for a while can put you back there?"

"Well?" he said. "Isn't that why you're here?"

"So that's what you're doing then. That's why you're here. That's why you keep coming back," she said, more to herself than him.

"I just don't think it goes away ... just because your life moves past it. That's what I realized. I think we forget about it. I think we let it go to the back of our minds somewhere and that most of us don't pull it out again, but I don't think it ever goes away. I think it's still there."

"What? What's still there?" she half-shouted.

"You," he said and curled his lips under, like he was trying to swallow back the word.

"Look—we were in love back then. I know that. I know that because anytime I smell coconut suntan lotion, I'm right back in that room with you."

"Suntan lotion?"

"Don't you remember ... that body wash I used to have that you said smelled like a tropical vacation right in the middle of Marshall? Don't you remember buying me a dozen bottles of it when it was being clearanced out, how you said you could just bury yourself in my skin and all the coldness outside would just go away? Don't you remember?"

"Of course I remember," he said and stepped toward her.

"But ... the thing is," she started and took a step back from him. "I didn't want to remember. After you ended it with me–that night–I threw the last bottles of the body wash away, but I couldn't stand the idea that the smell would still exist in a heap of trash somewhere, so I took the bottles out of the garbage and emptied them, one by one, down the drain in the dorm bathroom. And I remember how mad I was the next day when I went to brush my teeth, and I could still smell the coconut in the drain ... and how it hurt even more when I went back later and the smell was gone, when it was completely taken over by that generic soap smell of the hand soap by the sink."

"That's crazy," he said. "I didn't remember that."

"Of course not. You weren't there. We weren't together anymore. It was right after—"

"No," he said, cutting her off. "I mean, I didn't remember buying all those bottles of it, all at once, and I didn't even remember the body wash at all until you brought it up, but now it's all coming back, and I can even smell it. Isn't that crazy? I can smell something from almost twenty years ago just because of the way it sounds when your specific voice says the word *coconut*. And this is what I'm talking about. It's like I'm losing my own past, like the path that leads back there is growing over with weeds, like you're the only one who can help me clear it all away and get back there again," he said with an obvious tension in his voice. "And I didn't know that, didn't realize it until I saw you at that game, and then it all started coming back, and the path back to it all was there again ... but only when I was with you."

"But maybe the path isn't supposed to be visible anymore. Maybe that's the whole point of life. Maybe the beauty of it is that all the pain of the past can eventually grow over," she said and bit her lower lip. "And ... the thing is ... even if I could go back there, I wouldn't want to." Even as she was saying it, she knew it wasn't true.

"But look where we are. We're middle-aged, but we're in this room again, and we're snowed in again, and it's just like that first night again."

"But that's the thing," she said, looking at the snow swirling in the wind outside her window. "It's not the same. We're not the same. You don't know me anymore. You know that other version of me, and I'm not her anymore."

"So I know the better version," he said. "I know the version who doesn't have to try to feel something. I know the version who can hear a new song and feel what it means, who doesn't have to turn the volume way up on her own damn life to see what's around her," he said.

"So you're gonna do that now? You're gonna use what I said against me?"

"Look—you came up to me. You could've just left the game, could've just left, and it would've been like I was never there. But you came up to me. You made that happen, so here we are, and at first I hated it. I didn't want to talk to the girl I almost married in college. Trust me—I didn't want to face that shit again ... because I had an expectation of what it would be like, had an expectation of some horrible small talk and an awkward goodbye in a parking lot somewhere."

"And that's what happened," she said.

"I know, but it was more than that. It was—"

"I can't do this. You being here ... I can't do this. You're gonna have to sleep in Bert's room or something. I'm sorry, but this is bad ... this isn't a good idea."

"Why?"

She sat down on the bed and pulled at a loose thread in her floral pillowcase. But Anton didn't sit down. Instead he continued to stand above her, hovering over her like an impatient interrogation officer waiting for an answer. "Okay," she started. "The truth is ... I don't know how to do this anymore."

"Do what?"

"This," she said and spread her arms out in front of her. "I don't know how to do any of this, and it's worse with you. It's worse because I used to know how to do this with you, and somehow that makes it all so much more uncomfortable." She sighed into the momentary silence between them. "The last year I was married, my husband never touched me, never even held my hand, and honestly, I didn't mind because I knew. I knew he wasn't attracted to me anymore. I knew he just saw me as this woman who was keeping him away from all the stuff he wanted to be doing. And I remember going to my cousin's wedding in Iowa City right before I got divorced. I was staying alone in this hotel downtown—that's how bad it was between us. He didn't even want to go to a wedding with me, so I was there all alone, and I was in one of those rooms way high up where you don't even need to close the drapes because no one below can see you anyway. And there was this office building across the way, and I remember wishing that there was a man still working in one of those offices when I got back to my room after the wedding. It's humiliating to say this, but I'm just gonna say it. The truth is I really wanted to take my dress off in front of that window. I really wanted for some stranger across the way to see me, to just watch me undress, to just watch me."

"Why? As a way to get back at your husband?" he asked.

"No, it had nothing to do with him, not really anyway. It was more than that. It was the fact that it just suddenly occurred to me that that wasn't ever going to happen again, that no man, for the rest of my life, would watch me undress and react to it, that it was over, and I just wanted to have that feeling one last time. And doing it for some anonymous person somehow seemed innocent, like I wasn't really doing anything wrong ... not that it was even really that wrong. Our marriage was basically over already. It's just so weird, as a woman, to reach that point when compliments don't come in a steady stream anymore, when they trickle in less and less. It's weird knowing that soon they won't come at all. When I was in college, I couldn't be out in public for more than an hour without someone telling me I was beautiful, without at least a small comment about it. I'm not bragging. That's just the way it was," she said and shrugged.

"I remember," he said and laughed.

"And now I'm just a teacher."

"You're still beautiful, Lyla." Hearing her name in his mouth sent a shockwave rushing through her body.

"But is it because I am now or because you're remembering me then?"

"I don't think it matters," he said, and maybe he was right. Maybe it didn't matter. Maybe they had already traveled back to that time where they first met because, in that moment, all she could see was the twenty-two-year-old version of Anton. All she could see was the boy with the searching eyes and soft voice, the boy with the long dark hair, the boy her college friends used to call her Norwegian prince. She couldn't see the path back to their past anymore because they were already there, and when he sat down on the bed and leaned over to kiss her again, she already knew the outcome, already knew all the pains and pleasures that were waiting for her up ahead, but it didn't matter anymore. There was no longer any way to stop it.

Chapter Twenty-two

Waking to a winter wonderland outside and a day of no classes inside was a dream come true for the students in the rooms surrounding Joy, but for her the blizzard was not a welcome break from the routine of classes. For her the blizzard was interfering with the important appointment she had at the Marshall Community Center with the wedding coordinator.

"Hi, Shelly," Joy said into the phone, with a hint of caution in her voice.

"I think ... I'm thinking with the weather the way it is this morning ... I'm thinking that we better just reschedule," Shelly said.

"But didn't the director of the community center say she lives right next door? Don't you think she could just walk over? I mean—she wouldn't want to lose the booking, right? I can't imagine there are many opportunities to host weddings in the winter, right?" Joy asked.

"That's all well and good, but how am I supposed to get there? I live three miles out of town, and there's no way my husband's letting me drive in this craziness."

"Okay," Joy said and sighed into the phone. "I'll just call her and cancel."

And she did call, but she didn't cancel. Instead she threatened to move her reception to a different location unless the woman who ran the place could still meet with her during the blizzard.

With the dorm building less than a mile away from the center, Joy decided she could easily walk to the appointment. After all, what was a little walk in blowing snow compared to a lifetime of love with Miles?

*

In a dorm room across the building, Bert was working his way through a stack of math homework assignments when a huge thud startled him so severely that he accidentally spilled coffee all over the ungraded pages. "Damn it," he said aloud to no one. "What the hell was that?"

He thought about just tossing the papers in the trash and giving everyone who had bothered to turn in the assignment full credit. He could pass it off as a kind gesture toward the students who were still doing their daily homework in November (the point in the semester where the serious students had fully separated from the ones who were only there to party).

He grabbed an old towel and started to soak up the coffee but didn't finish. Looking at that soggy stack of papers, he knew he couldn't possibly pass them back. He knew that no amount of cleaning could erase the shame he would feel when explaining that a loud noise had startled the coffee cup right out of his hands. Somehow the thought of passing back coffee-stained papers seemed more embarrassing now that he was living in the dorms, like the mistake was amplified by the fact that he lived where his students lived, heard them having sex on the other side of his walls, saw them in boxer shorts brushing their teeth before morning classes. He could no longer blame all coffee related homework incidents on his cat's unruly tail. They knew where he was living, and they knew you couldn't have a cat there.

Bert was not surprised when he heard a knock on the door, and he was even less surprised to see Juanita Jane standing there. "Did you hear it?" she asked.

"What *was* that? It kinda sounded like last winter when we had that really big storm and the roof of my garage caved in, and

Jean was somehow furious with me over it, like it was somehow *my* fault that the roof couldn't hold the weight of all that snow, like I was supposed to be camped out on the roof all night shoveling it clean while she slept in the house, like I was somehow supposed to—"

"Interesting story, but nope. That's not what happened this time. What happened this time is that Josh Sawyer got so wasted last night, after they announced that classes were officially off, that the poor bastard fell out of his bunk, and we're not talking bottom bunk here. Poor bastard. Nope—we're talking this dipshit somehow slid out the back of it or somehow made it over the side rail in his sleep and landed right on his back."

"Oh, my God," Bert said and scratched his head the way he did when contemplating a complex math problem. "Is he okay?"

"Of course he's okay. Isn't that the crazy shit of life? You fall while walking at eighty, and you're done for—gone—dead in a week, a couple a months if you're lucky. But you fall from the top of the room at eighteen, and you just get up and shake yourself off. Crazy," she said and shook her head wildly.

"So how did you find out about it?" Bert asked.

Juanita Jane pushed past him, pulled him by the arm into his room, slammed the door, and said, "Let's just say that Josh wasn't the only one who got drunk and fucked up last night."

"You slept with my neighbor again?"

"Oh, that? Yes. But that's not the fuck up. That's been fairly ongoing, truth be told. But it wasn't the sex that's the problem. No, no, it wasn't the sex. That was great. That's always pretty damn great, truth be told," she said and slapped Bert's shoulder. "It was what happened *before* the sex. That was the problem, and it was *really* what happened after," she said and shrugged with a smile on her face that betrayed her attempt to sound concerned.

"What happened?"

"Before or after?"

"Both."

"Donny was bugging the shit out of me. He thinks that just

because he got me a plane ticket to come to Billings over Thanksgiving that he can rule my life, thinks I should always be available to chat with him on Facebook day and night, thinks that a four-hundred dollar ticket means he owns my ass, and I was sick to hell of that shit, so I told him to fuck off," she said and nodded at Bert.

"And you regret that?"

"No."

"Then what's the problem?" he asked.

"I realized it last night as I was trying to shove my ass into a pair of Margie's jeans."

"Realized what?"

"That I might be falling for all of this."

"All of what?" he asked.

"Look around you—this—this is a fantasy. This isn't real. You think you're in this world because you live here for a couple of months, but you're not ... not even close. They're all the way in it—the students, I mean—but you—you barely have your toe in the water. And what the hell am I doing? What are any of us doing? Sure, Mr. Administration thinks this is about retention, thinks this is some faculty-student relationship development bullshit, thinks that he can put this feather in his cap if it happens to coincide with higher enrollments in the spring, if we happen to register more students than the numbers they got last year. But he doesn't know what's really going on, doesn't know the psychological warfare that's raging inside all of us down here in the trenches. Think about it—last night I'm in bed with a college kid, and I'm thinking *I love him*, and then I'm thinking *no, no I don't love him. I love the idea of what he represents—love the idea of somehow holding onto those last shreds of the person we all used to be*. And I suddenly realized that, as it turns out, I'm actually living in a ridiculous version of *carpe diem* gone horribly, horribly wrong, and what a fucking embarrassment that is. I mean, I teach this shit, right? How many poems scream at us from the page *live in the moment ... seize the day*? But those poems never talk about what happens to us after—no. Poets never give that bit of insight, do they?"

"So what is it?" he asked. "What happens after?"

"What happens after is that your fifty-year-old ass is naked in bed next to a nineteen-year-old the morning after when Josh Sawyer bursts into the room—the room that your sexy nineteen-year-old forgot to lock the night before—and Josh Sawyer looks both horrified and excited as he shares the news of his spectacular fall to his naked English professor and her quasi-boyfriend that he went to high school with."

"Oh no," Bert said. "He saw you?"

"Oh, he saw me. He saw *all* of me," she said and laughed. "And for a moment I forgot. Isn't that crazy? For a moment I forgot who I was ... or rather *where* I was."

"You mean you thought you were in your own room?"

"No. Oh, no. I knew where I was in space. I just forgot where I was in my life." Suddenly the animation in her face dropped, and, for the first time in weeks, she looked to him the way she had those first days in the dorms before he knew the possibility of excitement that resided behind the aging exterior. He noticed again the pattern of tiny lines across her thin lips and wondered what it felt like for a teenager to kiss them. He noticed the slight sag of her makeup-smudged eyes and the way the skin over her nose was redder than the rest of her face.

"Do you think he'll tell anyone?" he asked.

"Anyone? I don't think he'll tell *anyone*. I think he'll tell *everyone*," she said, and for some reason, the smile was back on her face. "But I'm not sure if I care. I mean, first of all, who's gonna believe him anyway? He's Josh Sawyer—the dipshit who fell out of the top bunk. This is literally the perfect time to blame information on a possible head injury. And second of all, so what if he does? Nineteen is legal age, and the guy's not even in my class, and would it really be the worst thing to have the reputation of being the professor who slept with a hot student? Would that even be so bad?" she asked.

Bert shrugged, but maybe she was right. Maybe the whole thing wasn't such a big deal. After all, the chair of his department had once said that the only two paths to job termination after tenure were sleeping with an under-aged student or acts of physical violence. Other things could get you out of the classroom and reassigned to some soul-sucking administrative work, but they couldn't make you lose your job.

*

There was nothing more beautiful, and there was nothing more lonely, than the day after a blizzard on the prairie—the way everything stood still for a moment as schools and businesses closed down, the roads that were too heavy with snowfall for cars to move over them, the absence of music on the radio as long lists of the day's closures were read repeatedly, and the typical sounds of winter birds hushed as they hunkered down somewhere hidden from view. And there was a strange freedom in the feeling of being trapped, a strange weightlessness in being untied from the day's scheduled activities.

When Margie knocked on Lyla's door a little before noon to see if she wanted to have lunch in the dining hall, Lyla opened the door just enough to be seen through the narrow opening and whispered, "I can't today. Anton's here."

"What? Really? Oh, my God. Really? So you guys are, like, snowed-in together? That's so romantic, like a movie or something."

"Yeah, something like that. I'll come see you later," Lyla said and winked at Margie before shutting the door.

"Who was that?" Anton asked.

"Just Margie. You know—the girl I was at the game with."

He nodded and said, "Remember what we always used to do on snow days in college?"

"Yeah—stay in bed late and have sex all morning—just like today."

"Yeah, that's a given, but I'm talking about the other thing," he said and stood up to grab his jacket.

"Go for a long walk and talk about how great it is to not worry about watching for cars?"

"Yeah, that thing. Remember the time we walked all the way to County Market just to buy candy bars and gummy bears? My parents would've been so pissed if they knew how I spent their emergency fund cash," he said.

"Well," she said with a smirk on her face. "Today might be your lucky day because the older version of me has plenty of cash for candy bars."

*

Joy's trudge through snow to get to the Marshall Community Center was much harder than she had anticipated. With occasional wind gusts of over forty miles per hour, she kept her face down as she walked, trying hard to prevent the blotchy-cheeked look of windburn that so many Minnesotans wore in the winter months, a look that was sure to prompt questions from Miles since she was anything but outdoorsy.

Because it wasn't particularly cold with the temperature in the mid-twenties, it didn't take long for Joy to feel sweat beading beneath her bra and on the lower part of her back. She wondered if it would have been better to just wait the extra day or two to talk to the venue's director about her preferred table linens, centerpieces, and background dinner music, wondered if her solitary snowy trek was more foolish than romantic. But there was something heroic about the whole thing, something almost cinematic about a woman walking alone down the middle of an abandoned street, something that made her feel strong as she inhaled the cold air and struggled with each step through the deep snow, something that she could tell her grandchildren someday when they asked why their grandmother planned her wedding alone. And when she thought about all the future sacrifices Miles would certainly make for her—the late nights taking care of sick children, the thousands of times he would mow the lawn at their future home, all the furniture sets he would put together, the hot summer days when he'd wake up early to paint the house, all the meals he'd cook, all the laundry he'd do, all the dishes he would scrub, the huge accumulation of tasks married life would require—a walk to the community center didn't seem like a big deal at all.

When she got to the community center, she had to pull the front door hard to dislodge the hill of snow that had drifted over the entryway. "Hello?" she yelled out to the dark room inside. There was no answer. "Hello?" she yelled again. Nothing.

She stomped her feet on the entry rug to get the snow off her boots, shook her shoulders and brushed the snow off her green ski jacket. She removed her black hat and matching mittens and shook them over the rug too before shoving them into her coat pockets. "Hello?" she yelled a third time. Still no response. "Oh, well," she whispered and flicked the light switch on.

The community center didn't look the way it was pictured on the website. Without the decorated tables, without the perfectly posed people in their best dress clothes, without the white chairs with brightly colored bows on their backs, without the tiny white lights bordering skirted tables filled with desserts and family photographs, without all the expected elements of a wedding venue, the community center's reception room looked more like a place to play basketball than a place to celebrate a wedding. Still, Joy knew that indoor weddings were always this way. This was why she wanted the ceremony portion of the day to be outside because, even in December, the natural beauty of the outdoors would serve as a better backdrop for the beginning of her life with Miles.

Just as she began to wonder exactly where she would be standing when Miles fed her a bite of wedding cake, the back door flung open. "I'm so sorry, so, so sorry," the woman across the room shouted. "I'd like to be able to blame it on traffic. Ha! But that's a clear lie today, isn't it? Honestly, the only person we can really blame is Dr. Phil. You wouldn't believe this episode," she said while speed walking toward Joy. Joy felt slightly disgusted. *The woman she was entrusting her wedding reception with was late because of an episode of Dr. Phil?* For a moment, she thought about telling the woman to just forget about it, thought about telling her she'd like to find a different place to feed her friends after the wedding. But then she remembered Shelly saying that the community center was "basically free in the winter months" and decided she'd give the woman a chance.

"So Shelly spoke with you about my vision?" Joy asked.

"She did. She did indeed, and I think we can get it all done for four. Three if you want to give them the cheap food and skip the twinkle lights," she said.

Joy did the math in her head. Even with the dress, cake, officiant, flowers, makeup, hair, photographer, and the courthouse wedding they'd have to do a few weeks later to make it all legal, the wedding would definitely come in under ten thousand. "No, I definitely don't want to skip the twinkle lights. I definitely want those," Joy said with a huge smile spreading across her wind-chapped face.

"Okay, then. Let's get you all set up."

Chapter Twenty-three

The Happy Chef was almost full at one in the morning on a mid-November Saturday in Marshall. Desperate college students studied all night over pancakes and pots of stale coffee, trying to somehow salvage a semester of academic neglect and apathy. Drunks from the bars downtown staggered in, searching for the kinds of conversations that can only be had after a night of heavy drinking, the kinds of conversations that go well with a plate of greasy hash browns and a cold glass of flat coke. Waitresses with tired faces and outdated hairstyles rushed from one table to the next, trying to keep up with the late-night rush and still maintain the relatively pleasant demeanor that was expected of Midwesterners. Joy and Miles sat in a booth by the bathrooms.

"I've been thinking," Joy started. "I'd like to do something really awesome for your birthday."

"Why?" Miles asked and took a sip of his coffee.

"I just think it would be fun."

"Okay," he said and leaned back in the booth.

"And I'd like to invite a few people," she said.

"What do you mean?"

"I mean—when's the last time you had a party—a party for you—a party with your friends and family?"

"Friends and family?" he said and sat up straight. "What are you talking about? You want to throw a party for my twenty-eighth birthday and invite my *family*?" The way he said the word *family* made her wonder if his familial relationships were strained in some way.

"I just thought it would be nice," she said and forced a smile.

"But who throws a party for turning twenty-eight? Thirty—sure. Twenty-one—of course. But twenty-eight? Who does that?"

"But maybe that's the fun of it, right?"

"I'm pretty drunk right now, and you look pretty hot in that green sweater, so I'll meet you in the middle on this, okay?" he said.

"What do you mean?"

"I'll let you do this, but you're not inviting my family. I'm not signing off on that shit."

"Then who can I invite?" she asked.

"How about a few guys from the bar?"

"That's not enough people."

"Can we talk about this later?" he asked. "Work was a bitch tonight, and I'm pretty spent."

"Okay, but just promise me you won't make any plans for your birthday. I've got it all covered," she said.

"Sure, why the hell not?"

*

"How's the wedding coming?" Juanita Jane asked Joy as she sat down beside Joy at the dining hall.

"Shhh, we're in public," Joy whispered.

"Oh, come on. Do you really think any of these people give a shit about our drama? Trust me–they don't. They have their own shit to worry about," Juanita Jane said. Joy looked around at the tables filled with students who appeared to be fully engrossed in their own conversations. Maybe Juanita Jane was right. Why would the students care about what was going on in her life? She wouldn't have cared about the personal lives of her professors. And so what if they did? Maybe it didn't matter anyway. After all, she'd be a married woman next semester, so what did it matter if a few students in the dining hall heard about the wedding planning?

"Everything's pretty much in order," Joy said.

"Pretty much? We're like three weeks out. What's left? And please don't tell me you need help making a thousand paper grasshoppers or something."

"No, nothing like that."

"Well, then what?" Juanita Jane asked.

"I'm just having a bit of a hiccup with the invitation part."

"What do you mean?" Juanita Jane asked and leaned way over the table toward Joy.

"I mean ... I was gonna send out those birthday invites, remember? But Miles feels weird about all the attention and won't give me any addresses, so now I'm gonna have to just send messages to people he's friends with on Facebook and tell them about the party that way. The only problem is ... well ... I don't really know who his real friends *are*. I mean ... I know some of his friends, of course, and I remember his mom's name ... I remember that, but I don't know about the rest of the people. You know how Facebook is—you could have a thousand Facebook friends and only want to see a handful of those people in your real life."

"You're planning a wedding for this guy, and you don't even know his friends?"

"I know some of them. Of course I know some of them, but I don't know enough to make up half of a wedding list, and it doesn't seem fair, right, to have most of the guests be people on my side, right? No, that doesn't seem fair at all."

"How many people *do* you know?" Juanita Jane asked.

"Honestly? Not that many. With his mom and sister, maybe eight, and that's assuming everyone can make it, but it's okay because I think I figured it out. I was thinking about something Bert said the other day—you know, when he was going off about how underutilized math is in our current curriculum, about how students can get a degree now and just take that Friendly Formulas class—and I realized that maybe I've been overlooking math too, that maybe everything really can be solved by math."

"What do you mean?"

"I mean maybe all I have to do is count the likes."

"Count the likes?" Juanita Jane asked.

"Yeah—on Facebook. I was thinking I can just make up a chart of how many times different people like the stuff he posts on Facebook. That should give me a pretty good idea about how close someone is to him. Don't you think?"

"You think a guy in his late-twenties who works in a shitty bar in Marshall is getting likes on Facebook from his true-blue besties?"

"You don't know him like I do. Everyone thinks they have this idea of who he is, but they just don't know," Joy said.

"Okay. Go ahead. Make your chart, but don't be too shocked if your surprise wedding is populated by dope dealers and women who want to fuck the mysterious-looking bartender."

"Trust me. I know what I'm doing," Joy said and stabbed a soggy green bean with her fork.

"These potatoes are horrible," Juanita Jane said. "Where do they get this shit? I bet you twenty bucks they're using that boxed crap. I bet you twenty bucks that if we went back there, if we went through the kitchen trash right now, we wouldn't find one damn potato peel anywhere."

"Speaking of potatoes—I need to plan some kind of honeymoon."

"How is that *speaking of potatoes?*"

"My parents went to Idaho for their honeymoon."

"You were raised by people who went to *Idaho* for a honeymoon? No wonder you're a little fucked up," Juanita Jane said and winked at Joy. "And what are you talking about *plan a honeymoon*? This is starting to reach a level of insanity that I can just barely condone anymore."

"We can't just get married and hang out in Marshall after. We can't do *that.*"

"Doesn't he have to work?"

"I took care of that," Joy said.

"You told his boss about your crazy plan?"

"No, of course not. I just asked Max if he could cover Miles' shifts for a couple of days so I can take him on a surprise birthday trip."

"So where is this honeymoon-slash-surprise-birthday-trip going to be?"

"That's the tricky part. I'm not sure," Joy said and bit her bottom lip. "The thing is ... with all the wedding expenses and everything ... it's going to have to be budget friendly ... *very* budget friendly, and besides, I don't know how to spell Miles' middle name, so I can't book a flight anyway."

"You're planning a wedding, and you don't even know the guy's middle name?"

"I know it. I just don't know how to spell it," Joy said, but the truth was that she didn't know his middle name, wasn't even sure he had a middle name. The one time she asked him about it, he told her he had officially outgrown the need for a middle name, told her he would never again get himself into the kind of trouble that warranted the first-middle-last name call-out, told her he'd go to the courthouse right then and remove the pointless name if he had the extra money, said he never liked it anyway so why'd she have to bring it up. She thought about going through his wallet to look at his license, but he had a strange routine of sleeping with the wallet under his pillow, a habit he developed back when he had a roommate who frequently brought women home who weren't looking for sex as much as they were looking for something good to steal.

"So what's it gonna be then? A couple a nights in Minneapolis?" Juanita Jane asked.

"There's a cute little bed and breakfast in Okoboji that looks nice. It might be fun to stay there a couple nights."

"Iowa? You're strong-arming this guy into getting married and then dragging his ass to a tiny town in Iowa to sit by a fireplace with a bunch of elderly people?"

"I think it'll be romantic. We can rent snowshoes and have hot cocoa in bed. The town's website says they're Iowa's winter jewel." As Joy spoke, her pink cheeks glowed under the florescent lights of the dining hall. "And I need to schedule a haircut and a pedicure. I'm thinking I might go a little different with the hair for the wedding. Maybe keep it chin-length in the front and a little shorter in the back, so the stylist can pull the sides up away from my face and stack some tight curls in the back. Like this," she said and pulled the front sections of her hair up over her forehead. "What d'ya think?"

"Just be careful. I know you've got this all played out in your mind, but you can't control what *he's* gonna do. And trust me—no amount of planning can keep that piece on the chess board, no amount of planning can force someone not to run," Juanita Jane said and saw a flash of her former self driving alone through Iowa, driving away from the wedding Kyle had so carefully planned, speeding away from the life she never wanted in the first place, the life she was too rooted in to easily free herself from.

Chapter Twenty-four

"Are you sure I can have *all* of these?" Margie asked Juanita Jane. "This has to be like a thousand dollars' worth of perfumes."

"Hell yeah, I'm sure. They're just not doing it for me anymore. With all these bullshit pre-menopausal pheromones I've got going on, they're just not cutting it anymore. It's like my skin is just instantly soaking up the smells now, and the only one that seems to stick is this Gingerbread Whorehouse perfume oil I got in New Orleans last year."

"So that's why you smell like Christmas lately."

"Christmas with a hint of sex," Juanita Jane said and winked at Margie.

"Just as Christmas was always intended to be," Margie said and laughed. "But seriously—are you sure I can have all these? I feel bad. Maybe I should just take one or two."

"Nope—have at 'em," she said. There they were—a decade's worth of perfume purchases spread out on Juanita Jane's bedspread. There were floral scents and earthy scents, fruity scents and seasonal scents. There were scents for dates, scents for work, scents for one-night stands, and scents for trips back home to Louisiana. Juanita Jane's mother had taught her that a person's smell is a person's true identity, so what did it mean that the only scent that stuck now was a perfume called Gingerbread Whorehouse? What did it mean that the alternative was smelling like the musty fabric of those old quilts she cuddled under as a child at her grandmother's house? It didn't make any sense. She had spent her whole life searching for the perfect scent—that ideal combination of perfume notes that would transform her life into the one she'd always wanted; but even the search wasn't working anymore. Her body was becoming resistant to it all, like her skin was almost ready to surrender to the smell of aging, and only the sweet scent of a Gingerbread Whorehouse could even attempt to stop it.

*

"Are you gonna live here next semester?" Mark asked Juanita Jane and passed the bottle of whiskey back to her.

"I'm not sure yet. It all depends on what Mr. Administration wants us to do."

"I hope you do," he said and licked his thick lips.

After-midnight visits to Mark's dorm room were becoming what Juanita Jane lived for. Behind his door was a world of music Juanita Jane had never heard, walls covered with postcards of places he hadn't been yet, the familiar earthy scent of marijuana, and shelves lined with books about painters and photographers long dead. As they smoked weed and sipped cheap whiskey, she stared at the postcards from Santorini—postcards he'd bought at the Barnes & Noble in Sioux Falls—and she wondered what it would be like to take him there. Logistically it wouldn't be so hard to do. She had more than enough money in her checking after a semester of free meals and lodging, and winter break was coming up. She could probably still get airline tickets and book a decent hotel. "We should go," she said and nodded in the direction of the postcards above the bed.

"Go where?"

"Greece. We should go to Greece."

"Is that a sex thing, some older slang I don't know about?" he asked.

"No, Greece. Greece the country. You have all these postcards. I'll take you there, and you can take pictures in person.

Wouldn't that be fucking amazing?" she said and grabbed his hand.

"I'm nineteen," he said and pulled his hand away from hers. "Of course I haven't been there yet. I kind of like that, you know? It's just fun to think about going."

"But what if you never go?"

"Then I don't. No biggie," he said and grabbed the whiskey for another slug.

"But it is, though. It is big. What if you live your whole life, and you never see it? What if all you ever do is imagine it? Wouldn't that be fucking tragic?"

"Not really. Sometimes imaging stuff is better than being there anyway."

"I'm just saying ... look ... you brought the music back to my stale existence ... that night you were playing, and I heard you through the door ... remember that night? I know you might not understand this yet, might not understand what I'm saying for years still, but someday you will ... see what I mean? Someday you'll be doing something mundane in your life, and you'll suddenly remember something I said to you, and it'll all just click for a second, just click right into place ... just like that. And what I'm telling you now is that if someone gives you an opportunity to see something new, to go somewhere you might never step foot in otherwise, you just go. You don't sit in a room and look at postcards for years. You just go."

"It's a really nice offer, but I can't let you spend a bunch of money on me. That's where I draw the line. My friends are already giving me enough shit about this," he said and started unbuttoning his jeans. "Let's just keep the focus on what we do best, okay?"

She looked at him and thought about what it would be like to exist somewhere outside of that room with him. In Marshall it was impossible, but in Greece they could walk together freely down narrow roads much older than either of them. They could dine in tiny cliff-side cafes and drink wine with locals who laughed at America's irrational drinking-age laws. In Greece they could finally be honest about their feelings, finally say that it wasn't just about the convenience of sex, that it wasn't just about the thrill of doing something culturally forbidden, that it was so much deeper than all of that. "At least consider it," she said.

"Not gonna happen," he said and started to pull her skirt down off her waist.

"But why not? What do we have to lose? All I'm asking is for one week, one week out of a five-week break, one week to get away from everything and go see something you obviously want to see anyway. Why not just do it?" she said and pulled her skirt back up. "Why not just take the chance?"

"The chance for what?"

"To see what happens."

"I have everything I want to see happening right here. I don't need to fuck you in another country. This one's just fine," he said and smiled. "Besides, what would I tell my parents—that I'm going on vacation with the professor I've been fucking around with all semester? I don't think so."

"Just tell your parents you're going with a friend."

"But then they'll ask where I'm getting the cash for the trip. They know I don't work, and it'll just lead back to the old arguments about selling weed in high school, and there's no way in hell I'm stepping into that shit storm again—no way in hell."

"We'll think of something," she said.

"Look—this is really fun—what we're doing right now, and I don't want to stop doing this yet, but I don't want to go to Greece with you."

"What do you mean *with me*?" she asked.

"I just don't think it's a good idea."

"Why not? Why isn't it a good idea?" she pressed.

"It just doesn't make any sense."

"So what? What are you saying? So I'm good enough to fuck but not good enough to accompany on a free vacation? Is that what you're saying?" she shouted.

"Are you trying to wake up everyone on the floor?" he said through clenched teeth.

"So what if I am? Other couples in the building have fights. Other couples in the building get—"

"Other *couples? Other couples?* Is that what you think's going on? Are you completely insane?"

"Well ... what do *you* think is going on?" she asked. "What the hell do *you* think we're doing here? Because if you think that continuous sex with the same person over and over again is just a goof, just a funny story to tell your friends when you're sixty and your life is boring as shit, then you obviously don't know what the hell you're talking about." She was shouting as she stood up. Looking down at him sitting on the twin bed with his back against the cinder block wall—he suddenly didn't look so attractive. For the first time, the tiny pimples spread out across the delicate skin under his eyes and the day-old blonde stubble at the bottom of his chin made him look a little like Charles Soderman, that high school kid who spent Juanita Jane's entire senior year relentlessly pestering her to just give him one chance, just one date, but she never did. Was it possible that her hot nineteen-year-old wasn't so hot after all? Was it possible that Mark was, in fact, just a guy who couldn't get any from the girls his own age and was forced to satisfy his raging sex drive in an unusual way?

"What did you think was gonna happen?" he yelled. "Did you think we'd fall madly in love and get married or something? Is that what you thought? Because that's completely insane. You know that? Completely crazy, you know. You're older than my mom by like ten years. This isn't what's supposed to happen."

"Then why'd you let it happen?" she shouted.

"I don't know," he said, suddenly softer. "I guess I just wanted to know ... you know ... wanted to know what it'd feel like."

"To sleep with an older woman?"

"To sleep with any woman," he said.

"Oh," she said. "Oh ... no ... is that what you mean? You mean you'd never done this before? You'd never done ... any of this ... with anyone?" she almost whispered and sat back down on the bed beside him.

"Yeah. I thought you knew that."

"No, I didn't know," she said and sighed.

"You were like my teacher, you know? It was like I was taking another class, but it wasn't a class I was paying for. It wasn't a class on my official schedule, you know. But it was my favorite class this semester," he said and smiled at her.

Something about this enraged Juanita Jane. Who did this kid think he was anyway? She wasn't his teacher. This wasn't a class. She was his lover. "So that's it then? You got your first fuck out of the way, and now you're ready to move on to greener pussies. Is that it then?" she shouted and stood back up.

"I guess so," he said and nodded at the door.

"You guess so? *You guess so?* What the hell kind of a break-up is that? You can't even put any inflection in your voice? You're not even twenty yet, and you can't even be bothered to say something real at the end of a three-month long affair? Trust me, kid. This does not bode well for your life going forward. It's all going to be a long slide into death for you if this is how you talk to your first lover."

"Maybe it will," he said and didn't look up at her.

"Fuck you," she said calmly, grabbed her red purse with the rhinestones on the strap, and walked out of Mark's dorm room.

*

"I'm back with Donny," Juanita Jane said to a very sleepy Bert.

"You woke me up at two in the morning to tell me that?"

"It's actually three," she said and pushed past him and into his dark dorm room. "Let's get a light on in here. This might take a bit," she said and plopped down on his still-warm bed.

Bert flipped the light on and sighed. "Can't we do this at a more civilized hour? I have a class at nine."

Chapter Twenty-four

"We *can*, but we won't. I need to talk this shit out, and no one else is even considering a conversation right now."

"Well ... I'm up now, so let's just get into it," he said and moved the thermostat dial up to seventy. "What happened?"

"Things kind of came to a head with Mark. Let's just say it's done. Finito. That fat lady was singing so loud she nearly woke up the whole damn town," she said and slapped Bert on the knee.

"So it's back to Donny—just like that?"

"What can I say? I moved into the dorms and kinda got caught up in the whole thing. And who wouldn't, right? How the hell are we supposed to remember our plot in life when the stage is decorated for a different story? How the hell are we supposed to keep that shit straight? And someone really needs to discuss this with Mr. Administration before they do another round of this shit. Someone needs to make sure the next group isn't just thrown to the wolves like this. And look what I did—I almost ruined it with a perfectly good man just for the chance to spend a couple a weeks in Greece with a hot nineteen-year-old, and then where'd we be?"

"Greece?" Bert asked, suddenly more awake.

"Yeah, the kid wanted to go, and I thought about it ... I did. But ... in the end, it just seemed like I'd be prolonging the inevitable, and I have to be the adult here. I have to be the one to shove that kid back to where he belongs. And Donny. What the hell was I doing with Donny? I can't believe I almost gave up Thanksgiving in Billings for a pointless affair with a teenager. What the hell was I thinking?"

"So *you* ended it with Mark? You're the one who called it all off?" he asked.

"Here's the thing," she said and slowly ran her fingers over the gold ruffle at the bottom of her green knee-length skirt. "I used to only wear black."

"Really?" he asked with the tone of shock in his voice one would expect to accompany the confession of a murder, not a former fashion choice.

"Yeah ... really ... spent most of my thirties in nothing but black clothes. You see—I loved that contrast, loved that look of black next to blonde. It's really an iconic look. Trust me. All you have to do is look at the old magazines, the old movies. They're all gonna tell you the same thing—nothing sexier than a woman in a tight black dress with red lips and blonde hair. Nothing. So I filled my closet with all things black—black heels, black blouses and skirts, sexy little black slips with tiny bits of lace on the straps. I wanted all of it, all of it to make myself into this vision of perfection. And I was. Believe me. I was. And, sure, I threw in a little color now and again—a red sweater here, a blue belt there—but I felt most like myself back then on those days when I dressed myself head-to-toe in nothing but black."

"So what changed?" he asked.

"It just didn't feel like me anymore. I don't know why. I just woke up one morning in my mid-forties and couldn't put that shit on my body anymore, like it didn't fit anymore. Well, it still fit my body, but it didn't fit *me* anymore. You know what I mean?" But she didn't give him a chance to answer. "So I opened a bottle of wine and raced to the closet and just started tearing all those colorless clothes up."

"You don't mean you literally tore the clothes, right? You don't mean that?" he asked.

"Yeah. That's what I mean."

"You mean you didn't bag them up and donate them to charity or something?" he asked.

"No, I didn't *bag* them up. No ... no I didn't do that. Just trust me—I could feel it. Those clothes had some seriously bad juju all over them, and I wasn't putting that shit on someone else. Oh, no. If it wasn't working for me anymore, why would it work for someone else? I couldn't risk it—no. So I spent all morning ripping the fabric into shreds with my bare hands, and for the clothes that were too thick to shred by hand, I got out the scissors. I can still see it all, how I sheared the shit out of that black wool jacket, how I cut so hard I wore that brand new sewing scissors down to nothing, how my hands were beat up and raw from all that ripping. But that's what I did, what I had to do. Sometimes it's like that, you know?"

"Wow."

"And the next day I drove to Sioux Falls and bought the brightest clothes I could find, and that's been me ever since. But the point I'm trying to make is this—I didn't know any of that was coming. I didn't know I'd wake up one morning and feel suffocated by the thought of putting those black clothes on, didn't know I'd have to destroy all of it to figure out where the fuck I was going next. I didn't know that. And Mark doesn't know where he's going next, and I didn't want to be there to find out. That's the thing. I don't want to be there when he cuts that beautiful hair off, don't want to be there when he stops playing guitar in a dorm room, and I sure as shit don't want to be there when he sheds every piece of himself over and over again to make way for something new. There's just not room for me in any of that, and I know that now."

"And there is with Donny?" Bert asked.

"I don't know. Probably not, but I'm willing to try to find out with him," she said and shook her head.

"So it's Billings for Thanksgiving then?"

"Yeah. Sure, I guess it is. Why the hell not?" she said and gripped her hand tightly around Bert's shoulder for just a moment before standing up to head for the door.

Chapter Twenty-five

"I can't believe he called a meeting today," Juanita Jane said to Joy. "Doesn't this dipshit know it's the day before Thanksgiving break? I had like three students in my afternoon class, and he expects us to meet with him at *four*? What the hell is this guy thinking?"

"What d'ya think he's gonna talk about?" Joy asked and took out a notebook and pencil.

"Fuck if I know, but it better be fast because I have to leave for the airport at six, and I haven't even packed yet."

"Man, you cut things close to the bone," Joy said.

"This from the one whose wedding is less than two weeks away and hasn't even told the groom yet."

"Shhh. Bert's coming," Joy whispered.

"Trust me—I think he can handle it."

"What coat are you bringing to Billings?" Joy asked in an attempt to reroute the conversation as Bert entered the dorm lounge.

"I'm thinking I'll wear that orange velvet one with the purple flowers on the pockets. That oughta stand out in Billings ... because there's one thing you don't want when you're meeting a guy for the first time, a guy you've had months of lead-up with, a guy you could really see yourself with long term. There's one thing you sure as shit don't want to do."

"And what's that?" Joy asked.

"You don't want to blend. You don't want to be one of a hundred women standing there in a brown coat. You wanna tell him to look for the woman in the orange velvet coat. You wanna come off that plane like a blaze of light rushing straight into his lonely existence. You wanna shine, shine, shine."

Bert smiled at Juanita Jane and wondered what this Donny guy would think of her.

"Where's Lyla?" Joy asked. "The meeting starts in three minutes. She's always ten minutes early."

"I think she's a little preoccupied these days," Juanita Jane said. "She's with that guy a lot now."

"I hope it works out for those two," Bert said.

"Yeah, there's hoping, and there's real life, and I think we both know which one always wins out with shit like this. Am I right?" Juanita Jane asked and threw her head forward and back again to give her freshly-curled hair a bit more volume before the meeting started.

"Here she is," Joy said as Lyla rushed into the room right in front of Mr. Administration.

"Holy shit. You're wearing a suit today too?" Juanita Jane said to Mr. Administration as he approached the FDD group. "It's an hour before Thanksgiving break, and your damn tie matches your socks. No wonder they pay you the big money."

"Thank you, Doctor Ruckler, for your kind words," he said and nodded at Juanita Jane. "I think today we should move the meeting to the conference room in Berry Hall. We'll be discussing some private matters that shouldn't be spoken about in an open area like this."

"Why don't we just move to my room?" Juanita Jane said. "Three can fit on the bed, one on the office chair, and Joy can sit on a pillow on the floor."

"Oh, no. No, that won't be necessary. We'll just walk over to the conference room," he said.

"But it's cold as shit today, and we'd have to all go back to our rooms and get our coats. Let's just go to my room," Juanita Jane pressed and stood up.

"That's not a viable—or appropriate—option, Miss Ruckler." Juanita Jane noticed that Mr. Administration seemed to always make the switch from *Doctor* to *Miss* when he was scolding a female faculty member.

"Appropriate? What the hell do you think is gonna happen? What kind of crazy scenario is playing out in your head? Are you worried about an orgy breaking out? Is that what it is, because, trust me, that's not gonna happen. Nobody's starting an orgy with you wearing that suit. Am I right?" she said and looked at Joy.

"We'll meet you there in five minutes," Bert said and started for his dorm room to retrieve a coat.

"Fine, but this better be a short meeting because I have a plane to catch," Juanita Jane said and stomped off to her room like an angry child, a look that was made more ridiculous by the huge snag in her black pantyhose, a snag that started at the back of her knee and disappeared somewhere in her hot pink heels.

*

"Here's the thing," Mr. Administration started. "We don't have the numbers yet, don't have the official enrollment records for spring semester yet, won't have them until early January, but something has happened ... something unforeseen ... something that's, frankly, a bit shocking."

"Come on. Out with it," Juanita Jane said, sitting directly across from Mr. Administration at the oval conference table.

He looked at the table, scratched his chin a bit too long to fake the appearance of a legitimate itch, ran his thin finger down the bridge of his sharply pointed nose, and exhaled audibly into the small room.

"Well?" Juanita Jane said and pointed to the blue clock on the wall behind him.

"Legally speaking ... I can't name names, can't get into any real specifics, but I thought the four of you should be informed of the fact that this program will not be renewed next semester. We received the official word from the provost this morning, that there will be no funding for any new FDD cohorts." Bert felt himself sinking down in the uncomfortable straight-backed black chair, and he had the sudden urge to run out of the room, down the hallway, out of the building, down the street, and away from campus. He imagined himself crashing down into a pile of snow somewhere, imagined shoving handfuls of sticky snow down his sweater, imagined the relief of the cold lumps melting against his skin. But he didn't move.

"What happened?" Joy asked.

"Like I said, I can't get into specifics with you right now."

"So get into non-specifics," Juanita Jane said. "Just give us the vague outline."

"There was a rumor ... well, a report, shall we say ... an email ... that alluded to inappropriate contact between a member of the FDD program and a student in the dorms."

"So the program's getting canned because I slept with a student?" Juanita Jane blurted out, surprising everyone, even herself.

"Miss Ruckler, I said we weren't going to get into any specifics right now," Mr. Administration said with a clear tone of exasperation.

"I'm so tired of living on the periphery of truth," Juanita Jane said and stared straight at Mr. Administration. "We all know that's what it is. That's the source of the issue, and it's just the five of us sitting here, and I've brought these three people into my life this semester, shared all the inner-circle shit with them, and back the other way around, so why can't we just have a real conversation? Because *you* know, and I know, that nothing I did was illegal, that I'm still sitting safely in that solid web of tenure, that I couldn't possibly be—"

"Let's just let him speak," Lyla said in an attempt to cut off Juanita Jane.

"Oh, he can speak. He can speak all right, but it's not quite his turn yet. Just because he's got the suit and I've got the JC Penney clearance dress, it doesn't mean I don't get a turn when it's warranted. And, trust me, it's warranted. Here's the thing," Juanita Jane said and put her elbows up on the table so that she leaned forward a bit. "You're sitting there judging me, judging all of us really, but what did you think was gonna happen? What did you honestly think this would come to? Did you really think you could just drop us off with no real direction and have some optimal outcome, fill out some bullshit spreadsheet with just the right numbers to get you in the provost's good graces? Because, believe me, you'd have been just the same as the rest of us if given half the chance. You'd have been running wild down there too, and wasn't that really the point anyway? Isn't that what you said that first meeting, that we should all just live in the dorms, just like the students, that we shouldn't alter our behavior in any way, that we should just let the crazy storm of life circle around us? Because that's what they're doing, you know. That's what the students are doing every damn day, so if you—"

"I'm going to stop you right there," Mr. Administration said and put his own elbows up on the table to lean into her a bit. "I specifically told you *not* to sleep with the students. That was on the agenda the very first meeting. I have the minutes back in my office, as a matter of fact."

"But you said to just do what they do, and, trust me, there's some sex going on over there. You might want to bury your head in the sand on that one, but trust me, it's happening. And let me just speak for all of us and say that the contradictory information you gave us on day one really threw us off course, but wasn't that the point anyway? Wasn't this really more about shaking the dust off the faculty a bit, so to speak? Wasn't the real intent to make our own existence a bit more exciting, to put the sexuality and the impulsiveness and the thrill of youth back into our own lives at the university, to remind us of the other side of things, the student side of things? Wasn't that what this was really all about?" Juanita Jane asked.

"No. No, it was absolutely not about any of that. The point, as I've stated all along, was to improve retention and enrollment by creating the idea of an accessible and approachable faculty presence."

"But what the hell does that even mean?" Juanita Jane asked.

"My initial response would be that if you, or anyone else in the program—or any program at the university, for that matter—felt like you didn't understand the intended outcomes, or how to get to those outcomes, that the best thing to do would have been to talk with me and reach some clarity on the issue."

"But that's what we're doing now," Juanita Jane said.

"And don't you think it's a bit late for that now? Don't you think this conversation would have been more appropriate *before* the incident occurred?" he asked.

"No, no I don't. I don't think so at all," she said.

"And why is that?" he asked through lips so pursed they practically curled under.

"Because then it wouldn't have happened ... because haven't you ever done anything fucked up in your life only to realize that somewhere, in the middle of the mess, you were staring at something so beautiful you couldn't imagine ever putting it down, couldn't in a million years ever imagine taking it back?"

He just sat there stunned.

"Because that's what it was for me. Sure, now it all looks so awful. Now it's all so clear sitting in the brightly lit conference room with the walnut table at four in the afternoon, but you've got to understand that we don't all live in this reality, that some of us don't even want to," she said and nodded at Bert. "You've got to understand that some of us actually want to sit in the smoky room after midnight and feel that beautiful blurring of reality and expectations, that some of us are actually doing our damnedest to figure out a way to just get into that room. And I figured it out. I got in, and I can tell you it was everything I expected it to be. It was everything I remembered from those moments so long ago when I used to practically live in that room, when I could so easily waltz in and out without any real effort on my part. And *he* was everything I remembered, those feelings of lust and longing that were never quite satisfied. And I know I'm not supposed to say any of this shit to you, but what the hell does it matter anyway? Who do we really think we are to continue to speak so formally about an experience that was so insane?"

"I think the best thing to do ... the only thing to do really ... at this point ... is to refocus our attention a bit," Mr. Administration said.

"And what does that mean?" Bert asked.

"The damage has been done, so to speak. Parents are concerned. There's talk of the newspaper running some kind of story. Upper administration is working on damage assessment so we can start to implement the necessary recovery efforts to get things back to where they were before this mess," Mr. Administration said with a look of concern on his face.

"Recovery efforts? Damage control? Are you serious right now? I slept with a guy who was so into it he couldn't get enough, and we're sitting here busting out the post-hurricane terminology? That's where we are now? I'm sorry, but I just can't fall down to this, just can't do it. I mean, this is supposed to be a place of higher learning, for God's sakes, and you're sitting there acting like a little sex has destroyed the school," Juanita Jane said.

"That's the tricky part," he said.

"What do you mean?" she asked.

"As I stated at the beginning of the meeting, we don't know the numbers yet, can't really assess the true outcome of the incident at this juncture, can't really know if—"

"You mean there's a chance the incident will actually improve enrollment?" Bert asked with a slight smirk on his face.

"Well ... studies have shown that when something like this occurs with a male professor, the university's reputation often experiences a slight decline that can take up to six months for full recovery. But we just don't have the data on female professors, so we just don't know."

"So there's a real possibility that this is a classic example of the 'sex sells' advertising model, that we may actually see an increase in male enrollment because of the incident?" Bert asked.

"To speak frankly—yes. There is that possibility," Mr. Administration said.

"But, regardless of the outcome, the FDD program is definitely still dead?" Bert asked and pressed his fingernails into the skin behind his ear, a nervous habit he had developed as a kid when his parents shouted at each other right in front of him.

"Oh, yeah. The program is definitely dead," Mr. Administration said without looking back at Bert. Instead he was still staring straight ahead into the surprisingly calm light blue eyes of Juanita Jane.

Chapter Twenty-six

After the meeting, Lyla walked alone to the library, took the elevator up to the top floor, found a seat by a window looking west, and watched as the sun slowly sank down beneath the long expanse of snow-filled fields below. She had always wanted to see those picturesque sunsets of Hawaii and Iceland and the upper coast of Maine, but she knew that it was all likely to be a huge disappointment, that it was completely possible that the best sunsets were right there, sitting by the fourth floor window of the Prairie State Library, the highest place in Marshall, the same place she had sat all those years before when she last lived on campus.

During that year she lived alone after her divorce, she never would have stayed on campus late like this, never would have seen the way the sun left coral-colored streaks across the navy sky long after it disappeared from view. Instead she would have jumped in her car right after classes, raced home to watch the Mankato five o'clock news while she heated up a frozen dinner and checked her email. She would have sat in front of the TV for hours, flipping from one channel to the next, always searching for the perfect show, always disappointed that it couldn't be found. She would have called her mom, called her sister, scrolled through her Facebook news feed, planned intricate details for trips she might never take—all of it just to avoid thinking about her actual life.

Something about living on campus had allowed her to stay

in one place long enough to let the old pleasures back in. She didn't want to say anything at the meeting, but she understood exactly what Juanita Jane was talking about. She had assumed that moving back to the dorms was a huge mistake, that the embarrassment of it all might eat her alive, but maybe it really was the mistakes that led her right back to the place where she was happiest.

She pulled out her phone to take a picture of the bright sky, and there it was—a text from Anton.

Call me when you see this.

Normally she would walk back to her room before calling him back. Normally the top floor of the library was a strict study zone, a place of no talking or loud noises. But it was an hour before the library closed up for the long Thanksgiving weekend ahead, and she was pretty sure she was the only person on the entire floor, maybe the only patron left in the entire building.

"Hey," he said after just one ring.

"Hey, yourself. What's up?"

"What are you doing right now?"

"Just got out of the meeting. Just killing time. Why?"

"I need you to do something for me," he said.

"What's that?"

"I need you to meet me in Graceville ... tonight."

"Graceland tonight? Are you insane? Why do you want to meet at Graceland, and how would we even get there tonight? How could that possibly work, and do you even like Elvis? I could've sworn you said—"

"No, not Grace*land*. Grace*ville*—you know—that tiny town halfway between Fargo and Marshall. Remember? We used to stop there on the way back from my parents' house sometimes. They had that little ice cream shack with the really good strawberry soft serve," he said.

"Oh, yeah. I do remember—that little town on the lake – but it's like twenty degrees outside right now. I'm pretty sure that place is closed for the winter. I'm pretty sure it's—"

"This isn't about ice cream, Lyla. I just need to see you, and I can't drive all the way down and back before tomorrow. I promised my mom I'd be at the house early to help with the cooking, and I'd invite you to come up here, but I think it would be too much of a shock to everyone if I tried to reintroduce my college girlfriend to the whole extended family on a major holiday. I just think it would—"

"Oh, yeah ... no ... I get it ... of course not. But can't I just see you this weekend, though? Wouldn't that make more sense? I mean, I'm more than happy to drive up on Friday. I don't have any plans, and it's—"

"But that's the whole thing," he started.

"What?"

"That's what I'm sick of doing, what I've been doing ... at least until that day I saw you at the game. I'm always doing what's easiest in the moment, what makes the most sense, and it's all bullshit."

"So what? You want each of us to drive two hours each way to do what? Sit by a frozen lake and ... what?"

"I just want to talk to you," he said.

"But we're talking now."

"I just want to talk to you ... there. I don't know why, but it just feels like that's where I'm supposed to be tonight, like I'm supposed to be back in Graceville with you. And haven't you ever wanted something, wanted to be somewhere with someone, and you didn't know why, but you knew that if you didn't drive there right then that everything might be different in the morning, that everything that could've happened will somehow vanish?" he asked.

And she did. She knew exactly what he was talking about. The last summer they were together, Anton had a job in road construction that required him to travel across Minnesota, sometimes staying at a work site for weeks and sometimes only a few days. She hadn't seen him since spring semester, and they kept in contact through long emails where he told her funny stories about the uncivilized men he worked beside, and she complained about crabby customers who made her life miserable at the grocery store where she worked over the summer. At the end of July, Anton was working for a few days with a crew in Olivia, a town just an hour east of Marshall, and Lyla thought about making the drive out to see him, but she didn't do it. Instead she let the whole summer slip by with nothing more than written contact and a few scattered phone calls here and there, and after their break-up the following year, she often wondered what it would have been like, what kind of day they could have had if she had only made the drive out to see him the summer before. "Okay, I'll meet you there," she said.

"Really? You'll do it?"

"Yeah, sure. Why not? I just have to run back to my room and change first."

"Graceville is almost right in the middle of Fargo and Marshall," he said. "You leave there in thirty minutes, and I'll leave here in a couple minutes, and I should get there a little bit before you. Meet me in the parking lot of Lake View Park. I'll bring a flashlight," he said.

"This is crazy. You know that, right?"

"Yeah, I know, but I still wanna do it," he said.

*

Traffic on Highway 75 in Western Minnesota was almost nonexistent the night before Thanksgiving. With nothing but tiny towns and long stretches of rural highway between Marshall and Graceville, the dark drive made her feel like there was nothing in the world beyond the beam from the headlights of her little car. As she drove, she thought about how crazy it all was and couldn't quite believe she was doing something like this at thirty-eight, couldn't quite believe she was driving two hours to a tiny town just because Anton had to tell her something face-to-face and couldn't possibly wait the two days to do so. She wondered what would happen next semester, wondered if he would still make the long drive down to see her without the safety of the dorm room, that place where they first met, that place that was still so familiar that it could temporarily lull them into believing nothing had really changed at all. Most of all she wondered what it was that he wanted to talk to her about, wondered why there was a sense of pleading urgency in his voice when he asked her to come, even wondered what it was that made her say yes so quickly after all the past pain he had put her through.

As she pulled into Graceville, a rush of memories seemed to seep into the car and sit in the seat beside her—Anton's long brown hair spread out in the grass by the lake the day they took a nap outside after ice cream, the way his kisses tasted like sugar-laced strawberries, the faraway sound of an old man strumming a guitar on the picnic table across the water, the mallards slowly making their way down the shoreline, the way it felt like perfect afternoons would always be so easily found. All of it was there in the car with her, but outside everything looked so different. Outside even the population sign was half covered in snow, obscuring everything but the very tops of the town letters. Outside the town seemed buttoned up and put away for the long winter ahead. There was no one on the streets, no one in the gas station parking lot, no one standing in their yards talking to neighbors, no real sign of life anywhere except for a few illuminated porch lights here and there.

She drove through town, took a left toward the lake, pulled into the vacant parking lot, and waited. So as not to call attention to herself, she turned the car off and sat in silence inside the still-warm confines of her car. She checked her phone for messages. *Nothing. Why wasn't he there yet? Didn't he say he'd get there first? What was she doing? What if he didn't even show up? What if she waited all night by that cold lake, and he still never came? How long should she wait before giving up and heading back to Marshall, back to the security of her small room where she was surrounded by people and wouldn't have to worry about freezing to death far from home?*

And what if he did show up? What then? Every time she said goodbye to him at the dorm door over the past two months, she told herself it was the last time, told herself that there was no possibility of real forward motion with a guy like Anton, told herself that *she* should call him the next day and politely call the whole thing off, that she should be the one to end whatever it was that they were doing. But she never did. Instead she pulled out that old picture of the two of them from sophomore year of college, the one taken right after the first snowfall of the year, the one where he stood snuggled up right beside her with his arms wrapped tightly around her waist and one hand tucked up beneath her soft blue sweater.

She saw headlights approaching the parking lot, quickly pulled the box of breath mints out of her purse, and popped one in her mouth. But the car kept going, past the parking lot and down the street heading away from the lake. *Was it really possible that he wasn't coming? Would he really send her out into the cold night all alone to wait for him when he had no intention of meeting her there? And why would he do this? Was it possible that he started driving, changed his mind about the whole thing, and turned back? Was this all just an elaborate game he was playing for his own sick pleasure? Was he sitting at a bar with friends in Fargo laughing about his crazy ex-girlfriend from college who was waiting alone in a car for something that was never going to happen?* She checked her phone again for messages. Still nothing.

Her mind raced through the huge rolodex of memories from college. She found herself sifting through old images she had almost forgotten, those seemingly insignificant fragments of the past, like the way he always held her hand a little tighter as they ran from the dorm building to the dining hall without coats on in winter, an old trick Prairie State students still used in order to avoid lugging the heavy coat around while standing in line at the hot food stations. She could still see him sitting there, that younger version of Anton, staring at her across the table, offering her a taste of his overcooked pepperoni pizza, telling her that someday they'd drive to Chicago and find out what real pizza should taste like. She could still remember so many tiny details—the way his brown wool hat smelled like pine needles, how he always started a semester with a package of new pencils and threw out the old ones, that he sometimes pushed CDs under her dorm door with a note telling her which song she just had to listen to, that he loved to sleep with the window cracked open on the coldest nights just to feel that stark contrast between the winter outside and the heat of his body under the blankets.

She looked at her phone again. Still nothing. She wondered what she'd say if he ever called to apologize, wondered if she'd even pick up the phone or let it go straight to voicemail. She wondered if he'd even have the courage to make such a phone call. After all, what could he possibly say, and why would it matter anyway?

She hated herself for agreeing to come, hated herself for all the nights she let Anton walk through her dorm door, hated herself for letting a college kid talk her into approaching him at the homecoming game, and hated herself most of all for letting the ridiculous FDD program completely dismantle her sensible and structured life.

She heard her phone ring, quickly snatched it up off the passenger seat, saw that it was her mom calling, and hit the button to ignore the call.

It was starting to get cold in the car.

She thought about how difficult Thanksgiving would be the next day, how she'd have to politely endure lengthy conversations about her uncle's gnome collection while pretending to like the soupy orange Jell-O salad with cottage cheese her aunt always brought. She thought about how ridiculous and humiliating it was that the natural thing to ask a divorced woman nearing forty was the always-dreaded relationship-status question—a question she would have to answer over and over again to those smug-sounding relatives who had married young and somehow stayed right where they started out. She thought about herself at twenty, the way Thanksgivings back then were so easy, the way she floated from conversation to conversation with the ease of youthful arrogance as she explained again and again that Anton would propose in the middle of senior year, that they would be engaged for half a year and then marry at the Lutheran church in Granite Falls at the end of that summer.

She looked at her phone again. Still nothing!

She turned on the car, turned the heat and radio on, and told herself she'd give it just three more minutes, and then she'd head back to Marshall and likely never speak to Anton again. She'd waited two hours for her ex-husband to show up to a work party once, and she wasn't about to wait thirty minutes for Anton to show up to an empty parking lot. The radio DJ talked about how this Thanksgiving would be the coldest one on record in over twenty years, talked about how excited he was to get his hands on some of Grandma's chocolate pudding pie, talked about how turkey was the most overrated of the meats, talked about how hopeful he was that this would finally be a good year for the Vikings. And as the deep voice of the DJ filled Lyla's car with the pretend companionship of a one-way conversation, she suddenly couldn't hear anything he was saying.

She squinted as the headlights turned into the parking lot, trying hard to see if it was Anton's red truck pulling up beside her, and then everything came into focus. There he was—turning off the car, opening the door, waving over at her with a smile spread out across his face. There he was—this man she hadn't stopped loving since college, this man who had somehow stumbled back into her circle after so many years outside of it. And there she was—stepping out of the car, pulling her purple pea coat tightly around her, shouting to him as he approached her, "I thought you weren't coming. I was about to leave. I waited and waited, but I thought you weren't going to show. I thought you said you'd get here before me. I thought you were just—"

"I'm sorry. I got caught up for a moment. I just had to—"

"Caught up for a moment? You got caught up for a moment?

Chapter Twenty-six

Are you kidding me? I drove two hours, waited in a cold car the night before Thanksgiving, waited and waited, just like the shit my ex used to put me through, and all because you begged me to come out here, all because you—"

"It's fine. Lyla, it's fine. I'm here now. I just had to—"

"No, it's not fine," she shouted and took a step away from him. "I have to stop doing this. I have to. You basically ruined years of my life in my twenties because I couldn't put myself back on the tracks after it happened. I was just sort of stuck for a long time, doing nothing, because I couldn't take a step one way or the other ... and now ... now I should be better than that. At this point in my life, I should be somehow past the paralysis of waiting around to figure out what the hell you're doing ... because my own life is—"

"Lyla, I know. That's not what I'm trying to—" he said.

"And I'm always the one. I'm always the one putting all the effort in, always the one thinking—"

"*You're* the one putting all the effort in? *You're* the one? Are you serious? Who drove to Marshall all those times? Who—"

"But that's not the point," she said. "That's not what I'm talking about. I'm not just talking about tanks of gas and time in a car. I'm talking about—"

"You think that's all it is for me? Tanks of gas? You think this is about money?"

"How do you think I felt—waiting in my car tonight, knowing you weren't really going to show up, knowing you weren't—"

"But I'm here," he said. "I did show up. I'm standing right here."

"Yeah, *this time. This time* you're here, but what about the time when you don't show up? What about the time when you suddenly realize you have to—"

"Lyla, stop. Just stop talking for a minute. Just give me a chance to think for a minute. Can we just go sit by the lake for a bit?" he asked.

She wanted to tell him no, that they couldn't go sit by the lake for a minute, that she couldn't just keep sitting somewhere with him for a minute, that she had to get on with things in her own life now, that now that the FDD program was ending it was time for her to finally end this relationship that he walked away from all those years ago. But instead she just said, "Okay, that's fine."

They walked through ankle-deep snow to the picnic table by the frozen lake. Anton brushed the snow off the bench, and they sat down beside each other. "It's strange being here in the winter," he said.

She didn't look at him and just said, "Yeah, I know."

"But I'm glad we are. It feels like we changed something, you know. Like we finally figured out how to get to the other side of something together."

"Yeah, I know what you mean," she said, but she had no idea what any of it meant.

He grabbed her hand, but she couldn't feel the warmth of his skin through her mittens. "Are you going to your mom's for Thanksgiving tomorrow?" he asked.

"What? No ... I mean, yes ... yes, I'm going there tomorrow, but no ... no, we're not doing this."

"Doing what?"

"I didn't drive all the way here to talk about Thanksgiving. I didn't drive all the way here to—"

"Okay, okay."

"And why did it have to be outside? Why couldn't we be sitting in that bar I passed on the way here? Why couldn't we—"

"Don't you remember?" he asked and turned to face her. She turned her body toward him, pulled her hand away, and put her legs up on the bench so that her knees became a shield propped up between them.

"Remember what?" she asked.

"Don't you remember where we were the first time I told you?"

"Told me what?"

"That I loved you," he said.

Of course she remembered. It was her freshman year, and

it was starting to get cold outside, but Anton insisted on going for a walk. They walked all the way from Marshall to Lynd, a tiny town seven miles out of Marshall. She thought he might be crazy, but her attraction to him was so strong that she would have followed him almost anywhere. Because rural Minnesota was definitely not pedestrian friendly, they had to walk on the shallow shoulder of the highway and move over to the grass when a car or semi approached. When they got to Lynd, he kept talking about how it might be the last day before the snow came, how he wanted to tell her something before everything outside died, how he wanted to say it in a place that could belong to just the two of them. They walked past the population sign, past rows of modest one-story houses, past the only café in Lynd, and finally stopped walking when they reached the railroad tracks on the south side of town. He talked about how often he heard the train whistles from his bedroom in Fargo growing up, talked about how that sound would always have a strange comfort for him, how it would always remind him of that feeling of being safe at home. And then he told her. He looked her straight in the eyes and told her that he loved her, that he didn't know yet where it was all headed, but that he knew for sure, in that moment, that he loved her. She told him that she loved him too, and they kissed on the empty railroad tracks before they made the long walk back to Marshall, and that night they had sex in his dorm bed for the first time. And early the next morning, the snow started to fall.

"Yeah, I remember," she said with no emotion in her voice.

"It's always like that for me, you know ... how I can't say the big things in familiar places, how I have to be outside of it all in order to—"

"So what is it? What is it you wanted to say?" she yelled at him. "What is so important you had to—"

"I still love you," he yelled back at her. "I still fucking love you, Lyla, and I don't want it to stop this time. I don't want it to—"

"What are you saying?" she yelled. "What are you trying to

say to me? What are you—"

"Would you just let me talk for a minute, for just one second? Would you just let me—"

"What? Let you what?" she yelled.

"Would you just let me ask you something?" he said.

"Ask me what?"

"I can't believe you're doing this right now. I can't believe you're yelling at me while I'm trying to—"

"You can't believe *I'm* doing this? Me? *You're* the one who asked me to drive all the way out here to talk about something and won't tell me what it is. You're the one who—"

"I wanted to ask you to marry me, okay? I wanted to—"

"Wanted to?" she asked. "You *wanted* to? You mean it's past tense? You mean you changed—"

"No, I didn't change my mind. And no, it's not past tense. I just thought it might be nice to ask you in a way that didn't involve a shouting match. I just thought it might be—"

"So you're asking me to marry you?" she asked, her voice suddenly softer.

"Yes."

"Really?"

"Yeah."

"Wow," she said, and for a moment there was silence. "Yeah ... sure. Let's do it," she said and started to laugh. "Is there a ring? Did you have a whole thing planned, a whole speech and everything? Were you going to—"

"I thought you should pick out your own ring. I thought we could—"

"Yeah, that's good. I always wanted to—"

"I know. I remember," he said.

"So we're getting married?"

"Yeah."

"You and me?" she asked.

He pulled her mitten off, kissed the palm of her warm hand, and held her hand to his cold cheek for a moment before pulling her to him for a long kiss. "You and me," he said.

"After all this time?"

"Yeah," he said.

"Where would we live?"

"I thought I'd move to Marshall. That way you can keep teaching, and it's not like I love my job in Fargo anyway. I'm sure I can find something in the area."

"That sounds good."

For a long time they just sat and stared at the frozen shoreline they had visited once so many years back. With only the dim glow of the parking lot lights behind them, it was easier to remember it in the summer than to see it for what it was that night. She knew there was a water tower somewhere on the other side of the lake, but she couldn't see it. She knew there was a stretch of sandy beach hidden beneath the snow and darkness, but it would be months until it reemerged for those regional visitors looking for a place to swim and savor the few hot stretches of a northern summer. She knew the flocks of white pelicans would come back in early spring, knew the lake water would stay cool all summer, knew the dead trees beside the lake would once again become radiant green canopies of branches waving out over the water.

But she couldn't see the future seasons up ahead with Anton, didn't know if their marriage could fill in all the colorless spaces of so much time away from where they first stood, didn't know if she'd ever really trust him to stick it out when the boredom of everyday life started to seep back in. She thought about the FDD program, thought about the way Mr. Administration had said to spend the semester living like a college student, thought about how stupid it all sounded at the beginning of the semester. But maybe the FDD program was exactly what she needed. Maybe the only way to move forward in her life was to spend a semester living back in that place again, back in that tiny dorm room that seemed so far removed from her middle-aged life, back in that place the younger version of herself had known so well.

Chapter Twenty-seven

The night before Thanksgiving was a flurry of activity at Bert's house as Jean kneaded dough for dinner rolls and Bert peeled and cut apples into tiny cubes for the pies they'd serve to Jean's parents the next day. "Do you think we could listen to some music or something?" he asked Jean.

"Music? You want to listen to music? Since when do you want music on while you're cooking?" she asked. There she was—his wife—standing at the kitchen table wearing her faded green nightgown again and those red fuzzy socks with the snowflakes all over them. He just wanted to grab the keys off the hook by the door and drive back to the dorm room where he could hear something outside of that tired kitchen with the old oven that hummed softly as it warmed up.

"Never mind," he said and threw a handful of apple cores in the waste basket. "It's fine."

"I just don't understand you anymore. I just don't understand why you all-of-a-sudden want to—" she started, but the ringing of Bert's cell phone cut her off. He looked at the phone. It was Juanita Jane.

"I'm just gonna take this for a minute," he said to Jean, hit the accept-call button, and walked toward the back bedroom. "Hey," he said into the phone and closed the bedroom door. "What's up? Aren't you supposed to be with Donny by now?"

"You're not gonna believe this shit," she said.

"What? What happened?"

"He didn't show."

"What do you mean 'he didn't show'?" he asked and sat down on the bed. "Didn't he pay for the ticket? Why the hell would he pay for your plane ticket and then not show up?"

"I know, right? That's the crazy shit. He's the one that funded the whole damn thing, and then he didn't show."

"Do you think he's okay? Do you think maybe he got into an accident or something? Do you think maybe he—"

"Oh, no. No, he's fine. He's perfectly okay. He's just fucking fine sitting in his living room somewhere, watching a movie with his wife in some fucking living room somewhere. No, he's fine. Trust me—he's as fine as fine can be."

"His wife?" Bert asked. "I wouldn't jump to any conclusions just yet."

"Oh, I'm not jumping. There's no jumping over here. No, I'm not jumping. Get this shit—I got off the plane, turned on my phone, and there it was—a voicemail from the fucker—confessed the whole thing, said he thought he could, you know, all that shit, but he just couldn't do it. He just couldn't tell his wife that he was off working somewhere, just couldn't have her picturing him driving in his stupid truck somewhere while he was really shacked up with me in some rental house he was trying to pass off as his own. He just couldn't go through with it. And the really crazy part is the way his voice sounded—like *he* was such a great guy for pulling the plug while I was halfway to Billings up in the sky somewhere, like he was the great *hero* of the situation. Can you believe that?"

"Wow," Bert said. "So that's it then?"

"Seems to be."

"So now you're trapped in Billings all weekend?"

"Yeah, and that's the really crazy part, you know, the fact that this fucker had to be from the one place in the country where you can't get a decent bottle of Pinot to save your soul."

"So what are you gonna do?"

"I don't know ... maybe just finally admit to myself, you know—the big fucking admission ... you know, face the facts that this might be where the road of colorful Juanita Jane lets off, that maybe it's time to just go by Jane, cut all my hair off, let it go gray, start wearing the neutral tones of grandmas and dental secretaries ... that maybe last month I could fuck a nineteen-year-old, but this month I can't get a married trucker who's sick to shit of his life to shack up with me for a few days. Maybe I just finally slammed up against the wall of no-more-options. Maybe I'm done for ... or maybe it's just a run of bad luck ... who knows."

"I meant this weekend. I meant—what are you gonna do for the rest of the weekend? Are you staying somewhere in Billings?"

"Of course I'm staying somewhere in Billings. What the hell else could I do? I have a return flight on Sunday. I'm not about to pay out the ass for a last-minute plane ticket because some asshole pulled the rug out from under me. Hell, no. I'm at the Boothill Inn & Suites by the airport—booked a room no problem ... no surprise this place isn't exactly filled to the max this weekend ... probably never is. But it's not bad here—cable TV and rooms that smell like this sea breeze perfume my aunt used to wear. I'm not spending money on a rental car for this shit, but there's an Applebee's next door and a liquor store across the street, so I'll survive. Don't you worry about me."

"I'm really sorry that happened to you," he said, and he was, but he felt a strange surge of jealousy too as he pictured the weekend Juanita Jane would have and compared it to his own Thanksgiving plans. He would get up early the next day and head to Jean's parents' house where they'd spend all morning watching that horrible parade on TV while Jean's parents argued about which floats were the most impressive and which college bands had the best uniforms. He would eat lunch at exactly noon, help Jean's father with the dishes, eat a slice of pie an hour later, engage in dull conversation about the caloric disaster that every holiday was, play a few card games, and begin the long and carefully-composed process of politely saying goodbye before finally heading home. The idea of sitting in a hotel room in a strange city and watching the TV shows he liked while eating cold ribs out of a to-go box from Applebee's filled him with a sense of pleasure from just knowing the possibility existed.

"It sucks. I'm not gonna lie, but there are probably worse things I could be doing this weekend," she said, and he found himself nodding. "And the crazy thing is ... I don't really know why I was coming here anyway, don't really know what the hell I was hoping to find ... because we all know I'm not looking to permanently shack up with some guy from Billings who drives a truck around the country—if that's even really what he does—who the hell knows at this point ... so I'm just trying to figure out why I followed through with the trip in the first place ... what I was running from ... or running to. You know what I mean?" she asked.

And he did know. He knew exactly what she meant. That was the thing about Juanita Jane. She made absolutely no sense until she suddenly did. And Bert didn't know what he was running from either, didn't understand why he had to move back into a dorm room to escape a wife who had tried so hard to give him what he once thought he wanted, a wife who endured years of failed pregnancies, a wife who moved to a town she didn't want to live in just so he could have the career he wanted so badly. "I do," he said. "I know what you mean."

"I'm just gonna try to make the most of it. That's really all I can do," she said. "And who knows—maybe I'll have some fun here after all. Maybe I'll hook up with a hot waiter at the Applebee's. Maybe I'll buy some shit at the mall or check out some local museums—you know, make a real vacation out of this piece of shit situation ... or maybe I'll just get good and drunk and stay that way until it's time to cab it back to the airport on Sunday. Who knows ... but no matter what, no matter what else happens—and God knows what else is going to happen—I'm having a fucking piece of pie tomorrow. I'll knock on a stranger's door before I let this truck driving asshole take the pie out of my Thanksgiving.

You can bet your life on that."

"I was just making a pie when you called actually."

"Oh crap. I'm sorry. I can't believe my pathetic ass is calling you right now and ruining your Thanksgiving prep. I can't believe I'm pestering you with this shit on your holiday."

He wanted to tell her that she wasn't bothering him. He wanted to tell her that talking to her was actually the highlight of his evening, that it was the one interesting spot in the otherwise dull painting of his predictable weekend plans. He wanted to tell her that the thought of walking back into that kitchen and making the pie crust border with a tiny fork filled him with the same sense of dread he had felt the year before when he went in for his first colonoscopy. He wanted to ask her to stay on the phone just a little longer, but all he said was, "Oh, no, it's fine. I completely understand."

"I guess I just wanted something to happen, you know? I guess I just wanted a little excitement to get me through the rest of the semester ... you know—something to chew on a bit until the next thing hits—whatever that is."

"Yeah, that makes sense," he said.

"So I guess I'll see your ass back in Marshall. We've got to finish this FDD shit out strong, really burn the place to the ground on our way out. You know what I mean?"

He had no idea what she meant. "Yeah, definitely. We definitely need to do that."

After she ended the phone call, he just sat there on the bed in the spare room and stared at the tan quilt and the way the row of matching throw pillows perfectly lined up across the white headboard. He remembered the day Jean purchased the quilt and pillows at the Lucky Linens in Sioux Falls, the way she was immediately drawn to the simplest quilt in the store, how she said it was the practical choice to get something that would never be out of fashion. He remembered showing Jean the more expensive quilt, the one with a huge yellow and orange sun stitched on top of a bright blue background. He remembered how Jean laughed as though his selection was just a joke, as though there was no way her husband could make such a frivolous and stylistically risky choice. He remembered driving home that evening after a mediocre dinner at Red Lobster, how he could feel the tan quilt in the back seat sucking the energy out of the car, how he looked at the passengers in the other cars on the highway and wondered what their conversations were like, how he wished he could be somewhere else for just a couple of hours.

He thought about how the tan quilt had been in his life for over a decade, and there was no way to get back to that day in the store and convince Jean to make the other choice. And the FDD program would be ending soon. The red bedspread in his dorm room would be packed away in a forgotten closet, somewhere behind old suitcases and Christmas decorations they no longer used. He could feel it—the way the off-white walls of his old life were closing in around him again, and there was absolutely nothing he could do.

Chapter Twenty-eight

"I'm just a little confused," Miles said to Joy over the phone. "Why do you want me to meet you at the state park? I thought we were going somewhere to drink."

"We are. Don't worry. I just thought it'd be fun to be outside a bit first," Joy said.

"Why? Why would that be fun? It's really cold today."

"No, actually it's not. It's not cold at all today—not by my standards. Think about it—when I was a kid, we went winter hiking all the time, and it was a lot colder than this, really a lot colder. The high's like twenty today ... perfect weather if you just dress for it, and I know you have lots of good winter gear in your closet. I know you do. C'mon. I promise you this'll be so much fun," she pleaded.

"So you expect me to go hiking in the shitty woods outside Marshall before my birthday thing? That's what you wanna do? Is that place even open in the winter?"

"Yeah, I was just there last week."

"You were?" he asked.

"Yeah, it's great, and I heard the snowy owl is in the area right now, so, if we're really lucky, we might even get to see one of those guys. How great would that be on your birthday?"

"What? The snowy owl? What the hell are you talking about? You think I want to hike somewhere in cold weather, somewhere that sucks even in the summer, to see some stupid white bird?"

"It's not a stupid white bird. A lot of people say they're majestic. A lot of people swear that the experience of seeing one is similar to the feeling of stepping into the ocean for the first time or looking at a mountain range from the window of an airplane." *What was she doing?* She was supposed to be putting on her wedding dress and applying the final layer of lipstick before driving out to the state park to make sure everything was ready for the ceremony, but instead she was arguing with Miles about the significance of seeing a snowy owl?

"Look—I didn't want to do this birthday stuff in the first place, but I figured I'd let this one go since you gave me all those rides when my truck crapped out last year. But this is where I'm drawing the line. I'll go sit somewhere and drink some beers with people, but I'm not going hiking right now. It's just not gonna happen."

"I'll bring whiskey," she said and sucked in her breath while biting her lower lip.

"What kind?"

"I still have a bottle of that Norseman stuff you like."

"Fine, but I'm not staying out there for more than an hour."

*

Driving in a wedding dress was harder than Joy thought it would be. The day she bought the simple lace dress with beading down the back, the saleswoman explained that it was the best choice for a last-minute wedding since the only necessary alteration would be to take the hemline up an inch or two, but Joy hadn't factored in how the close-body fit of the sheath styled dress would make the leg movements required for driving so difficult to maneuver.

Driving alone to her own wedding was definitely not the fantasy she had invented in childhood years when she spent hours acting out wedding day schedules with Barbie dolls and Lego people. But there was a certain pleasure in it too, a sweetness in the

Chapter Twenty-eight

silence that gave her time to reflect on all the beauty that was waiting for her in the hours ahead.

As she pulled into the state park entrance, she looked at her face in the rearview mirror. Shelly was right. The woman she scheduled to do Joy's hair and makeup really had turned her normally pleasant but plain face into a painting of an exotic Disney princess. Her dark eyes were somehow bigger and brighter, her lips fuller, her skin the luminous hue of perfume ad models. Her dark hair was formed into loose waves with the pieces around her face pinned back to expose the tiny pearl earrings that matched the buttons on her dress. She couldn't wait for Miles to see her this way.

She parked her car next to Shelly's blue sedan, pulled the white satin wedding coat with the fur-trimmed hood out of the backseat, got out of the car, and carefully slipped her arms into the delicate fabric of the coat. She was ready.

With just twenty minutes left until the invitation's arrival time, she walked quickly to the open area where the white rental chairs, pink luminary bags, and altar table with a single vase of pink roses were all set up. Because it had snowed lightly the night before and the prairie skies over Marshall were unusually calm for a winter day, the tall trees behind the altar had that even layer of snow balancing on branches that Joy had envisioned for her wedding photo backdrop. Everything was perfect.

"What d'ya think?" Shelly asked.

"I can't quite believe it. I mean, really ... it's like a dream," Joy said and took a deep breath of winter air.

"You took a chance, and it paid off. What can I say? When you first came to me, I thought you might be crazy—a winter wedding outside in Marshall. What could go wrong? Oh, yeah—everything. Every single thing could go wrong, but look at you. You somehow managed to pick the perfect day to get away with this crazy plan. You just might be the luckiest woman alive right now. That's all I'm saying."

"It's exactly like I thought it could be," Joy said and smiled in that exaggerated way where she crinkled her nose up and squinted so hard her eyes almost closed, the kind of smile she reserved for only the very best moments.

"Now all we have to do is wait for the officiant, groom, and guests to get here," Shelly said.

"There's something I have to tell you," Joy started. "There's something you should probably know about ... about the groom."

*

Twenty minutes later, Joy was hiding in the state park office with the one park employee scheduled to be there for the day. After the initial shock of the surprise wedding news, Shelly had agreed that it would be better for Joy to stay out of sight while the guests arrived. That way Joy could emerge at the invitation's scheduled time and explain the plan to everyone all at once instead of enduring the tediousness of relaying the details to one guest at a time as they trickled in. While Joy was safely sequestered in the small office building, Shelly would pretend to be some kind of birthday scavenger hunt coordinator, keeping everyone close to the parking lot and away from the wedding set-up until it was time for the big reveal.

"So you don't want people to see you all gussied up before the ceremony? Is that it? Like a wedding dress superstition thing?" the park employee guy asked Joy.

"Yeah ... mostly don't want the groom to see. They say it's bad luck, right?"

"I guess so ... wouldn't really know ... haven't jumped off that cliff myself yet," he said and turned back to his laptop computer where he appeared to be playing a rudimentary version of the shoot-'em-up games Miles sometimes liked to play. "What time's this thing supposed to wrap up, you think?" he asked.

"It should be pretty quick. The ceremony I have planned is short—just the vows and a short reading, and then we'll take some

Chapter Twenty-eight   249

photos. The main event is at the community center after. We're doing a full meal and a dance and the whole thing," she said.

"Oh, okay."

"Hey, can I ask you something?"

"Okay," he said without looking up from his computer.

"If you didn't know you were getting married ... I know that sounds weird, but just imagine it, just for a second. Imagine you didn't know you were getting married today, and the bride looked like I do right now, and you were in love with her, but you hadn't ever actually said it out loud yet. I know this sounds really weird, right? But just imagine it. Imagine that you didn't know, but then you saw her. Suddenly she was standing there in a wedding dress, and she looked better than you ever knew she could look. What would you do?"

"I don't know," he said. "I've never really had that, never really had a girlfriend exactly ... not yet. I don't know." She looked at him, this middle-aged guy with the greasy brown hair and glasses that were in style twenty years ago. He was nothing like Miles. What could he know?

"That's okay. Never mind. It doesn't matter. I was just wondering."

*

As Joy walked from the office building to the parking lot, she could feel her legs shaking beneath the layers of silk and lace. This was it. This was the moment that four months of planning had been building up to. In less than an hour, she would be married to Miles. In less than an hour, they'd be taking pictures under the snow-covered trees, driving together to the reception hall, eating their first meal as a married couple, dancing all night to the songs Joy had so carefully selected when she met with the DJ the week before, leaving the reception to check in to their room at the Ramada where they'd make love in a king bed and sleep all night wrapped up in each other before leaving for the Iowa honeymoon the next morning. This was the last moment before everything changed, the last shred of her life as a single woman.

"Hey, guys," she half shouted as she approached the group. "It's good to see you all."

"Are you wearing a wedding get-up?" some guy she didn't recognize asked.

"I am," she said.

"I'm confused. I'm just a little confused. Is this some kind of costume party thing? Is that what's going on? Because I thought this was a birthday party thing—for Miles. I thought this was—" he started.

"It is," Joy said. "It is a birthday party ... but here's the thing," she said and looked over at Juanita Jane. "It's more than that too. The thing is ... as you know ... well, some of you ... some of you know ... that Miles and I have been dating for quite a while now, and the thing is ... the thing is I love him. I love him a lot. I do, and I know he loves me too. I know it. And I've been thinking a lot about birthdays, about what a birthday is, about what a birthday could be, about how it's a start of something new. And I thought about what I would want for my birthday, what I would rather have than some stupid thing in a box, and that's what I'm giving him," she said.

"I don't quite follow. What do you mean?" a different guy whom Joy didn't know asked.

"I mean I'm surprising Miles with the best birthday gift I could imagine. I'm surprising him with a wedding. I'm giving him the gift of a lifetime of love, and you're all here to celebrate with us," she said and clapped her hands together in an attempt to generate the kind of enthusiasm required for the plan to work.

"Oh, my goodness," shouted the woman Joy recognized from Facebook pictures as Miles' mom. "Oh, my goodness. I'm so happy. This is such happy news. I had no idea that Miles was thinking about marriage, didn't even know he was dating anyone, to tell you the truth. I had no idea you even existed, but here you are, and you look lovely, dear. You look absolutely lovely. My goodness. I can't hardly believe it. I can't. You have no idea how happy this makes me, how happy I am that my son is *finally* ready to grow up a little and settle down," she shouted and rushed toward Joy to pull her into an aggressive embrace. "I just wish we had known. Lord knows, I would have worn something else for this," she said. There she was—Miles' mom—wearing her second favorite pair of jeans and a black sweater, standing in a parking lot with a bunch of people she didn't know, about to watch her son get married to a woman he'd never even mentioned to her.

"It's okay. I think you look great," Joy said and smiled at her soon-to-be mother-in-law.

"So let me get this straight," said a guy with a poorly groomed goatee. "Miles has no idea about any of this? He's just going to show up and find out that it's his wedding day? Is that what you're talking about?"

Joy inhaled deeply and started to say something, but Juanita Jane spoke over her. "Yes," Juanita Jane said. "Yes, that's exactly what she's saying, and I'm assuming we don't have all day to stand around in a parking lot and play let's-judge-the-woman-in-the-wedding-dress, right?" she said and looked over at Joy. "So why don't we just let her say her piece, and let's get this damn thing up and running," Juanita Jane said.

"Okay—so this is how it's gonna work. Everyone needs to follow me," Joy said. "There's a ceremony space set up just over there, and Miles is supposed to be here in less than twenty minutes. My friend Shelly's going to stay here, and she'll walk him over when he gets here."

"I just don't think this is going to end well," the bad goatee guy said. "I know Miles, and I really don't see him going in for this crazy shit."

"Just give it a chance," Miles' mom said. "You never know what can happen until it does. Let's just give him a chance—let him decide for himself."

"I just don't think I can sit there and watch this thing blow up," goatee guy said. "I just don't think I can, in good conscience, sit there and watch what's about to happen. And I sure as hell don't want him thinking I have any part in this. No, no, I don't want him thinking that," he said, his head shaking. "I gotta go. I gotta get out of here," he said and headed through the crowd and back to his car.

"Does anyone else here feel the way he does?" Juanita Jane asked. "Because if you do, you better speak up now. If you do, you better state your piece before Miles gets here. If you're not full in it with Joy ... you better head on out of here just like that guy. You better head on down that highway so he doesn't feel your negative energy coming at him." No one spoke. "Okay then," Juanita Jane said. "Let's get over to those wedding seats and wait to see how this thing's gonna play out."

Chapter Twenty-nine

Joy posed alone for a few pre-ceremony photos while the guests waited for Miles to show up. "Hold the bouquet just under your nose and look down," the photographer told her. "It's a great shot. It'll look just like you're smelling the flowers." *I am smelling the flowers*, Joy thought. "Now turn to the side and stare at the first branch of that tree right there. No, don't smile. We want some good thinking poses, like you're picturing what life will be like after the wedding," he said. "Now put your chin on your left shoulder and your left hand on the hip and turn to the side with a soft smile. Yeah, good ... good ... like that."

Suddenly Joy's mom rushed into the shot. "I'm sorry. I'm sorry. I know you're trying to—well, honestly I don't know what you're trying to do. I mean, I know you're taking wedding pictures, but I don't know how this is happening, and I really wanted to say something earlier—standing over there—but I just couldn't even get myself to speak, and God knows your father wasn't going to say anything. God knows he's even more stunned than I am. We thought we were coming to a birthday gathering to meet your boyfriend, to finally meet this Miles you've been going on about for a year now, and now *this* is happening? I just can't even catch my breath right now. I just don't know what to think, and I'm worried about you right now. I am, and I'm sorry for not saying anything over there, but I just couldn't speak, and that loud woman was really running the show, wasn't she? I just couldn't even collect a thought. I couldn't."

"It's okay, Mom. I promise you—I know what I'm doing," Joy said.

"Why don't we take this opportunity to get a mother-daughter shot," the photographer said in an upbeat voice and motioned for them to move closer together. Joy took a step toward her mother and put her hand on her mother's back. "Let's see some happy smiles," he said, but Joy's mother couldn't quite do it. Instead her expression was more like the startled look of a baby trying broccoli or beets for the first time.

"I just hope you know what you're doing," Joy's mother said as the photographer snapped another photograph.

"Trust me. I do," Joy said.

"Because we're not rescuing you again this time. We're not. And this one is way out there—way beyond the branches of what's happened before," she said and spread her arms out wide in front of her. "I just want you to know—we're not picking up the pieces again if this thing goes down in flames. We're just not doing it."

"I know. Don't worry. He really loves me. He does. He's going to be here any minute, and he's going to be as happy about everything as I am. I just know he will be," Joy said.

"Okay. I hope you're right," her mother said and shook her head.

While Joy's mother returned to her seat and the photographer looked over his shot notes, Joy stared at the guests seated in front of her, trying to do what the wedding magazines always suggested, trying to have a silent moment of recognition before the ceremony began. Right there, seated in the middle of Miles' friends and relatives, were the members of the FDD program. Because there was no rational way to justify extended family invites to a birthday party for her boyfriend, Joy had only invited her parents and the FDD members to represent her side of the wedding guest list. She told herself that she would try hard to stay in contact with the FDD members after the program ended, that the shared experience of her wedding day could somehow keep them close long after they weren't living in the dorms together anymore.

"Alright, let's get a couple happy shots of the bride before the groom shows up," the photographer said. It was so easy to smile. In just a few moments, Miles would be there. In just a few moments, the officiant she'd only met once, that guy with the gray beard sitting in the front row with a black bible in his lap, would marry them. And after that everyone would stand up and cheer as Joy and Miles walked down the snow-dusted center aisle holding hands and beaming with the bliss of easy days ahead. "Okay, just hold your bouquet up as high as you can with your right hand, and give me a big smile ... yes ... just like that. Okay ... great ... now let's set the bouquet down for a minute and stand in front of the audience. I want to get a shot of you with everyone in the background. There you go ... good ... yes ... keep smiling just like that, a nice relaxed smile. Let's just get a couple more with—"

"There he is," a woman's voice shouted out. "He's coming."

Joy whipped around and saw Miles rushing toward the ceremony space with Shelly speed-walking behind him, struggling to catch up with him. He looked handsome in his worn brown leather jacket and the old pair of jeans he often wore at the bar. He raced down the center aisle with a serious look on his face, like a man determined to get married as quickly as possible.

"What the hell is this? What the hell is going on?" Miles yelled at Joy as he approached her by the altar table. "Is this a joke? Is this some elaborate birthday prank you've thought up to mess with me? Is this—"

"No, it's not a joke. Didn't Shelly explain? Shelly was supposed to—"

"Are you kidding me? Are you fucking kidding me? Is this really happening? You're standing there in a wedding dress? I'm not having some shit dream after a bad night at the bar? This is real?"

"I thought you'd—" Joy started.

"This is crazy. I knew it—knew you were one of the crazy ones

– knew I should've run away a long time ago—knew I should've never—"

"Just let the girl speak, will you? Just let her say what she needs to say—after all the effort she put into this. Just give her a chance," Miles' mom said.

"My *mom* is here?" he shouted. "Are you kidding me? Why is my mom here? And who the hell are all these people?"

"They're your friends," Joy said.

"What are you talking about? I don't know half these people," he shouted and squinted into the sun to try to identify who was sitting in the audience. "Is that ... is that the guy I worked with at the grocery store like six years ago for like two weeks? I don't even remember that guy's name. Why the hell is *he* here? Why are these people here?" he asked Joy in a softer voice.

"I invited them. I thought you'd want to have them here. They're the ones who commented on your stuff the most," Joy said with a shaky voice and felt her perfectly painted eyelashes filling with tears.

"My stuff? My stuff? What the hell are you talking about?" he said, his voice getting louder again.

"On Facebook."

"Facebook?"

"Yeah, they're the ones who showed the highest activity rates on your page. I came up with a basic algorithm to see—"

"Are you kidding me? This is fucking crazy—you know that? Absolutely crazy," Miles yelled. "And now I have this fucking black spot on my reputation—in this town. This is insane."

"I know you love me," Joy said through tears. "I know it. And if you'd just let me explain ... because I know this can work ... we can work. I know it ... and I just think you're scared—that's what it is ... because you've never been—"

"No," he yelled and faced the audience. "And I want *everyone* to hear this. I'm not scared. That's not what's going on here. I *never* told this crazy bitch that I love her—never. I never told her anything at all—nothing. And this is how crazy she is—this is what she did—for some insane reason, she invited the *other* woman I'm sleeping with, the one I'm actually pretty into, and she's sitting right over there—so thanks a lot for screwing *that* up," he shouted and turned back to look at Joy.

"So that's the end of it? I planned all of this for months for no reason? I spent all my savings to give you a dream wedding for no reason? I spent all my free time planning and thinking and—" Joy started.

"No one told you to do that," Miles said. "No one who even almost knows me would have told you to do this."

"I can't believe the goatee guy was right," Joy said.

"What goatee guy?" Miles asked.

"The guy who left earlier, the guy who swore this was a bad idea, the tall skinny guy with—"

"Zack? Zack was here? Is that why he kept calling me? He knew about this? Oh, my God. Is that why he was calling me? Did he know? God damn it, I should've answered my stupid phone. I had a feeling too – had a feeling about it—was ringing and ringing, but my stupid ass hit ignore. I can't believe this." There they were—arguing with each other in front of an audience of forty wedding guests who weren't going to see a wedding after all. Despite the intense heartbreak of knowing Miles would be out of her life for good as soon as he walked away from the ceremony space, the most painful part for Joy was the sense of shame she felt standing there in front of everyone wearing a wedding dress.

"Don't you think I look pretty?" she asked in a near whisper.

"I'm a twenty-eight-year-old guy who works in a bar. I'm not looking for pretty right now. I thought you knew that."

"I thought you'd be so happy. I thought—"

"Happy? You thought I'd be *happy*?" Miles yelled. "This is literally the worst day of my life. This is literally worse than the day I—"

"Okay," Juanita Jane yelled and stood up. "Okay, we get the point. We all get it—you're not going through with it. We get it. At least *I* had the decency to walk away from my situation. At least I had the decency to get in my car and just drive away, to not make a public scene of the whole thing ... not that my situation was the same ... it wasn't the same. No, it wasn't the same at all, but that's not the point. We're not here to compare me running from my wedding to you rejecting Joy's wedding. That's not the point. The thing is ... for the rest of her life," Juanita Jane started. She paused to look at Joy standing there, noticed the way she no longer carefully cradled the bouquet of pink roses but instead held them carelessly at her side, noticed the way her shoulders slumped down like an old woman's under that silk wedding coat. "For the rest of her life, she's going to remember what you said here. For the rest of her life, she's going to remember how she loved you and how it all went to shit. At least have the decency to say something nice to her, to say one good thing to her before you high-tail it out of here, leaving her to deal with the awkward shit-storm of how to handle the reception."

"Reception?" Miles yelled and turned to look at Joy. "There's a reception? Are you kidding me? Are you fucking *kidding* me? And is there anything *else* I should know about? Have you already paid for a honeymoon, put money down on a house, picked out the paint color for the baby's room? And we don't want to forget about the end, right? We don't want to forget about that. Why don't we do it right now? Why don't we decide *right now* what kind of casket I should get, where I should get buried, what kind of cake you should serve at my funeral ... because that's what you want, isn't it? Isn't that what you want—to plan my whole fucking life right now? Isn't that what you're trying to do?" he yelled.

"I thought you loved me," Joy said without looking at him.

"Loved you? You thought I *loved* you? Are you completely out of your mind? Are you completely—"

"Okay, enough," yelled Juanita Jane. "Enough already. Enough," she said and stood up again. "Why don't you just go and leave poor Joy Toy to fend for herself now. Why don't you just—"

"Happily," Miles yelled and started walking down the luminary-lined aisle.

"Wait," Joy yelled after him. "Wait just one second—just one second so I can at least explain—so I can at least—"

"Just let him go, dear," Miles' mother said and shook her head at Joy. "I'm embarrassed to admit he's not the kind of man who'll stay and let you explain anything ... not now at least. I think he's just a little bit shook by the whole thing, and can we blame him really? I don't know, but maybe later—maybe after he's had some time to think it all over—I don't know," she said and looked right at Joy with the kind of vacant stare reserved for the faces of disappointed women.

"He's an asshole," shouted the curly-haired voluptuous brunette in the back. "I'm sorry, but that's what he is. I got the invitation for this thing—a birthday party for the guy I thought was *my* boyfriend. I thought *you* must be his sister or something," she said and nodded at Joy. "He slept with me like three hours ago, has been telling me all the bullshit for months, the I-love-you and the I-can-really-see-this-going-somewhere-with-you and the I-promise-I-won't-be-working-at-this-bar-forever and the you're-the-exact-one-I've-been-looking-for ... all the lines, all that crap, and meanwhile *this* was going on, and I had no earthly clue, no earthly clue that there was even an idea of anyone else, much less all of *this*," she said.

"He told you he loved you?" Joy asked and couldn't understand how this stranger sitting in the back of her wedding ceremony set-up could possibly be telling the truth.

"Oh, he told me," she said. "He's been telling me for months. He's been—"

"I think we should all just take a minute to hit the pause button," the officiant said and stood up to face the crowd. "I can't say I have experience with this sort of thing ... well ... at least not at a wedding ... no, I can't say that, but I do feel that, as the one who was supposed to lead the ceremony here, that I have some responsibility in getting the ship straight again, at least as straight as we can expect to get it in circumstances such as these.

And I don't feel like this is productive. No, I don't," he said and turned to look at Joy for a moment. "I know that what you're going through—what so many of us are going through—is difficult. I'm sure there will be many conversations and likely some counseling sessions up ahead for some of us present today, but I don't think now is the time to have those conversations. I don't think now is the time when speaking about what happened here today is emotionally productive."

Joy nodded along as he spoke, but she couldn't concentrate on what he was saying. Despite the cold temperature and thin coat she wore, Joy felt the warmth of waves of nausea rushing through her, and she had a sudden urge to sit down in the snow to try to calm herself. "I just can't believe it happened," Joy told the officiant. "I just can't believe everything I've done for him—all the planning—that none of it mattered to him, that it didn't matter at all."

"And I understand that," the officiant said. "But we have some decisions to make right now. We have some hard choices to face, so you're going to have to put all of that aside for a minute to make some tough choices."

"I know," Joy said.

"You spent a lot of money to feed everyone here today, right? You have a whole reception planned with a meal and dessert and entertainment, right?" he asked.

Joy nodded.

"And you need to make a decision that you can live with. You need to—" he started.

"Do you think Miles would come?" Joy asked. "Do you think—that if I just called him and talked it out—that maybe he'd at least come and eat with us, that he'd at least—"

"No," the officiant said. "No, I don't think that's a realistic option. I think you need to just take him out of the equation and think about everybody else who's here."

"Joy's not going to this fucking reception hall to sit in a room with crappy catered food and a lemon wedding cake she picked out just because Miles likes the fucking flavor," Juanita Jane said to the officiant. "It's not gonna happen, so here's what we're gonna do," she said and walked up to the front to address the crowd. "If you want a free lunch, and you're one of the people here who has the stomach to choke it down after this disaster of a day, head over to the Marshall Community Center in an hour, but don't expect Joy to be there. Don't expect that ... because she and I are going for a drive. She and I are going to ditch that wedding get-up and find a field somewhere to burn that stupid wedding dress. She and I are going to scream all of our lives' disappointments in the middle of an empty road somewhere away from town. She and I are going to shake all the sadness out of her bones, if just for a second ... because we all know it's coming back. We all know exactly what the future looks like for her," she said and nodded at Joy. "But what about him? What about Miles? Where is he? Didn't even have the courage to stay and face her."

"But you asked him to go," Joy said.

"But did it really matter anyway?" Juanita Jane asked. "I mean, what difference would it make? Yeah—I asked him to go, but it didn't matter, and that's the thing ... the thing you have to see ... the thing you haven't been seeing for months. You think *I'm* the one who asked him to go? You think *I'm* the reason he's not still standing here? But even when he was standing here, he wasn't really here. That's the thing. Even when he was standing here, right in front of you, he was already driving away in his car. And the whole time—the whole time you thought knowing him was building up to something you wanted, he wasn't even there. He was moving past it, looking ahead to something else, running away from the plans he didn't even know you were making. That's the thing you're going to have to understand, the thing you're going to have to hold close to you so you can move on with your life—that he was *never* here, that he was always already gone."

Chapter Thirty

The Friday of finals week was the day selected by Mr. Administration as the official ending of the FDD program, a decision that was both illogical and inconvenient for the four faculty members who lived in the dorms that semester. Because finals didn't end until the following Tuesday and course grades were expected to be posted the next day, this meant the FDD faculty had to move all their stuff out of the dorm building right in the middle of that end-of-semester grading rush professors at Prairie State often referred to as Hell Week.

For Bert, the move was logistically easy. There would be no apartment hunting, no lease to sign, no roommate to secure, no furniture to purchase, nothing to retrieve from a storage locker somewhere. He'd simply pack the car with the same two suitcases and five boxes of belongings he'd arrived with four months earlier, sign his name on the underbelly of the wooden desk just like the ones who'd occupied the room before him had done, turn his keys in at the residence hall office across the way, and drive home to Jean to settle back into the life he'd lived before the FDD program.

Logistically it was all so easy, but somehow it seemed completely impossible. Somehow he wondered whether or not he could actually pull it off, wondered if he'd find himself veering way off course instead, wondered if he'd be able to turn the car down the streets that led back to his house, wondered if instead he'd keep driving and not stop until his eyes found something better.

He could do it, he told himself. He had options. He could just run away from it all, even if it was just for the month-long winter break. He could drive to a small Louisiana town and rent a cabin surrounded by those swamp trees with the curtains of moss Juanita Jane was always talking about. He could sit on that cabin porch alone and invent ways to bring the kind of freedom the FDD program had offered him back to his old life. He was a mathematics professor, after all—had spent his whole life learning to understand equations the general population considered too complicated to even care about.

But when it came to his own life, he couldn't seem to make the numbers match up, couldn't figure out the correct formula to keep the fifty-year-old version of himself comfortable in the choices he had made so many years ago. But if he just had some time alone, he told himself, maybe he *could* do it. Maybe he could finally figure out the missing parts of the equation. Maybe he could figure out a way to stay married to Jean and still feel like himself.

He stripped the sheets off the bed, threw them in a box with the pillows and comforter, and wondered who would be sleeping on the thin dorm mattress the next semester.

*

"Hey," Joy yelled down the hall as Lyla was leaving her dorm room with a suitcase full of clothes. "Juanita Jane just told me your news. Congratulations." Joy rushed toward Lyla.

"Thanks," Lyla said and pulled the door key out of her purse.

"Do you have a ring?"

"I do," Lyla said and held out her left hand so Joy could see the princess-cut emerald ring Anton had bought the week before.

"Oh, wow. I really like it. I don't think I've ever seen an emerald engagement ring before. It's really unique. I really like it," Joy said and smiled.

Chapter Thirty

"Thanks ... I'm sorry. I feel really bad ... having this conversation with you ... you know ... after everything you've been through. I feel really bad ... really awful."

"No, it's okay. Don't worry. It's okay. I'm fine. It was hard—yes, but I know it's not the end of the line for us. I know that. I had a couple of hard days—yes, but now that I've had more time to think about everything, I know it's not really over for us—not yet. I mean, look at you and Anton—look at you guys—everything you went through. Yes, I would've liked it better if it all came easy for us, but that's not always realistic, right? It doesn't always go like that. And, with Christmas coming up, I just know he's not going to be able to stand it," Joy said.

"What do you mean?"

"I mean, think about it—Christmas. What do they always say about the holidays? You know—all those sappy songs and all those movies and stuff. It's always the holidays that make people see things clearly, and I just know he's not gonna be able to get through the holidays without breaking down and calling me. I just know it."

"Did you guys spend last Christmas together?" Lyla asked while buttoning up her coat.

"Well, no, but that was right at the beginning, you know. That was before anything had really happened with us, before we even really knew each other. Think about it—yes, I'm sure I took him totally off guard. That's why he ran, you know. That's why he couldn't do the right thing for us, in that moment, but picture this—he's gonna be at one of those huge family gatherings for Christmas, and he's bound to have a cousin or something who's recently engaged. He's bound to. And he'll hear all about the engagement and the wedding plans, and he won't be able to stand it."

"What do you mean?" Lyla asked and leaned against the doorway.

"I mean ... look, here's the thing. I think sometimes you just have to be the one to feed the relationship, to keep it alive, even when the other person isn't doing anything—like how your parents totally take care of you when you're a little kid, like how you might love them and all, but that doesn't mean you're in a position to do anything for them, at that time. I think it's like that."

"But what about the other woman? What about the other woman he was seeing at the same time as you?"

"Well ... yeah ... I know. I keep forgetting about that," Joy said and exhaled loudly. "It's crazy, right? I just keep forgetting that she even exists—can't even remember what she looks like, even if I really try, but I know what you mean. I know. It's the one part of the mess that I'm not sure how to clean up yet, and maybe I can't. Maybe that's it. Maybe he was just a bad guy, and I fell for all of it because that's what we do ... that's what we have to do, right, if we really love someone? It's just hard to believe that the whole thing was so different for me than it was for him. It's just hard to square that concept up in my brain. It's just so hard to—" she started but stopped speaking as a group of male students approached her and Lyla in the hallway.

"Hey," one of them said to Joy. "I heard what happened to you. That was some fucked up shit—that guy leaving you at the altar like that—some really fucked up shit. And I just want you to know that we're not all like that, just want you to know that some of us are actually good guys, that some of us actually mean it when we ask a girl to get married, that some of us—"

"Oh, no—he didn't—" Joy started but stopped herself again and instead just said, "Thanks. I appreciate that."

"I just wanted you to know," he said and winked at her as he walked off with his friends.

"Juanita Jane," Joy said to Lyla and shook her head. "She promised me she'd find a way to spin this whole thing in my favor. The problem is ... it's only a matter of time ... you know? So many people were there, and it's only a matter of time before everyone in town knows exactly what happened, but still—I'm thankful she at least gave me some time, time to get my grades in and go away for a while, to get out of here for a while before everyone knows what really happened."

"It'll be something else by next semester. Something else just as crazy will happen, and everyone will forget all about it," Lyla said, but she knew it was a lie.

"You think I'm crazy?" Joy asked.

"No, no, not you. No, I don't think *you're* crazy. No, not at all. The situation ... I meant ... I think the situation is crazy, just a crazy story, but it'll all blow over."

"Maybe, or maybe it won't. Maybe he'll miss me over Christmas, or maybe I'll never hear from him again. Maybe everyone in Marshall will think I'm some crazy, psychotic woman who tried to force a guy into marriage, and maybe I'll have to go back on the job market before I get tenure here. Maybe I'll end up teaching at that community college on the north shore of Alaska, that horrible little place where they post polar bear warnings on their webpage and live in total darkness half the year. Maybe I'll—"

"It's gonna be okay," Lyla said and put her hand on Joy's arm. "Trust me—you'll feel a lot better in a week or two. You'll feel a lot better after you've had a chance to decompress a bit."

"Thanks. I hope so."

*

Despite the fact that it was almost dinner time on a Friday, the study lounge on the second floor of the dorm building was still half full with students desperately trying to memorize mountains of material for their exams on Monday. There they sat, stooped over wooden tables, scanning back and forth between books and notes, hoping they could remember it all at least long enough to get through the tests, hoping they could somehow salvage three months of not caring all that much, hoping for the kinds of miracles that weren't mathematically possible at a regional university that had to follow a state mandated rule that final exams could not account for more than twenty percent of a course's overall grade.

In the corner of the lounge stood a small Christmas tree decorated with generic ornaments, those boring red and green globes typically used in nursing homes and restaurants. The lop-sided dove clipped to the top of the tree looked like he was about to take a nosedive and get his feathers stuck in the few silver streams of tinsel haphazardly thrown over the artificial branches. Under the tree sat a few fake presents, empty boxes wrapped in outdated Mighty Mouse holiday paper and lightly coated with decades' worth of dust collected from previous years under the same tree.

But it didn't feel like Christmas yet. That was the strange thing about the end of fall semester on a college campus. Outside the world was ready for the holidays. Outside stores and houses and the main streets of small towns in Western Minnesota looked and sounded like Christmas. Outside the twinkling lights were in the trees, and the music of the season played through speakers in every grocery store and barbershop in the region, but on campus it wasn't Christmas yet. On campus nothing that was happening outside was real yet, not until those last finals were turned in, not until those final semester grades were posted. Everything at the university worked in cycles like that. There was no moving forward, nothing to celebrate until the semester was completely done and over with, and even the presence of a little Christmas tree here and there across campus couldn't do anything to change that.

"Marg," Juanita Jane whisper-shouted into the lounge. "Marg, what are you doing? I thought you had your last final already."

"I did," Margie whisper-shouted back to Juanita Jane where she stood in the doorway of the lounge. "It just seemed like a nice place to do some reading since it's finally quiet in here."

"Oh, my holy God. You're such a nerd, Marg," Juanita Jane said and motioned for Margie to follow her out of the dorm lounge and down the hallway to Juanita Jane's room.

Margie grabbed the silly novel she was enjoying about a gas station worker who was secretly a witch and shoved the book into her backpack before following Juanita Jane. "I thought you had

Chapter Thirty

to pack," she said.

"Done. It's all done, but I'm not cleaning that room out. Screw that. I'm not doing that shit, not after Mr. Administration made us move out before the semester's even over with ... some serious bullshit there, you know? And it's too bad really. It's too bad the guy's got such a huge stick up his ass because he seems like he'd actually be a good time, like he'd actually be a good guy to know if someone would just make him drop that crazy military-grade posture he's got going on, you know?"

"Wow, it looks so weird in here," Margie said as they entered Juanita Jane's room. "It's like it's naked or something. It feels so weird seeing it like this."

"Yours'll be the same way come spring, you know. They make you move all your shit out for the summer so they can have some band camp or some bullshit. Those camp kids stay on campus like four days, but you have to move all your stuff out and back in because of it," Juanita Jane said and sat down beside Margie on the bare mattress.

"Yeah, I heard about that," Margie said. "But the end of spring semester seems like a long time from now, like it's never really going to get here, and I keep telling myself that the summer's going to be the thing that glues my relationship with Chad back together, but now he's talking about taking some internship in D.C., and I just don't know if I can stand it. I just don't want anything to change. I just want to know that this summer will be the same as last summer, that he'll still come over for dinners, that we'll still go swimming all the time in Green Lake, that we're still going to stay together through college, just like he said. I just want to know it'll all be the same way he said it would be."

Suddenly there was a knock at the door. Juanita Jane recognized the knock-pattern. One muffled knock followed by two louder knocks. It was Mark.

She rushed to the door and opened it just enough to slip out of the room and into the hallway. "What's up, kid?" she asked him.

"My mom doesn't want me talking to you anymore, but I just wanted to say ... just wanted to tell you ... well ... that I had some fun this semester, a lot of fun this semester, with you, a lot of fun with you ... and I just wanted you to know that, so ... because I thought you should just know," he said without looking up at her face. It was hard to see him like that, standing there completely sober, standing there in clean clothes and a shorter haircut, standing there like a nervous child confessing to something, standing there like a stranger she used to know.

"I know," she said.

"I just wanted to make sure you knew ... just wanted to tell you thanks or something," he said.

"Anytime, kid," she said, and he looked up at her, looked her straight in the eyes and put his lips against hers, but it didn't feel like a kiss anymore. It didn't feel like anything.

"Have a good Christmas," he said. "I guess I'll see you around."

"You too," she said and slipped back into her room.

Margie was still sitting on Juanita Jane's bed, pulling at a loose string in the seam of the mattress. "Who was that?" she asked.

"Just a student who wanted to say thanks for my help this semester."

"That's nice," Margie said. "Do you have any lotion unpacked? My hands are so dry. They're killing me."

Juanita Jane dug down to the bottom of the hot pink zebra-patterned duffle bag and pulled out a bottle of rose scented lotion. "Here, keep it. I never liked this one anyway."

"Oh, no. I didn't mean—"

"Keep it. Consider it a parting gift."

"Okay—but you'll still come over next semester, right? We'll still hang out, right? It'll still be the same, right?" Margie asked.

"I'd love to tell you yes—that it'll all be the same, Marg, but the truth is—it won't be. That's the thing about life. That's the bullshit we all believe until we don't—that it's all gonna be the same, that the concept is even possible—that anything could ever really be the same. And the thing is ... I'm glad you still believe

Chapter Thirty 271

that because that's the beauty of life, isn't it? Isn't the real beauty in those moments when we still actually fucking believe something like that is possible, those moments *before* we're standing on the other side of it? And trust me, Marg—it would only be bad for you if we did still hang out like this ... because I don't want this for you. I don't want you to be on the other side of it yet, and you need to stand where you are in life with some other people who are still standing there too ... because you need to just be nineteen for a minute."

"So you're just gonna act like you don't know me if you see me? We're just supposed to act like none of this happened, like the semester didn't even happen, like we're not even friends?" Margie asked.

"No—of course not. Look, Marg—everything that happened happened, and I'm glad it happened, and I'd like to be at your wedding someday sitting in the audience, and I'd like to see your babies someday too. I would. The thing is—pretty soon everything's gonna start moving forward for you, and I'd like to see that, but I'm old enough to know that I'll be standing somewhere on the outside of it all. I'm old enough to know that when your life starts picking up speed, you're gonna be racing. You're gonna be fucking flying."

"But your life is exciting too," Margie said. "Look at all the stuff we did this semester. Look at all—"

"Oh, I know. Trust me, I know. I sure as hell didn't see this shit coming. I sure as hell didn't think I'd be living in a dorm room in my fifties, and I've no fucking idea what's coming around the corner next. Who the hell knows—sixty could be even crazier than this shit. But it's all a moment in time, Marg. That's the thing. It's all just a fucking moment in time."

"Just promise me we'll go get those chocolate chip pancakes at that diner in Pipestone next semester. Just promise me we'll go at least once. Just promise me that," Margie said and looked over at Juanita Jane.

"Sure, Marg. Sure, we'll try to do that."

*

As Bert placed the last box in the trunk of his car, the early winter winds of the Minnesota prairie whipped wildly against his face. He closed the trunk and looked back at the dorm building, that simple brick structure that held so much more life than his house across town ever could.

He thought about how, the year before, he had begged Jean to just let him paint the living room some color that wasn't a close neighbor to beige, thought about how they fought in the paint section of the Home Depot in Sioux Falls as she pulled paint sample cards from the display, only considering shades with names like *sunset sand* and *clean linen white*. He thought about how he had foolishly believed that coating the walls with *tangerine passion* or *midnight melody* would make any kind of a difference, how he had seriously considered calling in sick to work and driving back to that Home Depot to purchase the paint he really wanted, how he had imagined himself painting frantically to get it all done before Jean got home from work, how he had convinced himself that if she just saw the way the room looked, that if she could just stand there for a minute and see the splash of life on the walls, then she'd like the color too. But he knew it was pointless, knew she'd just make him paint over it all with that beige color anyway, knew that it would feel even worse because he'd have seen what it all could have looked like, what it all could have been if he'd just married a different woman.

The walls in the dorm building were all white. The hallways smelled of bleach and vinegar cleaning supplies, and the light fixtures were old standard-issue florescent tubes that buzzed and flickered when they were flipped on. All the bedrooms looked the same, and the shower stalls were lined with simple white tiles surrounded by shoddy grout-work. But none of that mattered because it was the place where Juanita Jane could knock on his door at three in the morning. It was the place where a guy could fall out of his bunk and send the whole building into a rush of

Chapter Thirty

wondering what happened. It was the place where he could hear music his ears didn't know yet. It was the place where the idea of sex still saturated every surface of the building, the place where he didn't need to think about things like changing the color of a wall to feel something. And for just that one semester, that one glorious and unexpected stretch of time there in the middle of his life, it was the place that made him remember what it would feel like, what it had felt like so many years before, to be young again.

CPSIA information can be obtained
at www.ICGtesting.com
Printed in the USA
LVHW010001250821
696050LV00010B/487